Remembering Christmas

Books by Tom Mendicino

PROBATION

Books by Frank Anthony Polito

BAND FAGS!
DRAMA QUEERS!

Books by Michael Salvatore

{BETWEEN} BOYFRIENDS

Published by Kensington Publishing Corporation

Remembering Christmas

Tom Mendicino
Frank Anthony Polito
Michael Salvatore

KENSINGTON PUBLISHING CORP.
www.kensingtonbooks.com

KENSINGTON BOOKS are published by

Kensington Publishing Corp.
119 West 40th Street
New York, NY 10018

"Away, in a Manger" originally appeared as a short story in a slightly different version in *Best Gay Romance 2011,* edited by Richard Labonte, Cleis Press.

All Kensington titles, imprints, and distributed lines are available at special quantity discounts for bulk purchases for sales promotion, premiums, fund-raising, and educational, or institutional use.

Special book excerpts or customized printings can also be created to fit specific needs. For details, write or phone the office of the Kensington Special Sales Manager: Kensington Publishing Corp., 119 West 40th Street, New York, NY 10018. Attn. Special Sales Department. Phone: 1-800-221-2647.

ISBN-13: 978-0-7582-6685-9
ISBN-10: 0-7582-6685-5

First Kensington Trade Paperback Printing: October 2011

10 9 8 7 6 5 4 3 2 1

Printed in the United States of America

Contents

Away, in a Manger

Tom Mendicino

For David McCaughey

And it came to pass in those days that a decree came forth from Berlin (Irving, not the city), echoed by a multitude of lesser tunesmiths, that all of the world should be burdened with the task of making-the-Yuletide-bright with the kith and kin of their blood, and each and all went to be taxed, hearts heavy with dread, everyone to his own city. And James also went down from the glittering canyons of Gotham through the savage wilderness of E-ZPass and diesel fumes, journeying to the humble city of Parkersburg to comfort the aged and lonely mother who called him Jimmy, and to pass four days, with only the companionship of his namesake (Stewart, James), in black-and-white without commercial interruption, to see him through the dark winter nights.

And so it was that his days were accomplished.

James couldn't remember the last time he could be found sitting in his office, waiting for the phone to ring, at 7:50 in the morning. The support staff, dragging their backpacks, wouldn't arrive for at least another hour, and the editors and sales managers they supported never began to meander in until after ten.

Solitude wasn't unpleasant, he decided, even briefly considering whether he ought to become a morning person. It was actually calming, having a few quiet moments to scan the titles of the volumes jammed into his bookshelves, a reminder of the relative importance of things, of the transitory nature of daily crises and urgent deadlines. Many of these books had once been well reviewed. Several had won prizes. More than a few had been prominently featured on best-seller lists. *Sic transit gloria mundi.* The few lucky ones, the award winners, now lived quiet, uneventful lives as paperback editions, languishing on the shelves of Barnes and Noble for years, waiting to attract a buyer's interest. The others had been banished to remainder tables or used-book bins, destined to be forgotten altogether. He jumped to grab the receiver as the phone shrieked, startling him from his reverie, and tipped a Starbucks Venti Morning Roast into his lap.

"Fuck!" he shouted, not exactly the warm greeting the highly respected but overbearing Washington D.C. super-agent expected from the editor who had won the bidding war to publish the as-yet-unwritten presidential campaign "autobiography" of his client, a charismatic and ambitious junior senator from a swing state rich in electoral votes.

"And a Merry Christmas to you too," the super-agent snorted.

"Sorry. Sorry," James apologized, trying to mop up the mess with a damp, wrinkled napkin. "I just spilled a cup of scalding hot coffee all over my pants."

"Ouch," the Senator snickered. "You've got to protect your most valuable assets."

James was taken aback at the unexpected sound of the voice he knew only from CNN and *Meet the Press*; the author-to-be, whom James had yet to meet, wasn't scheduled to be on the call. The leering undertone was clearly at odds with his reputation as a devout family man, the father of six, a husband admired for his deep, spiritual connection to his Episcopalian minister wife.

"No, no," James assured him. "No permanent damage."

But he couldn't shake the feeling this Starbucks catastrophe was an omen that this book wasn't fated to be one of defining successes of his career. By the age of forty-six, James had acquired and edited a long string of successful history and political books, including a former Secretary of State's Pulitzer Prize–winning chronicle of the democratization of the Balkan nations, a former President's literary memoir of his hardscrabble childhood, the definitive biography of William Howard Taft, and the autobiographies of an unsuccessful Democratic presidential nominee, a beloved First Lady, and a long-shot neophyte who had landed the vice presidential slot on a winning Republican ticket largely on the strength of the manuscript James had painstakingly coaxed out of him. The Senator was a prestigious addition to his stable of authors (though he wouldn't actually write a single word), and the bulk sales to his political action committee ensured at least a brief run on the *New York Times* bestseller list. Things had gone well so far, despite the super-agent's insistence on ungodly early meetings for scheduling convenience, his, not James's. James had engaged the perfect ghost to capture the Senator's colloquial style. He'd hired the best photographer in the industry for the cover shoot. And, thank God, the staffer the Senator had assigned to be James's primary contact seemed to be bright and responsive.

"So, what are your Christmas plans?" the Senator asked, clearly not interested, but feeling the need to make small talk.

"Going home to my mother's."

"Where's that?"

"West Virginia."

The Senator's interest was piqued. For one, brief, fleeting moment, James existed as something more than a faceless fungible unit in his campaign apparatus.

"I thought I detected an accent," the Senator claimed.

"I hope not! I've spent the last twenty-five years trying to clean up my hillbilly pronunciation!"

Big mistake, he quickly realized. The Senator spoke with a thick, musical drawl. James clearly was off his game, paying the price for rising before dawn with too little caffeine to kick-start his engine.

"Pure West Virginia, as Hannibal Lecter once observed about another native of the Mountain State. I always wanted a Carolina

Piedmont accent like yours," James said, effectively recovering the fumble.

He wandered out of his office after finishing the call, carrying several pages of handwritten notes for his assistant to type. The floor was still dark. The only signs of life were the burning lights in an office at the opposite end of the hall. Damn, he thought, remembering it was December 23, and that the holiday sabbatical had begun at five yesterday afternoon. He was officially on vacation now, having just completed the last meeting on his calendar for the year. He headed back to his computer, deciding to type the notes himself while his recollection was fresh, knowing he wouldn't be able to decipher his own chicken scratch when he returned in ten days, leaving him unable to translate for his frustrated assistant. After he finished, he answered the e-mails in his in-box and deleted his opened messages before shutting down his computer, determined to start the New Year with a clean slate, then turned off the lights and locked the door to his office.

It was all of nine-thirty as he walked to the elevator. The deserted offices and cubicles were decorated with dollar-store holiday trappings—red and green garland, plastic wreaths and holly, cutout Santas and snowflakes—that would be tossed into storage boxes or garbage pails when the occupants returned in January. He was tempted to steal a miniature Charlie Brown Christmas tree from a desktop to take home with him, but his good judgment prevented him from causing an innocent janitor to be fired for theft. To reach the elevator he had to pass the one brightly lit office, where Rhonda Brinkman, children's chapter book editor extraordinaire and workaholic, was chained to her desk, probably putting the final touches on the galleys of another Newbury Medal instant classic. She looked up and waved as he passed; he shrugged his shoulders and pointed at his watch, feigning urgent business, not wanting to waste an hour whining over their workloads, bitching about that year's meager annual bonus, and speculating over rumored editorial layoffs.

"See you next year," he hollered as the elevator door closed behind him.

Traffic, both street and foot, was light for a weekday morning at the corner of Broadway and Fifty-fifth. The city was slowing down for the holiday. Commuters from Westchester and New Jersey had taken vacation days to finish their shopping. The wind whipping through the concrete canyons was brisk; it was chilly on the shaded side of the street, but unseasonably warm in the sun. James was comfortable going coatless, wearing only a cashmere sweater and a scarf knotted around his neck, an accessory chosen for color rather than warmth at the last minute before leaving the apartment. He grabbed a *Daily News* from the newsstand and easily found a seat at the counter of his favorite coffee shop, a relic from a bygone era before fast-food franchises and the caffeine purveyor from Seattle conquered the world. He left a five-dollar tip on a twelve-dollar check for coffee and juice, a bowl of Special K, and an order of wheat toast, and decided to walk to Madison rather than taking a cab. He hadn't bought a gift for Ernst yet and had no intention of going to lunch that afternoon empty-handed.

Rockefeller Center was surprisingly, pleasantly, uncrowded, with just enough shoppers and skaters for it to seem a postcard-perfect holiday tableau. The women were well dressed, wearing leather coats and high, polished boots, and their children belonged in the glossy pages of high-end retail catalogues. The stampede of tourists in garish parkas and dirty sneakers had returned to their undesirable zip codes. Manhattan belonged to its residents again. James resented the hordes of slack-jawed visitors from Minnesota and Belgium, the lumpen masses staring through the lenses of their Nikons and clutching their tickets to the Christmas Spectacular at Radio City Music Hall. He missed the gritty and dangerous island of his youth, the Golden Era of Gotham when needles and broken bottles littered Ninth Avenue and six dead bolts on the door of his fourth-floor walkup never deterred the junkies from breaking in to steal his television two or three times a year. He paused to linger beside a sidewalk vendor, inhaling the aroma of roasting chestnuts (another dying tradition) and was surprised to hear himself humming along to the instrumental "Silver Bells" piped over an outdoor loudspeaker.

Why shouldn't he feel cheerful as the holiday approached? It was two days after the solstice, and here he was sauntering across Midtown wearing sunglasses, not needing a coat. Global warming certainly had its fringe benefits. One of these years the daytime highs would never dip below fifty and the nighttime lows would hover above freezing the entire winter. Wishful thinking, he knew, but definitely a possibility in his lifetime. He was young enough to expect to be alive when the environmental apocalypse finally arrived. He suddenly realized he'd squandered an hour doing nothing more productive than staring at the Saks window displays and cruising the college boys who had taken to the streets in cargo shorts and flip-flops, enjoying the benign December weather. He picked up the pace, his armpits damp with sweat as he charged the front door of Paul Stuart to choose a cravat (as Ernst, with European formality, insisted on calling a necktie) for his oldest (literally) New York friend. James still felt a thrill each time he entered the hushed cathedral of haberdashery and paused to admire the plush carpets and polished wood surfaces, the slouchy leather sofas, and the expertly crafted wares artfully displayed on the tables and racks.

A clerk, old enough to have been working the sales floor when Mary Martin headlined on Broadway, approached and led James directly to the ties. He considered and rejected an assortment of more traditional foulards and reps in standard reds and greens and blues. His eye was attracted to the more risqué selections, soft, rich silks of dazzling colors, cheeky plums and bold scarlets, arresting emeralds, and blinding sapphires. He finally settled on a brash blood orange, a small extravagance at two hundred dollars. Ernst, seventy-eight, bald as an egg and ugly as a box turtle, relied on an eccentric wardrobe to cut a dashing figure.

"Unusual color," the clerk commented as he rang up the sale.

"I'd like a bow for the box, if you don't mind," James asked, slightly perturbed by what he considered to be an intrusive remark.

The traffic uptown was heavier than he'd expected, and he fidgeted in the back seat of the taxi, knowing that Ernst demanded strict punctuality and that he could expect a cold greeting and biting remark at best if he arrived after the appointed hour. If the old man were in a particularly foul mood, James would receive a haughty dismissal by the maitre d' informing him that Monsieur Belcher had decided to leave when his guest was more than ten minutes late. Much to his relief, James had the good fortune to have entered the cab of a particularly aggressive Sikh driver and was delivered to the door of The Box Tree restaurant with six minutes to spare. He stood, finger on the bell under the brass nameplate, AUGUSTIN V. PAEGE, RESTAURATEUR, and despaired. How the fuck had he forgotten he wasn't wearing a jacket? He was sweating profusely as the door opened, expecting to be banished with a withering glance. But because of either the early hour or an abundance of forgiving holiday cheer, he was warmly greeted, his handsome scarf complimented as he was led to the table.

"Don't gawk, Jimmy. I know you better than you know yourself and as soon as you realize Betty Bacall is sitting at the next table, you're going to go all moonfaced and slack jawed and embarrass me to death."

James was pleased to find Ernst in a jovial mood, for him at least, and asked Severin their waiter, a man as austere and stern as his name, to bring him a bourbon and water, hoping for a quick buzz. Ernst was obviously on his second Tanqueray martini; these days he was blotto by four in the afternoon.

"Merry Christmas to you, too, you mean, cranky bastard," he teased the old man, knowing the septuagenarian reveled in his contrarian nature.

"Is that gift for me?" Ernst asked, his interest piqued by the box James had set on the table. "Don't make an old man crawl over the place settings to get it!"

"What makes you so sure it's yours?"

"Very funny, Jimmy. I suppose you want to pay for your own lunch, in which case I'm ordering the most expensive bottle of Cabernet in the cellar and having Severin charge it to you."

"You win. Your taste in Cabs would set me back two months of co-op maintenance fee. Please accept this small token of my affection," James laughed. "Merry Christmas, Ernst."

Ernst, like many gentlemen of means whose emotional attachments required significant financial support, took an almost childish delight in receiving gifts. He tore off the ribbon like a greedy boy and held up the tie to admire.

"Unusual," Severin commented, unimpressed by the loud, bright color.

James was shaken to hear the same critical judgment of his taste repeated within a single hour.

"Well, I love it!" Ernst declared, insisting Severin help him from his chair and lead him to the men's room so he could replace his own canary yellow cravat with James's gift.

James sipped his bourbon, potent as rocket fuel, and stared at the menu, not bothering to read it. He hated everything about this pretentious little bandbox, its Tiffany glass panels and Wedgewood china and Christofle silverware and, most of all, the haute-faggot affectation of a red rose at every place setting. He knew the lunch selections by heart; nothing ever changed here, nothing ever new, let alone, God forbid, *nouvelle,* on the menu. The routine never changed. Ernst would stuff himself with bread and butter, avoiding the wasteful extravagance of an appetizer because, despite his taste for luxury, he was, like many wealthy men, at heart a cheapskate. He would order the escargot, complaining they weren't as well-prepared as they had been his last meal here, and vow never to return until Augustin V. Paege himself descended on their table to flatter and mollycoddle him, soliciting Ernst's undying loyalty. James, as always, would order a salad, the sole, and a dessert.

Ernst wobbled back to the table, stopping to accept Betty Bacall's compliments on his marvelous tie. Severin poured the first glasses of a very good, not great, mid-list Bordeaux. James drained the last dregs of his bourbon before moving on to the wine, steeling himself for the annual accounting of Ernst's financial affairs, followed by the none-too-subtle warning about his continued expectation of James's unquestioning fealty. James was one of Ernst's three surviving long-term relationships; each had been promised an equal distribution of the considerable estate, built on the profits of his wine import business. Cody Parkinson, James's second successor, now a mergers and acquisitions lawyer at Davis Polk, knew for a fact the old man was delusional, that his business partners, his sister and her sons, had gone to great lengths to ensure the assets would never pass out of the family. But the three younger men were all genuinely fond of their old benefactor, and none of them wanted to hurt him by destroying any illusion that he still held complete power over their good fortunes. Plus, even though a cash endowment was out of the question, the personal effects—the furniture and the museum-quality tchotchkes and the artworks by minor painters—would be up for grabs when the old toad croaked. James had first dibs on a pair of sterling candlesticks and the German-language first editions of Thomas Mann.

But much to James's surprise, instead of delivering mildly veiled threats of being cut out of the will, Ernst wanted to spend the afternoon reminiscing, which in the past had always meant his repeating oft-told tales of notorious and celebrated homosexuals of the middle and late decades of the Twentieth Century, their scandalous behavior observed firsthand by Ernst in the discotheques of Manhattan and on the dunes of Fire Island. These anecdotes had been his currency, traded for invitations to the best dinner parties and weekends in country houses on the upper Hudson. Personal memories, however, were rarely shared, such indulgence being an affront to Ernst's deeply engrained Old World sense of privacy, so it was unsettling to James to hear the old man speaking sentimentally about their early years together.

"You were such a gawky boy, all knees and elbows. I remember Peter Orlovsky saying whoever took you home the night we met was going to wake up black-and-blue with bruises."

But fear of contusions hadn't deterred Ernst from descending on him in the basement of The Ninth Circle, where he had plied James with so many bottles of Budweiser he had to be carried up the stairs.

"I should have had you arrested the next morning for assault," James teased, delighting an old man who still took great pride in a well-earned reputation as an aggressive sexual predator.

"I still can hear your voice, Jimmy, protesting you were a top, though you were far too drunk to get it up. What a silly boy you were, thinking I would believe you had never been fucked before."

Ernst was clearly tipsy, his voice growing loud enough to offend the sensibilities of the legend lunching at the next table. But James was relieved to see Miss Bacall was too busy enjoying the ribald conversation of her own lunch companions to pay any attention to the embarrassing details of his youthful escapades.

"Do you recall that terrible shirt you were wearing that night? With those nasty little holes under your armpits?"

"That was my favorite shirt! I loved that shirt!"

And, indeed, James had worn his Patti Smith Group "Easter" Tour souvenir tee until the day it literally disintegrated in the wash cycle.

"I was so young and naïve in those days," James laughed. "I thought it meant you really loved me when you agreed to go see the Talking Heads with me at CBGB."

"Warhol was there that night," Ernst reminded him, always having perfect recall of even the briefest interaction with celebrity.

"At the next table."

Ernst took a deep breath and sighed, reaching across the table to grab James's hands with his own.

"We should spend one more Christmas in Munich. It's not too late, Jimmy. There is a night flight from JFK. My treat."

"You know my mother is expecting me in West Virginia tomorrow. It would break her heart," James laughed, expecting that this proposed spontaneous Christmas trip was nothing more than an old man's pipe dream and that the aged tightwad would never consider paying the walk-up price for two first-class tickets to Europe. "Besides Ernst, it's not like you to want to embark on sentimental journeys."

The little rube in the punk rock tee shirt had had pretensions to worldliness, but he'd never been issued a passport before meeting Ernst. Ernst had insisted they spend their first Christmas as a couple in Bavaria, making every effort to ensure the trip was memorable. James had studied his Baedeker's at breakfast, preparing for long mornings touring spectacular castles and cathedrals with Ernst as his guide. After a long, heavy lunch, they had meandered through the stalls of the Christmas Market with steaming cups of chocolate or spiced mulled wine. Come evening, they had dined in the ancient rathskellers, feasting on roasted slabs of pork and beef, pierced with the jagged ends of broken bones. And Ernst, being an experienced lover of much younger men, was wise enough to plead exhaustion and the need to retire to his comfortable bed after his nightcap, allowing James to explore the dance clubs and the cruise bars with their pitch-black, maze-like back rooms alone, undeterred by his patron's critical eye.

"I'll start working on my mother tomorrow to give her an entire year to prepare for the disappointment of spending her favorite holiday without her favorite son," James said, half-believing the two of them might escape to Europe for one last memorable holiday in the coming year.

"Oh, that hateful mother of yours will never give you permission to ruin her Christmas," Ernst said bitterly, rolling his eyes.

James relaxed as the conversation veered away from uncomfortable nostalgic reveries to the more familiar territory of resentful complaints. Momentary lapses into elegiac interludes must be an inevitable malady of old age, he expected, like macular degeneration and osteoporosis.

"My mother is very fond of you, Ernst, and you know it," he said, lying through his teeth.

"I am not so senile to have forgotten how your mother chose to have her guest rooms painted during my one and only visit to that wretched town, so that the two of us would have to stay at a hotel."

James had long accepted that Ernst was far too self-absorbed to understand why a woman of a certain age and place who was struggling to accept her son's uncomfortable "problem" could never have trusted an overbearing and controlling and much older gentleman who seemed to exercise an undue and most likely unwholesome influence over her child. He'd long suspected the real reason Ernst found his mother and his hometown repellently distasteful was that they reminded him of a far more provincial upbringing in rural Germany than he would ever deign to admit. James was starting to feel unpleasantly drunk after imbibing a cocktail and two glasses of Bordeaux. He hadn't been drinking much lately as overwork had left him too exhausted to pursue much of a social life. Even in his younger days, he'd never developed a taste for consuming alcoholic beverages before sunset, being pale eyed and prone to blinding headaches whenever he eventually needed to emerge into the sun. Ernst, greedy little bastard that he was, happily killed the bottle of Bordeaux and was about to order a brandy until James insisted he had to be in Chelsea for an appointment at half past three.

"With an hourly companion, I suppose," the old man snorted.

"Don't be ridiculous," James huffed, acting affronted by the assumption that he, a very well-preserved and youthful forty-six, with a body that still attracted appreciative glances in the locker room thank you very much, needed to pay for it. But Ernst's still uncanny instincts had correctly discerned that commercial trade was James's primary means of erotic release lately.

"What reason is there to go to Chelsea other than muscle boys or an overpriced meal at a bad neighborhood bistro?"

"None of your business. Just finish your wine."

"I would think that after my treating you to this lovely Christmas lunch you would have the courtesy to explain your reason for denying me a small brandy. It seems obvious the demands on your time are too pressing to indulge me in a pleasant afternoon of companionship and conversation."

The old man was slurring his words and sloshing the dregs of wine in his glass perilously close to the rim. James's better instincts told him to ignore the elderly despot, but the spirit of the resentful young pup he'd once been rose to the bait, provoking him to nip at the ankles of the master who had held the leash.

"Well, if you're so interested, I'm not going to Chelsea. I need to stop by Tiffany to buy a gift for Alex and Leo because I'm having dinner with them tonight," he announced, intending his words to be hurtful.

Ernst slumped in his seat, deflated, and James immediately regretted the unrestrained impulse to punish him for being such a demanding bastard. Severin quietly appeared behind Ernst's seat and helped him from his chair, but his offer to lead Ernst to the bathroom was gruffly rebuffed. While they waited for Ernst to return, Severin assured James that Monsieur's place of business would be invoiced for the meal. After helping the older man into his overcoat, the waiter graciously accepted the twenty-dollar bill James slipped into his palm for summoning the car.

"Merry Christmas, Severin," James said, as he led Ernst through the open door.

"And to you, sir," Severin answered, as he closed the door behind them.

The town car was waiting outside, a sleek black Mercedes, spit-polished and glistening in the bright midday sun. The chauffer ignored the honking horns of lesser vehicles and the curses of their drivers as they tried to squeeze past the parked obstacle blocking the narrow street. Ernst hesitated before climbing into the car, then turned and gave James a tight, affectionate hug.

"Please, Jimmy. Don't mention Germany to your mother tomorrow. There's no reason to upset her," he said, shockingly sober and coherent.

"It might be fun, Ernst. Another Christmas in Munich. We'll talk about it when I get back."

"No, Jimmy. I won't be able to go next year."

The sense of dread that had been looming in even the bright and sunniest stretches of the day came crashing down over James's head.

"It's pancreatic cancer, Jimmy. The doctor told me last week. I refuse to have the surgery. I will live the rest of my days as I see fit," he said, his words ennobling him, granting him stature, imposing and dignified as Rodin's Balzac, master of his fate. James stood speechless, too shocked to cry, as the door shut and the town car carried its doomed passenger down the street.

He rolled over on the bed and opened an eye, jumping off the mattress when he realized he'd overslept. He had exactly thirty-nine minutes to shower and dress and find a cab to slog through the last dregs of crosstown rush hour traffic and deposit him at the entrance of Alex and Leo's Central Park West co-op for a seven o'clock dinner invitation. He planted his feet on the floor, grabbed his head between his hands, and squeezed, trying to crush the throbbing pain in his skull. Why hadn't he popped three aspirin and chugged a bottle of spring water before he lay down to "rest his eyes"? He stumbled into the bathroom and was shocked by the haggard image that confronted him in the vanity mirror. His gray pallor and the dark rings under his puffy eyes made him look like the child of Lon Chaney's Phantom.

He thought about a last-minute cancellation, pleading a sudden attack of something vile and disgusting. He considered an elaborate alibi involving a gastrointestinal disaster since, after living with Alex for six years, enduring his nocturnal farts and his failure to flush the toilet, James was unconstrained by modesty and prudishness about bodily functions. But he also knew he'd brood if left to his own devices tonight. Sleep would be fitful if it came at all, and he would end up dosing himself with the Ambien he kept in reserve; come morning he'd be unable to drag himself out of bed for an early start for the ten-hour drive to Parkersburg. Besides, Alex Bedrossian was not Ernst Belcher. In Alex's book, punctuality wasn't a virtue, but the telltale sign of a pathetically open social calendar with no prior commitments forcing one to run behind schedule and arrive at the next destination fashionably late. James decided he had enough time for a soak in the tub instead of a quick shower and timed his arrival for sometime between seven forty-five and eight.

After drying off and gelling his hair, he grabbed a bottle of decent Merlot a guest had brought to dinner, slipping it into a Pottery Barn velvet gift stocking. He'd been too shaken by Ernst's announcement for last-minute shopping and, instead, had given the taxi driver the address of his home. He'd kicked off his shoes and gone straight to bed, not bothering to undress, hoping he would awake to discover the afternoon had only been a disturbing dream. Hours later, stuck in the snarling congestion at Columbus Circle, he was still struggling with the not entirely shocking news, mourning not just the sick old man, but also the wide-eyed boy he'd been when he'd arrived in New York, prone to spastic outbursts with each new experience, a young man for whom cynicism was still an affectation and not yet an affliction. Ernst was the last living witness to the opening era of his Manhattan life and, though the German was far from perfect, James had never considered him to be one of the many bad romantic decisions he'd made, a club with many current members and Alex Bedrossian as its president.

Not that he blamed Alex for the end of his relationship with Ernst. Even at his most naïve and inexperienced, James had never been a delusional romantic who believed in storybook romances and happily ever after. The vast age difference between him and Ernst and not a blinding infatuation with a dark and swarthy editorial assistant a few years his junior had been the reason James had finally worked up the courage to walk away and embark on a future without the reassuring training wheels of a controlling but indulgent mentor.

The taxi stopped in front of Alex and Leo's building and, after paying the fare, James impulsively yanked the velvet gift bag off the wine bottle and tossed it on the floor, knowing Leo would snicker that it was tacky. He stood on the sidewalk, hesitating before entering the building, reconsidering the wisdom of going upstairs when he heard a voice calling his name and knew the decision had been made for him.

"Oh, Jesus, James. Are you dreading this as much as I am?"

"More. You cannot believe the day I've had. I just want to go home and crawl into bed with a good book."

"Is that the fashionable euphemism for a two-hundred buck an hour hustler these days?"

Good grief, James wondered. Was the whole world privy to his deepest, darkest erotic secrets?

"I wonder if they think we don't realize they can never find time for us on their dance card the entire season, then insist we all gather for this horrid Christmas reunion to celebrate our undying friendship."

James had shared a house on the Island with Felix for sixteen years and was able to shut out his grating voice as easily as a man can turn off his nagging spouse.

"You know the only reason they ask us is to impress us with the ghastly new additions to their collection in the past year. I want to scream listening to Leo prattle on in that awful Forest Hills accent about the brushstrokes on whatever piece of shit he overpaid for."

James knew Felix, a curator of nineteenth-century painting at the Met, craved Leo's need for his approval of his acquisitions, that withholding his confirmation of the aesthetic value of Leo's expensive investments was the only power he could exert over a boy from Queens who'd amassed unfathomable wealth as a partner at Lazard.

"He bought a Cy Twombly he's dying to show off. Now act surprised when he makes the big announcement, or I'll spill the beans about what I caught you doing in the dunes at six in the morning during the Ascension party last summer," Felix threatened as the doorman signed them into the building.

The curator was clearly agitated as they stepped into the elevator, but, then again, Felix was always bitching about something. James was shocked by how old he looked in harsh lighting and close proximity; it was the ugly price Felix was paying for years of exposing his pale epidermis to carcinogenic ultraviolet rays on the sands of Fire Island and sealing himself in a tanning bed to maintain an unnatural hue throughout the off-season. James had never found Felix attractive, and now his weathered pixie features made him look like an evil imp.

"Is everything okay?" James asked, hoping to be reassured

that all was well. He'd never liked Felix well enough to be concerned about his many self-inflicted problems.

"Just ducky," Felix said sarcastically as they stepped off the elevator. "You may as well hear it from me first. Thomas isn't doing the share this year. And if we don't find someone to take his place, I won't be able to afford it. Maybe we should ask Leo to buy the house and let us stay there for free," he said bitterly, and only half-sarcastically, as they knocked on the door.

James's spirits suddenly lifted. He'd been dreading making his announcement, and now Thomas had done him the great favor of breaking the ice, ensuring that, at worst, his news that he had closed on a summer house in Woodstock would be greeted with resignation instead of anger and resentment. Truth be told, the inevitable breakup of what had once been an envied party house had only been postponed since the day, five years ago, that Leo used his obscenely large annual bonus, enough to justify a Bolshevik revolution, to purchase a Pines house of his own, a place where he and Alex could host fundraisers for GMHC and the Victory Fund and Lambda Legal that would catapult them to an exalted position among the celestial constellation of queer society. James believed the real reason Leo insisted on these annual Christmas reunions, the camaraderie growing more strained and forced with each passing year, was to rub the noses of the housemates, who had once patronized him for his outer borough tastes and loud enthusiasms, in the rewards of his success.

"Time to glitter and be gay!" Felix hissed, smiling through gritted teeth as they heard the dead bolt flipping and the door opened to greet them.

Leo and Alex always hired the most decorative help when entertaining. Aspiring underwear models and chorus boys between shows and even the occasional Juilliard student supplementing his income were always available to willingly, if not particularly skillfully, open doors and take coats and offer canapés. Armando, a tidy package with broad shoulders, a tiny waist, and a blinding smile (probably veneers), was a standard model in the dial-a-waiter catalogue.

"Oh, my God, I *love* your sweater," he gushed breathlessly as he greeted them at the door. "It's Marc Jacobs, isn't it?"

"Of course," Felix beamed, proudly.

James was irritated by Felix's preening, knowing that goddamn sweater had cost him at least eight hundred dollars. He bit his tongue, resisting the urge to remind Felix he might be able to afford his share in the house if he wasn't always maxing out his platinum card on wildly overpriced designer menswear. Armando took James's scarf without comment, causing James to stiffen, slightly indignant, and led them into the front room where the guests were having drinks.

James nodded and followed, though he would have preferred to linger a bit near the front door, in his favorite part of the apartment. Of all the rooms in this beautiful, sprawling, prewar co-op, this was the most impressive. More than the front room with its plaster ceiling and crown moldings and large windows with a view of the park. More than the dining room, large enough for a table that comfortably seated ten, with a magnificent Murano chandelier. More than the spacious kitchen with Sub-Zero appliances and granite counters, plenty of space for the catering staff to work without brushing elbows. This room was a foyer! A foyer, a genuine fucking foyer. A few square feet whose only purpose was to observe comings and goings, the ultimate luxury in the tight, confined living spaces of Manhattan.

"Get in here, you queens. You've got some catching up to do!"

Despite all they had been through, the fights and reconciliations, the betrayals and renewed pledges of emotional if not physical fidelity, after enough melodrama for a Joan Crawford marathon, James's heart still skipped a beat whenever he heard Alex's loud voice, a carnival barker's booming instrument more suited for subway platform conversations than cocktail chatter.

"Greetings, Felix," Alex drawled, his Southern upbringing requiring graciousness to even the most despised guests. "And, you," he said, turning to hug James. "I was afraid you weren't coming, oh love of my life. Armando, make sure these thirsty boys find something to drink."

"Just a club soda for me," James insisted. "Or a Diet Coke, if you have it."

"Don't be ridiculous, James. No one is leaving here sober tonight."

"I had a very liquid lunch with Ernst today at The Box Tree."

Alex scrunched his nose as if he'd been offered a particularly vile turd.

"Is that hideous place still in business? Do you have to be embalmed to get a reservation?"

"Just about," James admitted, debating whether this was the time and place to break the unhappy news of Ernst's illness.

"Scotch and soda, for me. Double malt," Felix ordered with exacting specificity, suspecting that the bartender had been instructed to save the top-shelf liquor for a more fashionable dinner party.

"I love your sweater, Felix. Is it Marc Jacobs?"

Felix smugly accepted the compliment, insisting it was just something he'd pulled out of his closet and thrown on, gloating over his small triumph. He might live in a tiny studio in Murray Hill, and none of his sweaters were paid for, but he could still pull off horizontal stripes with his David Barton–toned body, unlike the soft and lumpy Alex. Not that looking slightly ridiculous would deter Alex from buying and wearing an unflattering sweater or pair of skinny jeans. His utter self-confidence was endearing, to James at least, the reason he'd fallen in love with him.

"Come on in, everyone is dying to catch up with you."

Even the most jaded New Yorkers paused when entering this room, taking a moment to admire the quality and grandeur of the furnishings. Leo had entrusted the lavish appointment of his and Alex's home to the most sought-after professionals, experts in the decorative arts, scholars trained to appreciate the subtle nuances of Duncan Phyfe and English Regency cabinetmakers.

"I want to show you something," Alex said, in that sly, conspiratorial whisper James knew so well. Alex picked up his guest's hand and squeezed, a secret handshake acknowledging he shared a bond with James more significant than with anyone else in the room other than Leo.

"Leo had a fit about this, but I insisted. Look," he said, leading him to the impressive Christmas tree.

Sure enough, prominently displayed in a place of honor on the enormous long-needle pine was a cheap ornament, purchased in a Hallmark's card shop by James for Alex on their first Christmas together. All these years later, James cringed at the sentiment, FOREVER, painted on the glass ball, a tacky eyesore among the exquisite British and German antique ornaments acquired by the decorators. And, regrettably, standing in front of the tree, feeling desperately alone though Alex was by his side, James began to cry.

For all his faults and his many shortcomings, Alex always rose to the occasion in a crisis. He whisked James off to the kitchen without attracting attention and set him down among the busy caterers who were too protective of future lucrative engagements in the household to complain about the obstructions in their midst.

"Drink this," Alex said, handing him a shot of bourbon.

"I'm sorry. I can't believe I just did that."

"What the hell is going on with you?" Alex asked, the words far harsher than his comforting voice.

"Ernst. He has pancreatic cancer."

"Well, did you really think he was going to live forever? What is he? One hundred and six?"

"Don't be sarcastic."

"I'm not, James. For the life of me, I don't understand why you still talk to that nasty old shit."

"I don't know why I still talk to *you!*" he snorted, blowing his nose.

"Because I am utterly irresistible, and you are still madly in love with me," Alex teased, laying on the Blanche DuBois affectations for effect. "And, don't forget darlin', I love you too."

James laughed as he accepted the drink, no words needed to acknowledge that Alex had spoken the absolute truth.

Short and round, cursed even in his leanest youth with budding love handles that had blossomed into the comfy body of a plush toy, Alex Bedrossian would have been described as husky or stocky by the many who were charmed by him and fat by the less charitable, one of them being Felix. He certainly cut a distinctive figure among the chiseled, carbohydrate-starved bodies of his social set. He kept his dark, wiry hair cropped close to his skull after it began thinning in his late thirties. His thick, expressive eyebrows complimented his feral black eyes. He was no beauty, not by a long shot, and some even considered him ugly. But he crackled with energy, burst with enthusiasm, and was gloriously unconstrained by the caution and tentative self-confidence that James wore like a hair shirt. James loved Alex—who, according to the latest *Publishers Weekly,* had just successfully brokered a record-breaking advance from William Morrow for his brand-name-author client's next two military espionage thrillers—for being everything he wasn't.

"I like your hair, James," Alex said, playfully mussing James's still thick mane as James finished his drink. "Are you letting it grow longer?"

"No, I just need a haircut," James admitted, more pleased by the compliment than he should have been.

"Don't. Keep it longer. Silver daddies are all the rage these days. I can't believe you're . . . what? Forty-one? Forty-two?"

"I'm forty-six, and you know it. Which makes you . . ."

"Stop, stop! I can't bear it!" Alex shouted in mock horror, covering his ears with the palms of his hands. "You look much better with gray hair than Leo. He looks like his grandfather with that disgusting hair growing out of his nose. I keep begging him to have it colored, but he refuses. He says an outspoken faggot at Lazard can't afford to seem so trivial that he would care about the color of his hair."

Of course, a faggot at Lazard earning the GNP of a tiny third-world nation was perfectly free to indulge his narcissism in more acceptable, traditionally masculine ways, such as hiring a private trainer to arrive at his co-op at five in the morning, six days a week, to ensure that his waist size never exceeded thirty-two inches. Not that his weight or muscle tone mattered, since Leo's donkey dong and income just below the threshold for the Forbes 400 assured him his choice of the most desirable sexual partners. But Leo still needed to believe his conquests wanted to sleep with him because he was hot and not because he was powerful and almost unimaginably wealthy.

"We need to get back in there before Leo starts to suspect I'm doing you on the kitchen table," Alex laughed. "But I'm worried about you, James. I really am. What's wrong with you? I don't believe you're this down in the dumps because that evil old man is finally dying."

"He is NOT evil. I wish you wouldn't talk like that."

Alex, so used to charming people that even the ones he'd royally fucked asked him to dinner to thank him for his efforts, could only attribute his being the object of Ernst's undying scorn and derision to the old man's vile and corrupt nature. Ernst Belcher, a hoarder, avaricious to his core, had never forgiven Alex for stealing James from him. Never mind that James had grown beyond the age of Ernst's romantic interest and a younger, fairer, and more naïve understudy was already waiting in the wings: All that mattered was that a belonging of Ernst's had been taken from him.

"Have it your way," Alex said, dismissing the subject. "Just don't expect me to believe that the news that old bastard is dying is what put you in such a funk."

James refused to take the bait. Even Alex couldn't pry from him his nagging fear he was going to spend the rest of his life alone. Adolescents and widows might get sympathy for such a heartfelt confession of vulnerability, but a successful New York editor would be exposing himself to a chorus of ridicule and mockery for admitting he desperately missed falling asleep next to someone at night.

"Okay, be that way," Alex said, affectionately, knowing from long experience it was best not to pressure James when he slipped into the occasional miasma of doom and gloom. "Come on! I've got a surprise. Archie Duncan is here, and I've told him all about you."

"Who?"

"Don't go acting all snooty on me and pretending you don't know who Archie Duncan is."

The only Archies James knew were Veronica's boyfriend and Cary Grant.

"He was on that television series for years, the one about the basketball coach who has to take over the drama club. It was a really big hit. You know the one I mean. I loved that show!"

James had never developed Alex's appreciation for double takes and laugh tracks.

"Anyway, he's in New York now. He starts rehearsals for a revival of *Gypsy* in a couple of weeks. He's playing Herbie. You'll like him."

James's summer housemates were in the midst of auditioning for a one-night stand or maybe even something a bit more enduring, like an invitation to attend the opening night of *Gypsy* with the leading man. Felix, scowling by the fireplace, had obviously failed his tryout. Thomas, Philip, and Edward were still in the running, surrounding Archie Duncan in a half circle, laughing too loudly at every amusing syllable that tripped off his tongue.

"I'm not really in the mood for this," James announced to Alex and, instead, drifted over to pay his respects to Leo who was standing alone, admiring the tree.

James, the only one of the housemates with a legitimate reason to hate his host, was, in fact, the only one who genuinely liked him. His fellow refugees from unhappy adolescences in the Deep South or the Midwest openly sneered at the gritty native's slush-pile Queens accent and his roughshod table etiquette. Graduates of elite institutions of higher learning—the Yale School of Architecture, Johns Hopkins School of Medicine, the Rhode Island School of Design—they had come to New York with their polished pedigrees, claiming the city as their birthright, reserving a subtle contempt for the sons and daughters of the natives who had built the metropolis with their sweat and blood, preparing

Gotham for their arrival. Leo's coarse manners, unremarkable in the son of a labor organizer and a kindergarten teacher, hadn't deterred the Wharton School of Business from conferring a Masters of Business Administration on him or Goldman from offering him an entry-level position or the Lazard brethren from inviting him to join the fraternity after the financial press praised him as the reigning genius of derivatives. His former housemates, who had only voted Leo a share when one of the original number dropped out to take a job in Los Angeles, bitterly resented his galvanic rise in the larger world outside their isolated little bubble. Needing some excuse other than envy to justify their antipathy, they claimed to have never forgiven him for crimes against James, refusing to believe that James had actually been relieved when Alex moved into Leo's bedroom in the Island house, never to return to the one he'd long shared with James, knowing Leo was far better equipped to handle Alex's frequent mood swings and perpetual philandering. The longevity and happiness of their partnership was the proof in the pudding.

"What's the matter, buddy? You look like you've lost your best friend," Leo asked.

"Oh, please, don't you start too."

"I won't. I promise you. Now you better get on over there and get in on the action before one of those ugly bitches spoils Alex's carefully laid plans for you."

"I don't think I'm interested," James protested.

Archie Duncan (né Dombroski) was handsome enough in that bland, television leading man sort of way, like George Clooney, with that same studied, unthreatening, puckish twinkle.

"I agree," Leo conceded. "I don't know what all the fuss is about. He laid there like a dead fish when Alex and I had him after the Broadway Cares Christmas benefit last week."

"You probably said the same thing about me."

"Don't be rewriting history, baby. I was invited into *your* bed if I remember correctly. I don't think you were ever attracted to me at all."

"More than you ever knew, Leo. More than you ever knew."

"I expect you'll find yourself seated next to him at dinner, like it or not."

As if on cue, Armando entered the front room and, with great flourish and intonations worthy of the Great Bernhardt, announced that dinner was served.

Archie Duncan proved to be a far more charming dinner companion than his resume would have led James to believe. A proudly working class kid from a Polish and Ukrainian neighborhood in Northeast Philadelphia, he happily answered a fusillade of questions about what so-and-so and you-know-who was "really" like. Leo, sitting across the table from James, snickered and winked an eye, both of them enjoying the spectacle of a group of intellectually snobbish men, accomplished in the fields of architecture, neurology, museum conservatorship, and textile design, gushing over snippets of petty gossip about starlets and pretty boys.

"What about you, James? Isn't there some Hollywood legend whose deep, dark secrets you're dying to know?" Archie asked, soliciting James's opinion for the first time that evening.

James blushed, feeling slightly undeserving of the attentions of a man who had once had an audience of twenty-six million people a week.

"Uh, I don't know. I can't think of anyone."

"James is obsessed with Montgomery Clift," Edward, the neurologist, shouted from the opposite end of the table, competing for his moment in the spotlight.

"Before my time," Archie said.

"Sissy Spacek. James's favorite movie is *Coal Miner's Daughter,*" Philip, the textile designer, sneered, an inside joke about James's home state that went completely over Archie Duncan's head.

"I'm from West Virginia, not Kentucky, and my favorite movie is *The Miracle Worker,*" James protested, wondering how he'd survived so many summers living in close quarters with these vipers.

"The last time I saw Annie Bancroft was at the Golden Globes. She was complaining about her bunions," Archie confided.

"Ugh," James sighed, laughing. "You're destroying the illusion."

The wine—a very, very fine vintage—was starting to cast its spell on the evening. Voices grew louder, multiple conversations raging at once. James, still queasy after the long afternoon, was sipping his glass slowly and was nowhere near drunk, but the harsh edges were fading, and he found himself imagining himself lying in bed with Archie Duncan and how the handsome actor, another lonely soul starved for an emotional connection, would respond to his solicitous and affectionate touch, the antidote to Alex's and Leo's carnal cravings. Then again, maybe he was drunker than he thought, since he seemed to be slipping into sentimental quicksand.

"Okay, enough everybody," Alex announced, tapping his crystal wineglass with a dessert spoon, demanding their undivided attention. "I don't want Archie to go running back to Hollywood saying that all we New York fairies could talk about was Mrs. Robinson's feet. Armando, make sure everyone's glasses are full because now we're going to play a game."

"Oh, come on, Alex. Party games? *The Boys in the Band* was, what, forty years ago?" Thomas protested.

"The proper dramatic reference would be *Who's Afraid of Virginia Woolf?*" Alex sneered. "Here's how you play. Everyone has to tell the story of their worst Christmas ever. Leo, being Jewish, is disqualified, so he's going to be the judge. One rule. No tired old clichés about looking longingly at the Barbie dolls Santa left under the tree for your little sister. Now, who wants to start?"

The entire table was in revolt, preferring to gossip with a genuine Hollywood celebrity.

"Since I don't have any volunteers, I am electing Edward to go first. Proceed without further delay, please."

The neurologist's pathetic tale of witnessing his father back the station wagon over his beloved cocker spaniel Tip on Christmas morning would have been heartbreaking if the doctor, once upon a time a shy country boy from Ohio, could have told a story without sounding like he was reading a pathologist's report.

Felix volunteered to go next, expecting waves of sympathy for the tragic story of losing a fifteen hundred-dollar watch in his mother's garbage disposal trying to unclog the turkey grease in the drain.

"You try finding a plumber in Plano, Texas, willing to do emergency house calls in the middle of Christmas afternoon!" he huffed, after receiving a round of lusty boos for his story.

Thomas's tale of woe involved being stranded in O'Hare for seventy hours, sleeping on the floor and bathing in the sinks, waiting for the blizzard to subside so he could make a connection to Omaha, a story that wasn't even interesting, let alone epic. Archie Duncan had spent one Christmas Eve in the emergency room at Cedars-Sinai after an allergic reaction to peanut oil at Melissa Gilbert's—yes, THAT Melissa Gilbert's—Taste of Thailand holiday buffet. And Philip, whose catastrophes always involved a boyfriend, had arrived back in New York after a three-day visit to his parents' retirement community in Sarasota to discover his partner had changed the locks to the apartment while he was in Florida.

"Boring . . . Boring . . . Boring," Leo announced. "Doesn't anyone want to win the Loving Cup?"

"Buckle your seat belts, boys," Alex crowed. "You're about to hear about my worst Christmas ever, which also happens to be James's worst Christmas ever, but I'm better at telling it, so with your permission, James, I will proceed."

"By all means," James conceded.

"So, after five years of going our separate ways for Christmas, I was finally able to persuade James to come to Birmingham with me, pleading I needed his protection because my daddy was going to kill me when he found out I'd quit my job at Doubleday to try to make it as an agent. He could pop and spit like Mount Vesuvius once you got him irritated."

Unlike most of the men in their circle, who predictably kicked their families a rung or two up the social ladder in their provincial hometowns, Alex didn't exploit time and geography to recreate a more polished, serene, fictionalized version of his early years.

Alex insisted on portraying his Alabama childhood as a particularly raucous episode of *The Simpsons*. The colorful caricatures of a bulging-eyed, sputtering Armenian patriarch and his slightly daft, kindhearted wife bore no resemblance to his reserved and formal parents, the owners of a chain of Oriental rug emporiums, advertised on late-night television across north and central Alabama as perpetually "Going Out of Business, All Prices Slashed." Mom-bo-la and Pop-bo-la, as he'd christened them as a tongue-tied toddler, doted on their only son's every whim.

"So, I said to James after Christmas Eve dinner and a little too much sparkling wine, I have to admit, I said, 'James, I am going to die if we have to sit in this house the rest of the evening with Mom-bo-la and Pop-bo-la and fall asleep watching *White Christmas* on television.' And so we got in the car and drove downtown, where, of course, every bar and club was shuttered and the sidewalks pulled in, and I said, 'James, pull into the back lot, near that door with the red light over the entrance, I think we can find something to drink right there'."

"I wish you could have seen the look on his face when we walked into The Teddy Bear Lounge, scene of my earliest crimes against nature. Every drag queen in Alabama and half of Mississippi was in that tiny room, and the fabulous Miss Brandy Alexander was emcee of the midnight show, and a half dozen horse-hung dancers were shaking their weenies on the bar. I spotted him right away, before James. The most astonishingly beautiful man we had ever laid eyes on, the spitting image of Steve McQueen, military, rough, and masculine. He told us his name was Chance, right out of Tennessee Williams, perfect. . . ."

Actually, his name had been Chauncey, James recalled, but why ruin a good story?

"And I said to James, right then and there, 'That man is our Christmas present to each other.' James, always the practical one, pointed out that Chance was Air Force, on leave, staying with his sister, and, it being Christmas, the motels were full, you know, no room in the inn. . . ."

There were vacancies at every motel in Birmingham, but, again, the truth was rarely conducive to the creation of myth.

"I pointed out to James that Mom-bo-la and Pop-bo-la's room was ALL the way down a long hallway, and they were both heavy sleepers. . . ."

"Oh, God, you didn't! Please tell us you didn't!"

"We most certainly did. Several times, as a matter of fact. Though, it was a bit disappointing as Steve McQueen turned out not to be as impressive as hoped," Alex said, using the universal hand signal for tiny dick. "And not exactly the man we'd expected."

Alex, as always, had his audience eating out of his hand, begging for more.

"Well, Miss Helium Heels was an insatiable bottom, begging us to take turns, and God knows it was fun, until the heat of passion began to subside, and James and I realized that, unfortunately, Chance wasn't as *clean* as one would hope a boy with his particular sexual needs would be."

"Oh, God, stop! Stop! I can't stand it!" the adoring chorus pleaded.

Alex couldn't be deterred, and, in fact, was encouraged by the slapping of the table and the gasping-for-breath, gut-busting laughter.

"And I said to James, 'James, we are just going to have to suck it up and get this room April fresh and Laura Ashley perfect before Mom-bo-la wakes up in the morning.' "

James still recalled the panic striking his heart when he had emerged from the bathroom with an armful of towels and an aerosol can of air freshener and stood face–to-face with Mrs. Bedrossian standing in the hallway, modestly clutching her bathrobe at her neck as she politely inquired if James wanted some help. He thanked his quick wits for coming up with the plausible excuse that he had spilled a large glass of water on the comforter. To his great relief, she never asked why the crisis required a can of Glade Ocean Scent Room Freshener.

"And, after we got that boy all cleaned up to send him on his merry way, why he wrapped a bath towel around his waist and plopped in the armchair, and started waving his foot, announcing he hoped we hadn't finished because he was ready for some more. Just imagine that damn cracker, not having the good sense to stick his tail between his legs and sneak away in shame, luxuriating in my mama's easy chair and telling us he wanted more!"

Leo, of course, had heard this story a thousand times before, but it was still the obvious winner, as a tale of the sexual humiliation of a beautiful man was impossible to beat. After the hearty round of applause finally faded, and the tears of laughter were wiped from their cheeks, Leo stood and invited the group to the unveiling of his Cy Twombly, which had been set up on an easel beside the tree. Philip leaned over and whispered into James's ear, asking if these exhibitions didn't remind him of going to the showroom to look at the new Chevrolets. James was more forgiving, insisting he looked forward to the opportunity to view a great work of art outside the sterile confines of a museum.

Armando was soliciting orders for after-dinner drinks, which James politely declined. He was already plotting an early exit, pleading his monumental trek across the Appalachians in the morning. The closest bathroom was occupied, and he waited a few minutes, hopping from one leg to another, finally deciding Alex and Leo would prefer he invade the inner sanctum of the apartment searching for available plumbing rather than pee all over their hardwood floors.

He was taking one of those long, grateful-to-be-alive pisses when someone jiggled the doorknob, following with a light tapping on the door when their entrance was barred.

"Just a minute. I'm almost finished," James insisted, irritated by the rude impatience of the intruder.

"It's me. Open the door."

James unlocked the door, and Alex slipped inside quickly, his hands down James's pants in record time, his mouth eager for a kiss.

"Come on, Alex. Cut it out," James protested, amused by his

former lover's predictability. The opportunity for a little quickie with his old boyfriend while Leo was under the same roof, only a few rooms away, was too exciting for Alex to resist.

"Why?" Alex insisted, trying to force James's pants to his knees. "We haven't done it in, what? Forever?"

"I'll make a deal with you. If you find me so irresistible, then come over to my place one night next week, and we can get undressed and lie in bed and I'll make love to you without needing to worry about Leo's breaking down the door,"

"Okay," Alex sighed, disappointed.

James's fast thinking had gotten him off the hook without offending Alex, who he knew had no interest in leisurely lovemaking with no risk or possibility of being caught in the act.

"I have to pee anyway," Alex said, as James closed the door behind and walked down the hallway, where he encountered Archie Duncan peeking into doorways, searching for a place to empty his bladder.

"There you are, James. I was looking for you. I was worried you'd left."

"There's a bathroom at the end of the hall. The door's closed, but no one's in there. Just walk right in," James offered, chuckling at the thought of sending an innocent man into the mouth (literally) of danger.

"Be back in a minute," Archie promised, and James, without saying good-bye to anyone, asked Armando for his scarf and took the elevator six floors to the lobby where he found a cab conveniently waiting to take him away.

Tomorrow morning was hours away, and James wasn't quite ready to go home. He wanted to feel fresh and young and full of expectation, and, in Manhattan, there was only one place a middle-aged man in need of a drink could go to feel like chicken, so he gave the cabdriver the address of The Townhouse.

As usual, the bar was packed with gentleman of a certain age who looked to be out long past their bedtimes. They gathered in the piano lounge, sipping strong drinks through swizzle sticks, singing their blessed little hearts out. A quartet requested Irving Berlin's "Snow" and received an appreciative round of applause for a rendition that matched the classic movie version note-for-note. A dark-haired boy, conspicuous in an oversized, hooded parka, sidled up next to James, trying to make eye contact. James walked away, preferring to engage his hustlers through respectable agencies, and retreated to a quiet corner to be alone with his thoughts.

He'd had every intention of announcing his recent life-altering decision to become an Ulster County property owner to his soon-to-be former housemates tonight, but, somehow, the opportunity to casually introduce the subject into the dinner conversation never arose. He was going to have to take the coward's way out and present it to them in writing, something short and kind, the kind of correspondence he would want to receive if he was getting the grand kiss-off from someone he'd spent entire summers with for most of his adult life. It was probably for the better, breaking the news in a formal letter, delivering a controlled message that the time had arrived for new and different adventures. He didn't want to risk any hurtful casual words or remarks since, Felix aside, he was fond of each of them. But the truth was, they depressed him, them and the entire Fire Island scene. The nagging feeling that an era of his life had passed and it was time to move on had crystallized last summer as the sun rose on the beach and he found himself bobbing and weaving in a sea of dancing, shirtless men, many of a certain age, their hair closely cropped or shaved to camouflage telltale signs of graying or balding, their bodies shaped and defined by protein diets and free weights, their eyes, glazed by pharmaceuticals and exhaustion, squinting into the blinding rays of morning. Zombies, that's what they resembled. Zombie lemmings cursed by the desire for eternal youth and perpetual adolescence.

He could never hate the Island and still longed for the Cherry Grove of his youth, the magical place of quiet evenings in Ernst's tiny cottage, sitting Indian-style on the braided carpets in the soft glow of the kerosene lamps, listening to writers he had admired in college swap recipes for lamb biryani and argue the merits of the translators of the Russian masterworks. But age and mortality and exorbitant real estate prices had swept away the past like the winter storms that ravaged the dunes, and Fire Island Pines had become the playground of investment bankers and insurance executives and bankruptcy lawyers from Wall Street firms, a place where status was ranked by perfect abdomens and access to a supply of party drugs.

"So it was a success?"

James was shaken from his reverie by the sudden appearance of a vaguely familiar face.

"I beg your pardon?" he asked.

"The tie. Did your friend like the tie? Blood orange. Unusual color."

"I am so sorry. I didn't mean to be rude," James apologized, recognizing the clerk who had sold him Ernst's tie that morning.

"No apology necessary. Happens all the time. No one remembers me out of context," the clerk laughed.

"Yes. Yes. He loved it. He even took off the one around his neck so he could wear it. Thanks for your help."

"Don't thank me. I would have recommended something quieter, but you obviously know your friend's taste."

James refrained from commenting that the lavender cravat the sales clerk was wearing wasn't exactly subtle.

"I wouldn't have chosen it for myself, of course. A bright standard rep tie is my limit on outrageousness," James confessed, resenting being so insecure that he felt it necessary to defend his good taste to a supercilious stranger.

"Oh, my God, I don't believe it," the clerk gasped, his attention completely distracted. "I think that's Archie Duncan over at the bar. I read in the *Post* he's been cast in a revival of *Gypsy*."

It was the perfectly awful ending to a perfectly awful day. James wished he could fade into the wallpaper, an invisibility act worthy of a Marvel Comics superhero. With any luck, a swarm of fans would descend on Archie Duncan, demanding autographs and offering e-mail addresses and telephone numbers. James would slip by unnoticed and disappear into the night.

"James! James! Over here. Over here!"

The sales clerk was suitably impressed that the customer with the terrible taste in ties was on a first-name basis with Archie Duncan.

"You're going to introduce us I hope?" he asked, a demand masquerading as a question.

"Sorry, I can't," James said, wanting to slap down this presumptuous little ribbon clerk's hands. "I don't know your name."

"Damn, I didn't expect to see you here," Archie said, as James joined him at the bar. "I came looking for you, and they told me you'd left without saying good-bye."

"I apologize. My mother didn't bring me up to be rude. I've got no excuse for running off like that," James replied, feeling a bit childish for enjoying the envious glances he was receiving as a friend-of-Archie-Duncan.

"Why do I get this strange feeling you don't like me?"

James squirmed, wanting to be home in bed, sound asleep, the sheets pulled over his head.

"That's not true. I don't even know you. How could I not like you?"

"When you've been on television for, oh, a hundred years, people assume they know you."

"I've never even seen your show."

He regretted sounding incredibly snotty, like one of those culture snobs forever prattling on about high art—performances at Lincoln Center, gallery exhibitions, the latest releases from small university presses—while feigning complete and utter ignorance of the household names whose escapades are documented by *Entertainment Tonight* and *Us Weekly*. He felt a sudden urge to confess his addiction to *That '70s Show* to purge his conscience.

"Do you know Ashton Kutcher?" he blurted out.

Archie Duncan clearly had a sense of humor.

"It took you four hours to think of a celebrity to ask about, and that's who you could come up with?"

"Look," James said. "It had to be awkward for you, Alex practically pushing me onto your lap. I think he expected us to fuck under the dining room table. I know how he is. Believe me. No one likes having someone shoved down their throat, and I didn't want you to get the impression I'd been begging him for an introduction."

"That was sweet of you to be so considerate of my feelings."

"Not really."

"And funny."

"Why was it funny?"

"Because I asked Alex to introduce us."

James was stunned by the admission, it having been a long time since he had been an object of curiosity, let alone of desire.

"I invited them for a drink at the apartment I'm subletting after being introduced to them at a fundraiser. Come to think of it, I'm pretty sure they invited themselves after they tricked me into offering to share a cab with them. Alex picked up a book I'm reading and asked if I liked it."

James was pleasantly surprised Archie Duncan wasn't the type to volunteer the salacious details of the erotic conquest.

"I told him I loved it. It's a new American classic. He told me he knew the editor."

The gem of a memoir that had won the former President the National Book Award and selection as one of the *New York Times* Ten Best Books of the Year continued to reap rewards, none as unexpected as the interest of—yes, James would now concede under close, personal inspection—an extremely good-looking and charming man.

"I know what you're going to say. You didn't think anyone in Los Angeles knew how to read."

"No, I wasn't going to say that. I swear," James protested.

"I know you weren't," Archie Duncan teased, playfully squeezing James's arm.

"So what deep, dark secrets can I reveal about our beloved former Commander in Chief? What would you like to know?"

"Only what's in the book. Even a President is entitled to his privacy. Is he working on a second volume?"

James smiled cryptically, a look that could be interpreted as *can't talk about it yet.* The sad news was not yet public. In the first quarter of the New Year, the former First Lady would be announcing that the President's royalties had been donated to an Alzheimer's research foundation that would thereafter carry his name. James had never embraced the man's politics but had grown to love him and his careful precision with words and sentences; now the multi-volume epic they'd once envisioned, a work to stand beside the memoirs of Grant, would never be written.

Archie was far more erudite than James would have expected for a man who had earned a fortune by his impeccable comic timing and skillful delivery of punch lines. He'd read many of the popular biographies James had edited. His passion was American history, and he was particularly fascinated by the industrial titans of the late nineteenth and early twentieth century. His dream project, an epic-length history of the Homestead strike, had been in development for almost ten years and gone through five screenwriters and seven scripts.

"Thank God, I won't be too old to play Andrew Carnegie until I'm seventy-five," he laughed. "One more for the road?"

"I have a long drive ahead of me tomorrow."

"No excuse. So do I."

"Where are you going?"

"Philadelphia."

"Philadelphia! You can walk to Philadelphia from here!"

"Exactly. Which is why I'm in no rush."

"Well, I have to be on the road by seven."

"That's hours away. You can get into a lot of trouble between now and daybreak."

"I know. That's why I'm going to call it a day."

"I don't have to stay all night. You can kick me out after you've had your way with me."

Archie Duncan's smile could be interpreted several ways: either the comment was all in jest, a harmless bit of fun, or it was a formal declaration of interest. James felt himself wavering, intrigued by the possibility of a night of lust and passion with a television star. It was flattering. Hell, it was more than flattering; it was downright amazing that a man like Archie Duncan was interested in him. Then again, if ever there was an occasion to not be impulsive, this was it. They were middle-aged men, after all, and years of experience had taught James the sweet rewards to be gained by taking things slowly and exercising patience.

"I told you I was a stickler for good manners. I would never throw a guest out on the streets in the middle of the night. And I'm out of milk and coffee, and I'd hate to send you on your way without breakfast."

Archie laughed and grabbed a cocktail napkin off the bar and asked the bartender for a pen. He scribbled his number and shoved the rumpled paper in James's pocket.

"Let me give you mine," James said.

"Not necessary. Alex already gave it to me. So, are you free New Year's Eve?"

"Yes," he said, regretting his quick response, fearing it made him sound like a loser.

"I will pick you up at eight. And don't worry. I'll bring my own toothbrush so I taste all minty fresh when I kiss you good morning."

The good-night kiss was friendly, chaste. James certainly wasn't going to compromise a Page Six celebrity by swapping spit in the face of his curious public.

It was significantly colder on the street, as the temperature had dropped sharply after midnight. James pulled his scarf around his neck and shoved his hands in his pockets, stamping his feet for warmth as he waited for an empty cab. He looked at his watch. It was only twelve-thirty, hardly the witching hour. He felt old beyond his years, a middle-aged stick in the mud who had just passed up an opportunity to sleep with a bona fide leading man who was interested enough to have gotten his number from Alex. Was he so goddamn ancient he wouldn't be able to survive on three or four hours sleep tomorrow, especially knowing he could practically hibernate in West Virginia the rest of the week? Alex would be ashamed of him. Christ, he was ashamed of himself. What self-respecting gay man turned down an opportunity to have sex with Archie Duncan to ensure he got his proper beauty rest? He turned on his heels and marched back to The Townhouse, his face flush with anticipation, actually feeling the stirring of an erection in his pants, only to stop dead in his tracks halfway across the crowded barroom, seeing that Archie Duncan was otherwise occupied, locked in a tongue-chewing embrace with one of his adoring fans.

Whoever wrote there's no place like home for the holidays never had to travel more than a mile to reach the family hearth by Christmas morning. Year after year, James had made the annual pilgrimage to LaGuardia, watching the meter run while he sat in stalled traffic, shuffling through security, and rushing to the gate only to be slapped with the announcement of a three-hour delay. He could always count on United Airlines to lose his luggage or overbook the plane or seat him beside a screaming baby. Never again, he swore, after last year when he missed his connection at National and had to pay a king's ransom to upgrade to the only available seat on the last flight to Charleston, West Virginia, still a one-hour drive in a rental car to his final destination. Why not put the snappy little BMW 3 Series he kept in the city for summer weekend jaunts to the Fire Island ferries to good use? He would drive west through Jersey, dip south through Pennsylvania and Maryland, and be at his mother's house on the western side of West Virginia for dinner.

Clouds were massing on the horizon, chasing the early morning sunshine by the time he headed south on Interstate 81. But the gloomy skies couldn't dampen his soaring mood. He had John Fahey and Joanie Baez's Christmas albums on disc, records he had loved since college, and, with each mile, Ernst and Alex and the fates of old boyfriends faded further from his thoughts. It was the perfect opportunity to compose his New Year's resolutions. He had a marvelous idea, encouraged by the agent from whom he'd just bought a revisionist biography of James K. Polk; he would keep a journal about his restoration of his country cottage, with an eye toward publishing it as a memoir. He would spend his summer recording the life cycles of the insects that nested in the eaves of his new home rather than studying the mating habits of privileged, narcissistic men on a barrier island in the Atlantic. He would learn to embrace the pleasures of solitude, retiring early to bed with a book and rising to appreciate the sunrise with his first coffee of the morning. His weekend guests would be intelligent if not intellectual, curious, with surprising interests, men like Archie Duncan. They would drink more tea than liquor. The drive was passing pleasantly. He was making great time, way ahead of schedule, already miles beyond Harrisburg, Pennsylvania. It was the easiest Christmas sojourn ever, and he was absolutely convinced it was the best idea he'd ever had, right up to the minute the engine died on the Interstate 76, his punishment for ignoring the little red light, MAINTENANCE REQUIRED, that had been flashing on the dashboard since sometime after the Fourth of July.

Which is how James found himself in the passenger seat of a tow truck, sitting beside a three hundred pound ogre whose right earlobe looked like it had been chewed by a starving pit bull. His rescuer was wearing a filthy Steelers jersey, size sixteen boots, and a bright orange hunter's hat that provided some slight reassurance that small game, not human prey, had shed the blood that stained the floor of the truck.

"This goddamn weather is a fucking bitch," the driver growled as he squinted into the driving rain pounding against the windshield.

The exit ramp off the turnpike announced they were approaching Breezewood, Pennsylvania, the self-proclaimed Town of Motels.

"Guess I'm lucky, breaking down here instead of somewhere else," James said, trying to force a little holiday cheer into the gloom.

"Why's that?" the driver asked, fumbling in his shirt pocket for a pack of matches.

James decided it wouldn't be wise to ask him not to smoke.

"Not much chance anyone is going to tell me there's no room in the inn in the Town of Motels," he said.

The driver gave him a blank look, no wattage in his eyes, as if he'd never heard the tale of the Christ Child's birth.

"You know, like 'Away in a manger, no crib for his bed,'" James said, fumbling, wishing he'd kept his damn mouth shut.

The beast in the black and gold jersey scowled at the lame attempt at seasonal humor, his eyes narrowing into threatening slits, wary of being patronized by some suspiciously soft stranger driving a luxury car with a price tag higher than his annual salary.

"Where you from?" he asked in an accusing voice.

"West Virginia. Parkersburg. On the Ohio River. An hour north of Charleston," James answered truthfully, not lying about his place of birth.

"How come you have New York plates?" the driver demanded, determined to make his captive prisoner confess.

"When can someone look at the car?" James asked, trying to change the subject.

"Not until day after tomorrow. No one works on Christmas Day," he said, pulling a flask out of his pocket and, in the spirit of the season, offering James a nip. "So where you want me to drop you off?" he asked.

James could see the man was anxious to start celebrating a traditional redneck Christmas thirty-six-hour drinking marathon. He stared out the window at the phalanx of bright motel signs, each one promising cable TV, premium channels, and free continental breakfasts. Quality Court. Quality Inn. Red Roof Inn. Holiday Inn. Travelodge.

"That one," he said, pointing at the Howard Johnson's Motor Lodge up ahead to the right, seduced by happy memories of clam strips and peppermint-stick ice cream, wistfully longing for a roadside America that had vanished thirty years ago.

The driver snorted when James wished him Merry Christmas as he pulled away, dragging the fickle luxury vehicle behind him. The motel registration office was damp and moldy, and the lingering smell of industrial-strength cleaning solvents quickly doused the flickering flame of Ho Jo nostalgia. The Bengali matron at the front desk was polite yet insistent, somehow managing to seem deferential as she rushed him through check-in. Her sari was the traditional orange of a Howard Johnson's rooftop, but there was no sign of Simple Simon and the Pieman and no dining room or counter. She pointed to a pair of vending machines when he asked where he could get something to eat. The selection on the Christmas menu was barbecue chips, Butterfingers, and Diet Dr. Pepper.

"You don't have a restaurant?" he asked. He felt cheated, scammed, the victim of an unconscionable fraud. This was supposed to be Howard Johnson's! Where were the frankfurters grilled in butter and macaroni and cheese?

"Restaurant over there. One half mile," she said, pointing toward the front window and a soaring neon sign, high enough to be seen from the turnpike ridge, announcing that KAY'S KOZY KORNER was the place in town to EAT.

The rain was still coming down hard as he trudged to his room, but the temperature was dropping rapidly. Winter was arriving just ahead of Santa Claus, and he cursed himself for leaving his gloves and hat in the car.

It was almost seven o'clock when he called his mother to break the news he wouldn't be arriving for at least another day and a half. He complained about the shabby state of the hospitality industry, hoping for a little sympathy and maybe leniency for the unpardonable sin of having ruined her Christmas. It was obvious from the tone of her voice she wasn't buying his story and suspected he was actually still in the 10022 zip code area and on his way to a hoity-toity holiday party with his glamorous New York friends.

"Little Carol Ann will be devastated," she insisted.

"Little Carol Ann will somehow find the strength to survive."

Carol Ann, the daughter of James's sister, was hosting her first Christmas Day dinner as a married woman, a celebration guaranteed to be a *Martha Stewart Living* and Costco nightmare in the spirit of the ghastly wedding celebration he'd attended in June, with eleven attendants and enough pomp and circumstance for the betrothal of a Windsor.

"I'll be there as soon as I can," he promised, unable to convince her that, under the current circumstances at least, there was no place in the world he'd rather be than sitting down at his mother's table on Christmas Eve for country ham and ninety-proof eggnog.

"It won't be the same," she said, hanging up to pull her pumpkin pie from the oven.

He was too wired to sleep, so he showered and changed into dry clothes and ventured out on a scavenger hunt for something edible. The rain had changed to a steady snow that had quickly blanketed the streets and rooftops. The winter storm transformed the Town of Motels into a department store–window Enchanted Village. The inflatable Santas and Frostys and Rudolphs, their power cords buried in snowdrifts, seemed animated by magic. He took a short detour, making a pilgrimage to the illuminated crèche on the lawn of the First Lutheran Church. The town was perfectly still, the only sound the crunch of fresh snow under his feet. He shoved his freezing hands in his pockets and, through swirling gusts of snowflakes, headed toward the EAT sign, quietly singing "Away in a Manger."

The door flew open as he approached, and only his quick reflexes enabled him from narrowly escaping a broken nose. The tow truck ogre stumbled out of the restaurant, fumbling with his keys, staring at James wild-eyed, no glint of recognition on his face. James slipped past him, pitying anyone the man encountered on the icy roads tonight, and stepped into a thick fog of cigarette smoke. Christmas cheer was flowing from the beer taps. Holiday revelers, mugs in hand, already six sheets to the wind, were howling along to Springsteen's "Santa Claus is Coming to Town" on the jukebox. It was a rough-looking crowd, weathered by hard work and hard drinking. The girls wore Santa caps and NFL gear, and there was nothing jolly about the distended, swollen bellies of the men. A fight broke out at the pool table, and a tray of bottles and glasses shattered on the floor before a fierce-looking dyke in a snowflake sweatshirt could hustle the pugilists out the door.

"Merry Christmas," the boy behind the bar hollered. "What are you drinking?"

"Can I get a menu?" James shouted over the scalps of the drinkers hunkered down at the bar, arguing over the best way to eliminate the Muslim threat to their godly American way of life.

"You got a choice. Popcorn or pretzels," the kid laughed, pointing at the baskets of bar snacks. "The cook called out sick. It's on me," he said, refusing James's money as he handed him a shot of Crown Royal and a frosted mug of Bud Light.

The boy bounced along the bar, cheerfully pouring booze, taking bills, and handing back the change. He knew all the customers by name and smiled through the abuse that was heaped upon him whenever one of the regulars had to wait longer than twenty seconds for a drink. James was tired and hungry, and the whiskey went straight to his head. He set down his empty mug, ready to call it an early night, when another round appeared on the bar. He waved his palm and shook his head, but the young man insisted he accept the drinks. He figured he should at least tip the kid for his generosity, but the boy frowned and wagged his finger.

"Your money's no good here tonight. Can't accept it," he said, turning away to appease the loudmouthed drunk who was cursing him for neglecting his empty glass.

The motel was within stumbling distance, even in a blizzard, and James deserved to get a little buzz going after the shitty two days he'd had. He tipped the shot glass to his lips and let the whiskey burn his throat. The bartender looked like a college kid, barely legal drinking age, tall, square-jawed, with bright green eyes and a mop of floppy hair. He had the type of sharp features that would grow into a rugged masculinity as the soft layer of baby fat around his jaw and chin melted away with age. His voice, even when shouting, had an eager-to-please pitch that was slightly feminine, but his imposing size, six feet two or three, with broad shoulders, kept him from seeming swishy or gay. He winked when he caught James staring at him—nothing lascivious, just a friendly gesture, a secret message to a stranger who'd wandered into his bar that they were kindred spirits, fellow travelers, despite the obvious twenty or twenty-five-year differences in their ages.

"What's your name?" he asked, as he splashed Absolut and cranberry juice into a glass for a tough-looking babe who'd wedged herself into the crush of drinkers, staking her claim with an elbow planted firmly on the bar.

"What's his name, Jason?" she slurred, as she gave James the once-over, her piercing stare made even more unsettling by a lazy left eye.

"Jimmy," he said, surprising himself by using the name he'd been called in his Appalachian boyhood, the name that no one outside of West Virginia but Ernst had ever used.

"What did he say, Jason?"

"He said his name is Jimmy."

"Where's he from?" she asked, as she fumbled with a crumpled pack of cigarettes.

James, figuring he was safer admitting he was a New Yorker here than he would have been in the tow truck, had an odd, irresistible urge to impress the young bartender. "I live in New York," he said.

"La-di-da," the woman sneered, unimpressed. "You're too old for Jason, Mr. New York. You hear that, Jason? He's too old for you."

Something across the room caught her attention, and she suddenly lost interest, making a beeline for the jukebox where the dyke in the snowflake sweatshirt and a mullet-coiffed fireplug were looking awfully cozy, singing along to "Merry Christmas, Darling."

"Who's she? Your mother?" James joked, pretending to be miffed by the concerned intervention.

"Who? Wendy?" he laughed. "You got to be kidding. No. *That's* my mother," he said, pointing at Miss Snowflake Sweater. "Aunt Wendy's her girlfriend."

James figured he was stone drunk, hearing strange voices, and hallucinating that a lesbian militia had invaded this hillbilly backwater on Christmas Eve. He tossed back another shot—his third, or was it fourth?—and cradled a mug of beer while Jason placated the restless natives demanding another round.

"I love New York," the boy shouted as he worked the taps. "I'm gonna move there."

Sure you are kid, James snickered. Your senior class probably went to Manhattan for a field trip. Times Square was awesome, and *Wicked* changed your life. You're going to find a great apartment like Will's from *Will & Grace* and land a fabulous job as an assistant to a fashion designer or Broadway producer who will recognize you as a genius. In a year, maybe sooner, you'll be rich and famous and have an even richer and more famous boyfriend who will always be faithful and, after New York legalizes gay marriage, you'll have a beautiful wedding and an announcement in the Styles section of the Sunday *Times*. Christ almighty, he thought, shocked by his cruel cynicism; he was sounding like Felix and his bitter summer housemates. When did little Jimmy Hoffmann of Parkersburg, West Virginia, become such a misanthrope, he wondered?

"Right after I graduate," Jason declared.

"You know New York is pretty expensive. Maybe you should get a job first," James said, feeling oddly protective of this merry, open-faced boy. The booze was making him feel paternal toward this naïve kid and sentimental enough to romanticize the little hick from Parkersburg who spent his entire four years at UVA imagining his wonderful life in the bright lights of the magnificent island he had only seen on television and at the movies.

"Oh, I have a job. I interned in a recording studio last summer, and they offered me an apprentice engineer position. I start in June."

James couldn't picture this big country boy, handsome but unpolished, his vowels thickened by a mountain drawl, surviving the city. James was probably confused, hearing only bits and pieces of the conversation, distracted by the deafening racket of a packed barroom. . . . Did the kid say he'd been an intern? Where? Doing what? James had already forgotten. He was moving beyond a pleasant buzz, well on his way to becoming staggeringly drunk. Time to cut himself off and find his way back to the motel. But his new best friend behind the bar had different ideas.

"Cheers," the boy said, pouring two more Crown Royals and proposing a toast. "Nice to meet you, Jimmy. Merry Christmas and Happy New Year."

Jason swallowed his shot and winked again. His cheerful smile, all cheeks and bright, straight teeth, made it impossible for the gesture to look as dirty and suggestive as he intended.

"Don't you be disappearing on me, Jimmy. Mom says I have to close the bar tonight."

James stood by the bed, trying to steady himself, rocking on the balls of his feet.

"Okay, okay, I'm coming," he croaked, hoping to silence the persistent pounding that had roused him from blissful oblivion.

He opened the door and threw his forearm across his face, shielding his bloodshot eyes from the blinding sunlight reflected off the fresh, clean snowdrifts. He was greeted with a Merry Christmas and an awkward peck on the cheek as Jason swept past him, a large bottle of water in one hand and a paper cup of steaming coffee in the other.

"I figured you'd need these. And I wanted to make sure you were awake. You look like you could sleep through the day. Here, drink this first," he said, handing James the water.

He chugged the entire bottle without taking a breath. His dehydrated body could have absorbed three of the five Great Lakes.

"How's your head?" Jason asked.

Not bad actually, considering the amount of alcohol he'd consumed last night.

"You almost bit off my fingers when I forced you to swallow those aspirin last night."

"You know too much about hangovers for a kid," James protested, his raspy voice cracking and breaking like a pubescent boy's. Christ, had he been smoking last night too?

"My mother owns a bar. Remember?"

He did, vaguely. It was coming back into focus. The noise. The whiskey and the beer. Someone pulling a gun and waving it at a suspect girlfriend. Pissing on his shoes at the urinal. Something about Boston and the Berklee College of Music. "Rudolph the Red-Nosed Reindeer." James standing on the bar singing "Rudolph the Red-Nosed Reindeer." Falling on his ass on the ice. A pair of dykes laughing and swearing as they dragged him from the car and threw him on the bed. This boy, Jason, yanking off his pants and pulling the blanket up to his chin, wishing James sweet dreams as he gave him a chaste good-night kiss on the forehead. And, God, no, please, no, yes, yes, he did: James grabbing the kid by the arm and pulling him down on the mattress, pleading with him to spend the night, promising he wouldn't touch him, just sleep, all he wanted was to sleep with him.

"I gotta get back to church for eleven o'clock Mass. I'll pick you up around twelve-thirty. You didn't forget, did you?"

James must have looked perplexed.

"You're coming to my mom's for Christmas dinner. It'll be fun."

He grabbed James's unshaven cheeks and kissed him on his stale, sour mouth.

"I've been wanting to do that since the first minute I saw you," Jason said, blushing as he turned to leave, leaving James stunned, his knobby knees shaking and a boner stirring in the baggy crotch of his boxers.

* * *

According to Jason, three and half million cars exit the turnpike through Breezewood every year, but not a single soul actually lives there. They sped past the last stoplight at the edge of town and plunged into the wilderness, James's still bloodshot eyes protected from the snow glare by a pair of borrowed sunglasses.

"You're not kidnapping me, are you? I don't want to end up like *Texas Chainsaw Massacre*," he chuckled, joking of course, but slightly apprehensive about leaving the last evidence of civilization, such as it was, miles behind.

"Don't worry. You're in Pennsylvania. The serial killers are much cuter up here."

Jason reached over, squeezed James's knee, and growled, doing a damn good imitation of a buzzsaw.

"Do you have a boyfriend?" Jason asked.

"No, I don't have a boyfriend."

"Nice."

"Do you know how old I am?"

"Old enough to have a lot of gray hair."

Well, only since last summer, when he stopped coloring it after the famous cable news anchor he was blowing in the Meat Rack on the Island commented that James's hair was the same shade of purple as the bruise on his elbow.

"What makes you so sure I'm gay?" James challenged him, changing the subject.

"Um . . . could it have been . . . maybe . . . let me think . . . the P-town sweatshirt you were wearing last night?"

"What do you know about P-town?" he asked, sounding awfully petulant and irritated for a man who would be forty-seven on his next birthday. James actually hated Provincetown, but had grown attached to the baggy, comfortable sweatshirt the choir director he'd briefly dated had never reclaimed after the breakup.

"I told you last night. I live in Boston."

Yes, yes he did. Berklee College of Music. He was a dual major, studying music production and engineering, because he needed to make a living, and performance, because guitar was his passion, the most important thing in his life. He intended to support himself working in the studio and play at every open mike in every coffeehouse and dive bar in Manhattan and Brooklyn, Queens even, until he got his big break. James was ashamed at sneering at the dreams of this kid who was so much better prepared to take on New York than a certain naïve young alumnus of Charlottesville who'd arrived in Gotham with a degree in English and great ambitions only to discover that the hiring editors at Scribner's and Knopf weren't interested in anything on his resume except the score on his typing test.

"I'm glad you don't have a boyfriend," Jason said, his goofy grin illuminating his face. "I like older guys."

James smiled and shook his head no, discouraging him, then turned and stared at the pristine fields outside the window, thinking about Ernst, wondering how he was spending what was likely his last Christmas and remembering once being a boy who had liked older guys too.

Wendy was sprawled on the living room floor, her head and shoulders wedged between the wall and the Christmas tree.

"Flip the switch!" she shouted, apparently not passed out, then bounced up on her feet, mission accomplished, the locomotive of a classic Lionel Pennsylvania Flyer O-Gauge Freight Train set successfully relaunched after derailing off the platform.

"It never runs off the track where it's easy to reach," she sighed, resigned to the misfortunes of model railroading. It was a damn impressive display: two freight trains, the Pennsy and Chesapeake and Ohio lines, running on multiple level tracks through a scale model of the Town of Motels.

"Aunt Wendy, you remember my friend Jimmy from last night?"

She took a deep breath and drew herself up to full height, an impressive five two at best. She seemed a bit softer than she had last night in her fuzzy white holiday vest with red yarn candy canes embroidered on the panels, but her voice was as intimidating as it had been in the bar.

"He's still too old for you, Jason. But I'm not your mother," she said, her lazy eye drifting toward the train platform.

"Leave him alone," the lady of the house barked, setting a tray with an orange cheese ball and Ritz crackers on the coffee table.

James felt his heart jump in his chest, unfairly convicted and sentenced for a crime he hadn't committed. He panicked, worried she'd witnessed his embarrassing outburst while being tucked into bed.

"Look," he blurted, "I'm not planning on robbing any cradles."

Jason's mother cocked an eyebrow and grumbled in a low, threatening voice.

"What's the matter? Our Jason isn't good enough for you?"

"Ma," the boy pleaded. "She's just messing with you, Jimmy. Ma, leave him alone. It's Christmas."

She giggled apologetically, a tough woman turning unexpectedly shy and girlish as she capitulated to her child.

"Jason, why don't you tell your friend to have a seat."

"His name's Jimmy, Mama."

She extended her hand for a formal introduction.

"Kay Previc. Very nice to meet you. Again."

She cut a wedge of cheese and offered it to him on a cracker. Aunt Wendy poured out four glasses of sparkling cider and proposed a toast.

"I don't keep alcohol in the house," Kay announced. "We see enough of that at the bar. No need to bring it into our home."

James felt a bit defensive, suspecting she'd made a wrong assumption about his relationship with alcohol based on his completely out-of-character behavior the prior night.

"I'm not a big drinker anyway," he asserted.

"There's nothing wrong with being a drinker. That's how I put food on the table and gas in the tank."

He simply nodded, it being obvious that even his most conciliatory attempts at polite conversation would be challenged. Aunt Wendy tossed back her cider, twitchy and nervous, resigned to the imposition of Prohibition in the household.

"It's very nice you could join us today," Kay declared after a long, awkward silence.

"Thank you for having me," he mumbled, trying to swallow a mouthful of dry, salty cheddar.

The strain of trying to entertain her guest was exhausting, and Kay quickly abandoned any pretense of playing hostess and sank into an easy chair in front of the television, falling dead asleep during the second half of a Pistons / Mavericks holiday showdown. Jason suggested they go for a walk, obviously wanting to take advantage of this opportunity to spend a few moments alone. He lent James a wool cap and a pair of gloves and looped a scarf around his neck, pulling it gently, a maternal touch, solicitous. The borrowed rubber boots fit well enough over James's shoes, a little large maybe, but manageable.

The sun had lost its midday brilliance, and the afternoon had turned a soft, pale gray. Another storm was massing above the mountain range, and the wind was rising again, rustling through the naked tree branches.

"I think it's going to snow again," James said, worried about being stranded in this desolate outpost where snowplows seldom ventured, certainly never on Christmas Day.

"It will be real pretty when it does. Wait and see," Jason said, beckoning James to follow him down a steep, ice-crusted lane that descended through a thicket of soaring birch trees.

"Are you okay?" he asked, turning and reaching for James's hand.

"Sure," he said, his uncertain footing betraying his false bravado.

A dog barked in the distance, and some unseen creature bolted through the dense undergrowth. Jason was standing at the bottom of the hill, holding a broken branch like a staff. He lifted it above his head and brought it crashing back to earth, puncturing the sheath of ice beneath his feet. The water gurgled as it raced below the cracked frozen surface.

"Don't worry," he laughed. "It's only a shallow creek. No danger of drowning."

Still, the crunchy crush of yielding ice wasn't reassuring. James liked his toes too much to lose them to frostbite.

"We're standing on the Susquehanna watershed. When I was a little kid I dreamed about building a raft and taking it all the way to the ocean."

"Like Huckleberry Finn."

"Yeah," he laughed. "Except I've never read that book, but I think I saw the movie."

He took a lumbering step toward James, threw open his arms, and wrapped him in a tight bear hug. The dull white sun was barely visible behind a shroud of thin, hazy clouds.

"My dad shot himself down here when I was eight," he confided. "On the first day of school after Christmas. The ambulance was taking him away when the bus dropped me off. I burnt down the barn that summer. My mother always says it was an accident. But I started the fire on purpose."

He turned away, not wanting to see the expression on James's face, and ran back up the lane. He stopped when he reached the crest of the hill, waiting for James. Standing shoulder to shoulder, they turned to survey the horizon, range after range of the ancient Alleghenies still visible in the dying light, carpeted with hibernating hardwoods waiting, as ever, to blossom again in the spring. Snow was blowing in from the north, and the sun finally expired in a last gasp of bright violet streaks that trailed beyond the farthest visible mountain ridge. James thought for a moment the boy was crying, then realized it was only snowflakes melting on Jason's broad cheeks.

"It is pretty, isn't it?" he asked, his expectant face looking impossibly vulnerable, able to be easily wounded. "I wanted to tell you what I did so you would know from the beginning, just in case you might think you could like me."

The meal was simple. A turkey breast and sausage stuffing, candied yams, jellied cranberry. Aunt Wendy didn't seem to have much of an appetite except for the red velvet cake dessert; she excused herself, pleading fatigue, while James and his host cleared the table.

"Her diabetes is out of control," Kay fretted. "She refuses to take care of herself. Shoots up with insulin, then helps herself to a piece of lemon meringue pie."

James could see she was preparing to embark on her second widowhood, having given up on Wendy as a lost cause. He suspected the younger woman with the mullet was the insurance policy she'd taken out against a lonely future in this house high in the mountains and deep in the woods.

"You boys leave me to finish up in here. Go enjoy the rest of Christmas," she insisted, taking a scouring pad to the roasting pan.

"What's your favorite Christmas song?" Jason asked as they settled on the sofa, the only light the soft glow of the tree.

"Not Rudolph," James swore, cringing at the memory of last night.

"Good."

"The 'Hallelujah Chorus,' " James said. "It's my favorite."

Jason looked exasperated, shaking his head. "That's Easter! Everyone thinks it's Christmas music, but it's an Easter chorus! I had to play it as the recessional at eight-thirty and eleven o'clock Mass today. It was ridiculous!"

"Then why did you do it?"

"Because the Catholics pay me twenty-five bucks a service. That's fifty bucks. And the priest gave me an extra twenty-dollar tip. That's good money."

"But you like Handel?" James asked.

"I love Handel."

He jumped up and bolted from the room, returning with a guitar and sheet music.

"You're lucky. I've got a score, but it's arranged for a guitar quartet. A bunch of us whore ourselves out, doing crap like Sunday brunches at the Ritz. We don't even have to practice since no one really listens. They'd rather eat waffles and get shit-faced on mimosas. Hang on. It's gonna take me a minute to work this out."

He screwed his face into a pantomime of concentration as he studied the notes on the page, muttering instructions to himself. He ran his long, tapered fingers through his thick hair and announced he'd figured out how to play this solo. No promises, he said, but he was sure he could do a pretty decent job.

"Close your eyes and think of a full orchestra," he said, his voice brimming with quiet confidence. He tweaked the tuners and, finally satisfied, began to play.

The intensity of his focus, the power of his concentration was astonishing and unexpected. Only a brief moment ago he'd been a boy, awkward and eager to impress. His poise and command of his instrument was intimidating. His mastery of the neck was complete as his fingers coaxed a chorus of voices from the six strings.

"So? What do you think?" he asked, as the final note faded, seeking a sign of approval.

The question left James mystified and feeling inadequate, since any words of praise would seem facile, patronizing.

"But can you play 'Blue Christmas'?" he asked, retreating to the comfort zone where sarcasm was a brittle shield and a wry retort the best defense.

Jason smiled and strummed a few open chords as he sang the familiar lyrics. He didn't try any humorous attempts at Elvis-like vocal pyrotechnics, no campy gulps and throbs. His simple, sincere voice, direct and unaffected, was steeped in the all-too-familiar soul-crushing loneliness of a boy who feared he'd never be loved.

He played until long after midnight and, when it was finally time for bed, he sprawled on the sofa beside James, folding himself into the long crevices of James's body and gripping his hand through the night. James dozed in fits, never yielding to an aching arm or twisted knee lest he wake the boy. The man who longed to fall asleep beside a beating heart refused to yield to the sandman, knowing daybreak would arrive much too quickly, bringing this brief and unexpected interlude of peaceful contentment to its inevitable end.

* * *

The overnight accumulation measured an additional eleven inches. The Prevics, however, were undaunted by the challenge, and James, in his borrowed work gloves and boots, grabbed a shovel to aid in the cause. Mother and son took the wheels of their respective pickups and, working in perfect tandem, quickly plowed the long drive down the hill to the state highway. James and Wendy followed behind them on foot, clearing any residual clumps of frozen snow and ice scattered along the way.

Kay was in good spirits, promising a good, hot breakfast, though she was clearly distressed when Wendy insisted on soaking her Bisquick short stack with a half bottle of Log Cabin. James, unused to any physical labor other than moving heavy weights on the floor of his expensive gym, was convinced that muscle aches and pains from his strenuous efforts had already commenced. Jason was clearly nervous, making silly jokes and teasing his mother, trying to find some plausible excuse to postpone driving James back to Breezewood.

"Thank you very much for allowing me to share your Christmas in your home," James said, as he finished drying the breakfast dishes, knowing the time for good-byes had arrived.

"It was our pleasure, Jimmy," Kay said, with great sincerity and polite formality. James realized it was the first time since their introduction she had called him by his name. "Our Jason gets awfully lonely with no one but two old women for company, so I am very glad you could join us."

Some strange little beast was stirring in James's chest, whispering that maybe he could stay another night, or two. In the scheme of a lifetime, forty-eight hours was nothing.

"Wendy!" Kay shouted. "I'm leaving for the restaurant now. I got a sneaking suspicion that miserable little Mexican fry cook is still sleeping off his *Feliz Navidad* and I'm gonna be the kitchen for the lunch shift. You get your ass down there by three for the dinner shift. Where the hell did Jason go? Wendy, you tell him to be at work by eleven if he knows what's good for him."

"I'm here, Ma. I had to go look for something," he announced, clearly trying to hide whatever he had stuffed in the deep pocket of his coat.

"You run Jimmy over to where he's staying and hightail it over to the restaurant. I'm depending on you this morning."

A blizzard that would have paralyzed New York for three days hadn't inconvenienced the Prevics for more than an hour. Kay's truck bounced down the driveway and disappeared, hidden from sight by the towering banks of snow.

"You have any drugs on you?" Jason snickered, nodding at Wendy who was preoccupied with stacking the clean dishes in the cupboard. "Something that would knock her out so we can make out before I drive you back."

James laughed and ran his fingers through his dirty hair, still damp from sweating in his stocking cap.

"Jason, you take your friend upstairs and get him some dry socks before you drive him back to town. Them boots you loaned him was too big, and I know his feet must be soaking wet."

Jason beamed at his unexpected good fortune, this twist of fate in the form of a command to accompany James to a far corner of the house away from curious eyes and sensitive ears.

It was a standard issue boy's room, with a bed that likely had gone unmade since he'd arrived home from Boston and laundry scattered across the room. James assumed the clothes tossed on the floor were dirty and the ones piled on bureau and the bed were waiting to be folded. There were faded posters of Hendrix and Clapton and a newer one of the great Steeler Jerome Bettis on his walls. Jason brushed a stack of boxer shorts off the mattress so James could sit on the bed and found a pair of white tube socks, presumably clean, the type that come three pairs to a package, in his dresser drawer. James was sitting on the edge of the bed, barefoot, when Jason plopped down beside him and gave him an awkward kiss.

It was most definitely a boy's kiss, tentative, lacking confidence, with a shyness James hadn't tasted in years. Jason's mouth didn't resist James's tongue, and he whimpered softly as James took control and gently rolled him onto his back. But a loud creaking bedspring snapped James to attention, and he jumped to his feet, certain that Wendy would be charging up the stairs and that he was about to find himself staring down the barrel of a shotgun.

"I'll come stay with you tonight. In your motel. Just you and me," Jason said, looking impossibly young.

James knew he was likely to be stranded another day or two. The truck stop ogre was certain to have to order parts if not from Germany, then at least from a dealer in Pittsburgh. Twenty-four-hour delivery was the best case scenario, meaning James would be spending at least one more night before continuing his journey.

"We'll see," he said, doubting the wisdom of entertaining a young overnight guest in his Bollywood Ho Jo.

"Jason, you better get your ass in gear or your mother's gonna be really pissed off!" Wendy shouted from the bottom of the stairs.

Jason wasn't very talkative on the drive back to town. The silence made James uneasy, so he tried to make small talk about annual snowfall in the county and the incredible efficiency of the local plowing crews. He felt guilty, remembering how easy it was to break an inexperienced heart. Jason was a bright, perceptive boy and already knew James's answer. The innocent kiss in the bedroom was as far as James was going to go. James smiled, predicting the complete scenario. Today, tonight, Jason would feel as if his world had ended, that his one and only opportunity for true love and happiness had been lost forever, believing with all his heart that a feeling this rare and special could never, would never, repeat itself. And, in the darkest hours of the night, when it seemed the sun would never rise again, he would pick up his guitar and force it to sing a sad and lonely song, causing his mother, lying in bed with Wendy down the hall, to curse the callow stranger who had caused her baby such misery and pain. But, come morning, bright light streaming through his window, Jason would jump out of bed, eager to greet another day, forgetting for a moment that he was mourning his great, lost love. Resuming the requiem, he would trudge downstairs and mope into his oatmeal, utterly morose until Wendy, as usual, did something silly and he couldn't help laughing, and, soon enough, a week would have passed and he wouldn't be able to remember the color of James's eyes.

James's phone rang, the battery low from being left uncharged all night. The mechanic's news was brief and completely unexpected. The repair was done, and James could pick up the car whenever he liked. It was the alternator, an easy enough part to get from the dealer in Bedford.

"You can just drop me off at the garage," he told Jason. "I'll be fine from there."

It was awkward, saying good-bye, knowing they were unlikely to meet again. Jason shoved his hands in his pockets, making fists, trying not to cry and not succeeding.

"Can I e-mail you?" he asked.

"Of course. That's why I gave you my address."

"Here, this is for you," he said, pulling a CD from his pocket. "It's just okay. There are a few mistakes. Some of it's pretty good," he said, shyly.

James thanked him for the gift, grateful he would be spared being scrutinized by Jason's eager face as he listened to his clumsy, heartfelt love songs.

"It's Bach. Arranged for guitar."

Jason threw his arms around him and kissed him on the mouth, then turned and ran back to his truck. James turned to face the mechanic, expecting his wrath and fury. But the ogre merely handed him the bill and took his credit card, knowing to keep any unpleasant thoughts to himself, the man obviously smarter than he looked and wise enough not to incur the wrath of the proprietress of the KOZY KORNER, the best place in town to EAT.

Little Carol Ann's inaugural Christmas had been, of course, a disaster of Titanic proportions, forcing the overwhelmed bride to take to her bed sobbing when an overflowing toilet caused the dining room ceiling to collapse on her Perfect Holiday Table.

"Tragic, just tragic," James's mother declared in the most solemn of tones. "I just don't know if that poor child is ever going to recover from that catastrophe. You stop laughing, Jimmy, because it is not in the least bit funny."

James, of course, completely disagreed and was delighted by the thought of his hysterical niece, a young lady as histrionic as the most flamboyant Fire Island drama queen, pounding her mattress with her tight little fists and kicking the headboard with her tiny feet.

"Why don't you go find some nice Christmas music to listen to while we have our drinks in the living room?"

Adele Hoffmann had suffered through enough Bach arranged for guitar for one afternoon and was longing for more seasonal offerings from Bing and Elvis.

"Roy and his mama have been listening to 'White Christmas' at the mall since October. Maybe they want to hear something different."

"Jimmy, stop trying my patience. I'm already nervous enough without your getting me all worked up over nothing. Now take this out to the coffee table."

He carried her carefully arranged cheese board of Kroger's extra sharp cheddar and mild goat cheese to the living room, where he plopped into an easy chair and took his phone from his pocket, resisting the urge to place a call to Kay's Kozy Korner and ask to speak to the bartender.

"Jumping Jiminy, here they are, ringing the bell, and I'm not the least bit prepared!" his mother fretted, calling out from the kitchen. "Jimmy, go answer the door."

He knew his mother was sneaking a quick sip of white wine in the kitchen, anxious despite her perfect preparations: the roast in the oven perfectly timed to be served at precisely seven-thirty; the specialty of the house, her Green Goddess dressing, chilling in the refrigerator; a lovely frosted layer cake waiting to be served.

"James Hoffmann, I swear. You get better looking every Christmas," the matron in the ancient, full-length beaver coat insisted as he opened the door. "Doesn't he, Roy? Doesn't he get better looking every year?"

Roy Powers stood behind his mother Evelyn, smiling and rolling his eyes.

"Sure he does, Mama. He just gets better looking every year. I'm liking the silver fox look, Jimmy."

"Get your butts in here before Adele accuses me of letting you freeze to death on the front porch," James laughed, embracing the old woman and shaking the hand of her son. Funny world, he thought. In New York, he was forever kissing and hugging men he didn't even like, but here, on the threshold of his mother's home, etiquette demanded nothing more intimate than a formal handshake with the first man he had ever loved.

"Oh, Adele, just look at that beautiful tree," Evelyn declared as James helped her out of her coat. "Why I just can't believe they can make them so lifelike these days. I can practically smell the pinecones, I swear. Roy, next year we're going to get us one just like it and not bother with all the fuss and mess."

Adele wasn't quite certain she wasn't being insulted for not taking the time and effort to put up a real tree and decided, just in case, to defend herself with a show of bravado.

"Why thank you, Evelyn. I have to admit I just love my tree. It comes with the lights already on it. You know what you ought to do since you admire it? You should run down to Walmart tomorrow and buy this same tree half price now that Christmas is over."

Evelyn plopped her ample ass on the sofa, in easy reach of the cheese board, and helped herself to a generous serving of cheddar.

"One Dubonnet coming right up," James announced.

"James, you are so sweet to remember my beverage."

The only reason his mother kept a bottle of that nasty stuff in a kitchen cupboard was to be able to offer her closest friend her favorite drink whenever she dropped by for a visit.

"Roy?"

"Whatever you're having, so long as it's strong."

Roy smiled, his green eyes twinkling, and James was startled to see a striking resemblance to a certain young man in Pennsylvania. No, he decided on closer consideration. There was the obvious difference in their ages for one thing, and they looked nothing alike except for the color of their eyes and maybe the way they both threw back their heads, chins pointing to the sky, whenever they laughed.

Adele sat down beside her friend, and the Hoffmanns and their guests raised their glasses and offered a toast, wishing each other a very Merry Christmas and a healthy and happy New Year.

"Now, Jimmy. I want to hear all about the rich and famous people you've met since last Christmas," Evelyn announced.

She was confused by the identity of the Senator, mistaking him for the congressman who ran off with his mistress while his wife was on her deathbed with cancer. She nodded her head appreciatively when he mentioned meeting the cable news anchor during his summer vacation. But she saved her real enthusiasm for the news of the dinner he'd shared with Archie Duncan just several nights ago.

"I just loved that show of his. I wish they'd bring it back. I saw last week in *People* magazine he's dating that actress from *Everybody Loves Raymond*."

"The one who plays the mother?" he asked, sounding perfectly innocent.

James would have to severely reprimand Archie Duncan the next time their paths crossed for keeping this important information a secret.

"No, not the one who plays the mother. The other one. Oh, Jimmy, you are just too much," she roared, almost choking on her Dubonnet.

Roy smiled and sipped his Scotch, as usual not saying much.

"Oh, good Lord," Adele said, jumping off the sofa, preoccupied with fears of an impending culinary disaster. "I better get that roast out of the oven before it's burnt to a crisp!"

* * *

Times change. Fashions come and go. Tastes are fickle. The only loyalty was to the pursuit of the new, the novel, the yet to be discovered. In Manhattan the hot spot of the moment was likely to be shuttered the following week. But in Parkersburg, West Virginia, Scandals Lounge was eternal.

James sat in a time warp, nursing a beer. Aloysius, the bartender, had been serving drinks to the gay underworld of that small city on the Ohio River since long before Roy and James had first walked through the door, shaking with nerves as they presented their unconvincing fake IDs. He had told the boys they could stay only if they promised to hide in the basement in the event of a random police raid by members of Parkersburg's finest seeking to supplement their meager wages with a thick envelope stuffed with cash.

A frighteningly tall drag queen, a Kabuki Whitney Houston, was now engaged in a screaming match with a pair of young toughs from Marietta who were shouting racial epithets during her act. James was in a strange and unsettled mood, hoping to witness a fistfight, and jumped in his seat when a pair of beefy paws grabbed him by the shoulders.

"Sorry to keep you waiting. She had one Dubonnet too many, and I had to help her get undressed for bed."

All these years later, and James still both loved and hated Roy for his fierce devotion to his parents. He'd gotten a degree in pharmacy at WVU, a transportable skill, but had returned to his hometown where he made a very good living managing the retail pharmacies for a regional supermarket chain. He'd cared for his father while he was dying of prostate cancer and was a live-in companion to his dithering, demanding mother. James, on his most charitable days, thought Roy was noble. The rest of the time he thought he was a fool.

"I don't know why I let you talk me into this," James complained.

"You had better plans tonight?"

"Not really. I watched *It's a Wonderful Life* twice last night, and the only other DVD in my mother's house is the first season of *Touched by an Angel*."

Roy sat down beside him and ordered a round.

"What's the matter, Jimmy? You seem even sadder than usual."

James took umbrage at the comment, suspecting it was an unintended insult. "Ernst has pancreatic cancer."

"That's not good."

"No, it's not."

"Well, I'm very sorry to hear that."

It was ironic that the only note of sympathy and concern for the dying old man came from someone whose intelligence Ernst had insulted on his first trip to New York, attributing the shy manner and reticence of a young visitor from West Virginia, who was clearly intimidated by unfamiliar and overwhelming surroundings, to a mild form of autism.

"How are you dealing with it?" Roy asked.

James cringed at Roy's sincere solicitation, remembering how callously he'd broken his big, sweet heart all those many years ago. From the first awkward fumblings on boyhood sleepovers through the rushed, guilt-ridden ruttings in high school and on to the long, cramped nights on the narrow twin mattresses of college dormitory rooms, Roy had never considered a world without James, while James had dreamed of a different life, the stuff of books and movies, in the great city of New York.

James had departed for Manhattan after graduating and had been grateful to find a subsistence salary position typing correspondence and licking envelopes for a senior editor at Doubleday, earning barely enough to afford a tiny room in a struggling chorus boy's fourth-floor Ninth Avenue walk-up. By the time he had finally persuaded Roy to see Manhattan before making his final decision to sit for his pharmacy license in West Virginia and not New York, James had been seduced by expensive meals in restaurants he could never have afforded on his own and the open invitation to stay the weekend at his generous new friend's magical cabin on Fire Island. He had already regretted insisting on the visit as he greeted Roy at the airport gate, his cheap blue suitcase advertising the arrival of yet another bumpkin from the sticks. The clothes that had never bothered James in Morgantown or Charlottesville—the Ban-Lon shirt, the out-of-season corduroy trousers, the Hush Puppies desert boots and white sweat socks—embarrassed him in the West Village, blinding him to the appreciative glances the broad-shouldered, blond country boy received from the men cruising the available wares on Christopher Street. He had squirmed and resisted Roy's attempts to make love to him and sneered at his loud guffaws at Mickey Rooney's antics in *Sugar Babies*, rolling his eyes at Ernst, who smiled contentedly in the next seat, knowing the battle for James was over, the war had been won. James had cried all night after putting Roy in a cab for LaGuardia, regretting his bad behavior and the sad, confused look on Roy's face as they said good-bye, but relieved to be free at last of old obligations, finally able to truly begin his brand new life.

"I wish I'd never gone to New York, Roy. I should've stayed here in Parkersburg with you," he confessed, expecting Roy would wrap him in a bear hug and welcome him home, only to be surprised, and frankly a little pissed, when Roy laughed in his face.

"How many drinks did you have before I got here?"

"I hate you," James hissed, indignant over this unexpected rejection.

"Like hell you do," Roy said, amused by the sophisticated city boy's sentimental relapse. "I don't think you'd have many opportunities to have dinner with Archie Duncan in Parkersburg, and I can't picture you teaching the Romantic poets to high school kids destined for the Charleston State Correctional Institute."

"I'm moving back here, I swear. I should never have left. I was a stupid kid. I'm lonely and you're lonely, and it's all my fault that we're forty-six years old and both alone."

Aloysius, who had witnessed countless romantic epiphanies and moments of truth in his many years behind the bar, set up another round, this one on the house.

"I'm not lonely, Jimmy," Roy said, emphatically.

"Don't be ashamed to admit it, Roy. It's not a sin to be lonely."

"But I'm not."

James was growing irritated, remembering how obstinate and headstrong Roy could be.

"Roy, living with your mother is not a substitute for intimacy. Now admit it. You're lonely."

Roy sighed and threw his wallet on the bar, flipping it open to show him a photograph.

"This is Anh Vu. He's in Fresno spending Christmas with his parents. I'm picking him up at Pittsburgh International tomorrow night. Why don't you drive up with me?"

The young man was dressed for a formal portrait, in a jacket and tie, his serious grimace adding a year or two to his boyish face.

"I hired him out of pharmacy school to work in the Cairo store. He's working as the night manager in a Walgreen's branch in Vienna now because of the company's nepotism policy. Evelyn loves him. He takes better care of her than I do."

"Jesus Christ," James gasped, astonished by this unexpected revelation. "How old is he? Fourteen?"

"Very funny. He's twenty-six."

"And you'll be forty-seven on your next birthday."

"So?"

James struggled to find the right words to express his contempt without inflicting permanent damage to their friendship.

"You'll look ridiculous."

Roy tossed back a shot of Wild Turkey and ordered another round.

"You know, this isn't exactly the reaction I would have expected from a jaded and sophisticated man of the world like Jimmy, excuse me, James, Hoffmann."

"These things never work out in the end. You're going to get hurt," James insisted, his argument grounded as much in envy as in concern. "It can't last."

"Nothing lasts forever, Jimmy," Roy said, his green eyes brimming with kindness. "That doesn't mean we shouldn't appreciate what we have while we have it."

The altercation between the entertainment and her hecklers had reached a fever pitch. Punches were being thrown, and a microphone stand was being brandished as a lethal weapon. Aloysius calmly reached under the bar and retrieved a pistol, blowing on a whistle to make sure he had the entire room's undivided attention.

"If you boys think I won't use this, just turn around and count all the bullet holes in that wall," he said without raising his voice, taking aim over James's shoulder.

The two thugs, nasty little assholes with sexy jarhead buzz cuts, grumbled, mumbling vague threats as they shambled out the front door. The floor show resumed to appreciative catcalls and applause.

"You still get raided, Aloysius?" James asked, as the bartender poured a shot of Sambuca to reward himself for his cool head and steady aim.

"Naw," he said. "No one really gives a shit anymore. I miss them old days, don't you?"

Them old days didn't seem so different than these new days, at least during a light snowfall at one-thirty in the morning, the deserted streets of downtown Parkersburg illuminated by strings of Christmas lights. At high noon on a bright, sunny day, it was impossible to ignore that bail bondsmen and auto tag shops now leased the storefronts that had once been occupied by dress shops and bakeries and drugstores with soda fountain service. Commerce had moved out near the interstate exits where strip malls anchored by huge box stores offered acres of free parking. James flipped on the radio in the car, feeling lonely and wanting a bit of companionship. The AM band was wall-to-wall religious music—warbling gospel singers and treacly choirs and, worst of all, some abomination called Christian rock. The FM stations were solid classic rock, "Walk This Way" and Electric Light Orchestra. He slipped a disc in the player and drove home listening to Bach arranged for guitar.

Damn, he thought, cursing himself for his earlier brief lapse of judgment. What the hell had gotten into him, agreeing to make the trip to Pittsburgh International tomorrow night? The drive north would be torture. He would be a prisoner, forced to listen to candy-colored tales of Roy and Anh Vu shopping together for the perfect leather sofa, snuggling up on a Saturday night to watch *Four Weddings and a Funeral* on DVD, and planning their weekend escapes to the District of Columbia to see k.d. lang and Sarah Brightman in concert. The long ride home would be even worse, with James consigned to the backseat so that the reunited lovers, having been separated by an interminable seven days, could hold hands and rekindle the flame.

James pulled into his mother's driveway and sat in the heated car, turning up the volume and wallowing in self-pity and the sweet music of Jason's guitar. The house was dark except for the porch lamp and the brightly lit corner window on the second story, the bedroom that had been his sanctuary throughout his childhood. The room where, one rainy November afternoon, his mother and sister having gone to Charleston for an Ice Capades matinee, he and Roy, both just thirteen, had wrestled on his narrow mattress, their pants twisted around their ankles, grinding and moaning, caught unawares by a strange and remarkable pleasure. The same room where, many years later, on that first Thanksgiving after moving to New York, he had explained to Roy he wouldn't be coming home for Christmas, that he was going to Germany with his friend Ernst.

Roy's words still stung as if they had spoken only an hour ago.

"I'd change if I thought that would make you love me again."

Only now it was someone else's voice he recalled, from a different time and a different world, but laced with the same sad longing.

I wanted to tell you what I did so you would know from the beginning, just in case you might think you could like me.

It was after two when he finally poured a nightcap and settled into an easy chair, staring at his cell phone and resisting the temptation to call Pennsylvania under the pretense of thanking the Prevics for their hospitality. Good God, Adele, he chuckled, appalled by the huge, plastic pine tree that seemed to swallow an entire corner of the living room and remembering the seven-foot, fresh-cut blue spruces that had graced the house in his childhood, magnificent in memory, blazing with cheerful, enamel lights, branches bowed with bright glass ornaments and draped with silver tinsel. And the model railroad platform, with its trestle bridges and papier-mâché tunnels... *Damn!* he thought, jumping up from the chair, his knees wobbly, stricken by divine inspiration.

Adele was a hoarder; it was inconceivable any blessed artifacts would have been tossed in the trash. Downstairs in the basement, in storage boxes, that's where he would find what he was looking for. He carefully made his way down the steps, conceding he was slightly inebriated. Behind an old headboard and a cardboard wardrobe crammed with mothballed overcoats, he discovered three large boxes marked XMAS in bold black letters. The first box was stuffed with the dried and cracked wires of ancient Christmas lights and a set of old, tissue-wrapped, five-and-dime Nativity figures that hadn't seen the light of day in many years—a shepherd missing an arm, a headless magi, the Baby Jesus without a left hand. The treasure he was seeking was in the second carton: a Lionel locomotive, three Pennsylvania Railroad Vista Dome Passenger Cars with intricate skylights and the silhouettes of the passengers painted on the windows, and the matching baggage car, all in their original boxes.

The plan was brilliant, completely innocent seeming, nothing more than a kind gesture to thank a pair of model railroaders for a memorable holiday in their lovely home. He would take the train to Federal Express in the morning and ship it to Kay's Kozy Korner, then wait for Jason to write a short thank-you, maybe even call. He applauded himself for his ingenuity, the subtlety of his maneuver, for encouraging the boy's interest without making any commitment of reciprocation. His heart fluttered when he opened his laptop to search for the restaurant's address and found an unexpected message in his mailbox, a short note from Jason, wishing him a Happy New Year and saying he hoped he could call when he arrived in New York next summer. Three photos were attached. One was Jason's sweet face, grinning at the digital camera he held an arm's length away. The second was his thick, erect penis, and the third was an awkward shot, taken one-handed, of his bare ass.

I really, really like you, he signed off.

James arose early to break the news to his mother that he had to cut the West Virginia visit short, pleading a preposterous little white lie, saying the Senator had sent him a message saying he would be announcing his presidential ambitions in the first news cycle of the new year and needed an emergency editorial conference. He got a hundred-dollar ticket for speeding near Hancock, Maryland, and stopped only for gas and coffee and to empty his bladder. Aunt Wendy was the first to spot him as he walked through the door of the Kozy Korner. She whispered something to Kay, who tried to suppress a cautious smile as he approached her son's broad back. *Nothing lasts forever, Jimmy. That doesn't mean we shouldn't appreciate what we have while we have it,* he thought as he tapped Jason on the shoulder, remembering an angry, resigned face when he had announced he needed to be around people his own age, too much of a coward to admit what Ernst already suspected, that he was involved with the young Armenian editorial assistant in his office whose ass didn't sag and who didn't need forty minutes to get an erection.

It snowed off and on that entire holiday week, no more blizzards, just enough to keep the white blanket covering the countryside fresh and clean. Wendy was pleased with the peace offering of a classic Lionel, though she did complain that the faulty wiring of one of the Pennsylvania Railroad Passenger Cars caused the Vista Dome light to flicker off and on. Jason insisted on planning daytime adventures, trips across the mountains to visit Fallingwater and to hear the grand organ in a Somerset church; he fretted that James was bored and about to announce his imminent departure for New York, too young and insecure to recognize that his guest was perfectly content simply riding in his truck, drinking lousy coffee in a paper cup. Come evening, James sat at the bar, nowhere else in the world he would rather be, reading Stephen King paperbacks he borrowed from Kay while Jason poured drinks and bantered with the customers. James slept soundly at night, Jason lying naked in his arms, with the thermostat turned low, relying on body heat for warmth, the curtains thrown open and the bright light of the full moon outside the window flooding the motel room.

He rose early on the morning of the last day of the year to drive back to New York, expecting Jason to be heartbroken at being abandoned on New Year's Eve with no one to toast but the drunks at the Kozy Korner as the ball dropped in Times Square. But Jason surprised him by not protesting and promising to call when the clock struck twelve. James knew that Kay and Jason were driving Wendy to Erie on New Year's Day to see her son and grandchildren, but he was still disappointed, and a little miffed, to be allowed to depart so easily, without an argument to try to persuade him to change his mind. Jason looked puzzled and hurt when James wouldn't linger after they kissed good-bye; he was too trusting to believe he was being punished because James had spent the past few days allowing himself to indulge in a silly fantasy that he and Jason could be falling in love.

James expected the spell would be broken as he crossed the Hudson. He'd had every intention of canceling his plans with Archie Duncan, but kept finding excuses all week to delay making the call, finally deciding the wise and mature decision was to hedge his bets. This thing with Jason, lovely as it had been, was a folly, and the boy's capricious whims guaranteed an unhappy ending, with the foolish older lover wondering why he had been spurned. Archie was as good as his word, arriving to pick him up at 7:55 on New Year's Eve, carrying a ten-dollar bouquet of cut flowers he had bought from the Korean green grocer on the corner of James's block. He suggested a quiet evening, just the two of them, away from the noisy crowds, after a quick, obligatory stop at the New Year's celebration the production's Mama Rose was throwing for her supporting cast. Dispensation to leave wasn't granted until after two and, when they woke in the morning, they both knew it was over before it had begun, their single night of passion thwarted by the effects of alcohol consumption on the middle age libido and, truth be told, by James's nagging thoughts of lying on a lumpy sofa in a farmhouse in the mountains of Pennsylvania. He'd no sooner closed the door on Archie Duncan, sending him into the bright sunlight, when his telephone rang.

"I called you at midnight but you didn't answer," Jason said, trying, unsuccessfully, not to sound hurt. "I guess you were busy. I understand."

James knew he'd caused the boy a restless night, full of lurid fantasies of his faithless lover. This hadn't even started yet, this young romance, and he had already made his first mistake.

"I forgot to charge the phone in the car and the battery was dead. I should have sent you an e-mail, but it was a long drive back to New York and I was sound asleep by eleven."

"I thought that's what must have happened," Jason said, his voice brightening, refusing to suspect that James was capable of deceit and lies. His young heart was a fragile thing, capable of being easily bruised, and James understood it was time to choose between walking away or handling it with care.

Jason arrived in June, taking James up on the offer of a crash pad on the fashionable Upper East Side until he saved enough for a deposit on a hovel in Williamsburg or Jersey City. He stayed for seven years, until the inevitable conflicts between an excitable boy not yet thirty and a man in his fifties, settled in his ways, led to the fissures and tension that threatened to harden into intractable anger and resentment, and James knew it was time to set him free.

The cottage in Woodstock stands as a monument to their time together. Jason, forever the country boy, skilled with a hammer and saw, mentored James through its careful restoration. It's a home they still share, spending many weekends together, sleeping in separate bedrooms now, most often alone, sometimes with new companions who come and go, fresh audiences for oft-told dinner-table tales of their adventures reclaiming the old house from the ravages of time and weather. The memoir James published about their first two summers in the cottage won a literary prize and continues to sell, its readers inevitably disappointed to learn that the mismatched but happy couple are no longer together.

Their relationship has changed, but continues, and Jason never strays too far, always needing a safe place to retreat when his still vulnerable heart suffers yet another disappointment. Jason nitpicks, criticizing every quirk and each imperfection of James's new paramours; James bites his tongue, suffering silently through each declaration that Jason has found enduring love. Time is a precious commodity. James is busier than ever, and Jason's career has begun to take off. James is his biggest fan, never missing a performance, watching proudly as Jason's reputation as a musician and songwriter grows. Last summer was bittersweet, and James was often lonely in the cottage in Woodstock, even when the rooms were full with weekend guests, as Jason was off on tour, opening for Jackson Browne on the outdoor music festival circuit. Sometimes they're apart for weeks, occasionally for months, and James misses Jason's loud voice, the sound of his guitar in another room, the floorboards creaking under his heavy footsteps. They're always excited to see each other again, eager to hear all the news and updates, comfortable and secure in each other's presence. Jason's leery each time he returns, asking unsubtle questions, needing to be reassured another young man isn't lurking in the background, waiting to take his place. And every year, on Christmas Eve, he throws his bag in the trunk and tucks his guitar in the backseat of James's car and, together, they head west through New Jersey, and dip south through Pennsylvania, where they spend the night together in a farmhouse outside the Town of Motels before James pushes on in the morning, making the long drive to West Virginia alone.

A Christmas to Remember

Frank Anthony Polito

In memory of Patrick Liddy,
aka "Miss Peter"

DECEMBER 1991

All I Want

And it feels so close
Let it take me in . . .

—Toad the Wet Sprocket

Back when I used to be a Band Fag, all I ever wanted was to be *normal.*

O' the tears I shed, the years I squandered, trying to belong and be like everybody else. Now that I've come to accept—and appreciate—who I truly am, there's just one thing I'm asking Santa Claus to bring me this Christmas. . . .

My own boyfriend.

Imagine how the old man playing St. Nick at the Oakland Mall would feel if a twenty-one-year-old *guy* sat down on his lap and greeted him with this request. Not, "I'd like a Discman and the new De La Soul CD." Or "I'll take a gift certificate to the Gap, please." Or, in the immortal words of Charlie Brown's materialistic little sister, Sally: "Just send money. . . . How about tens and twenties?"

Nope. What I *really* desire more than anything, after spending the last five-plus years utterly and completely single, is to finally find the thing that I first heard Lionel Richie and Diana Ross singing about a decade ago. . . .

My Endless Love.

"Yo, Jack!"

The sound of someone shouting my name draws me out of my daydream.

"Sorry . . ."

Boiling water bubbles up and spills over onto the stovetop. Quickly, I pull the pot away and lower the blue flame on the burner. No harm done.

Time to add the angel hair!

He asks me, "What's-a-matter? . . . You wasted?"

To which I respond, "I didn't think so."

He grins, refilling my wineglass with white zinfandel. "Then drink up."

Damn that Kirk Bailey!

If I didn't know better, I'd say he's deliberately trying to get me drunk. But we're both aware that can't possibly be the case. . . . *Can it?*

Using the handy-dandy circle on the side of the box, I measure out two precise portions of pasta. Doesn't seem like nearly enough for the two growing college boys that we are, so I break off a few additional strands, submerging them into the steamy depths.

At the sound of the cracking semolina, Kirk gasps. "What are you doing?!"

Hesitating momentarily, I shoot him a look. "This is how my mom always does it."

"Yeah," he says, "but you're from Hazeltucky."

Har-dee har-har.

As if I haven't heard it all before. Hailing from the Detroit suburb situated between mile roads Eight and Ten, bordered by the newly "Fashionable Ferndale" on the west and "White Trash Warren" to the east, my hometown has been the butt of jokes for most of my new friends since they discovered I'm a hillbilly from Hazel Park. (Truthfully, I'm part Italian / Irish / German, part English / German / Canadian. Nobody in my family comes from Down South.) I don't know why. Lots of losers from HPHS end up here in East Lansing. It's not like we're at Harvard; this is Michigan State.

"How do they cook spaghetti in Center Line?"

This I ask still amazed at the fact that Kirk and I grew up a mere four miles apart, our paths never crossing until this past September 23rd on the first day of our senior year as Spartans. . . .

Deciding I'd try my hand at playwriting, I signed up for a course called Theatre Lab, being offered by (whom else?) the Department of Theatre. I'd attended a few plays during my days at Michigan State, most notably a production of *A Tale of Two Cities*, adapted from Dickens by the director, and *The Pirates of Penzance*. This one I especially wanted to take in as I grew up quite fond of the Kristy McNichol / Christopher Atkins parody, *The Pirate Movie*. But these shows, and the few others I'd seen, had all taken place over at the Wharton Center. I'd only set foot inside the Auditorium Building once before, freshman year, to attend a Sam Kinison concert ("Wild thing, I think I love you!"), despite its being located across the Red Cedar River directly behind my dorm.

The class itself consisted of actors, directors, and writers, all collaborating on different projects. Upon entering the room, I remember taking a good look around, asking myself, *Who's the cutest boy here?*, and then sitting down directly beside Mr. Bailey. Particularly was I smitten when Kirk got up in front of the class to present his audition monologue. The simple yet confident way he introduced himself—"Hello, my name is Kirk Bailey. My selection is from *Burn This*, by Lanford Wilson"—and the fact that, in the first line of the piece his character asks if we've ever been to a *gay* New Year's Eve party . . . like Calgon, it took me away.

Over the next six weeks we got acquainted working together weekly. But even more so when Bobbie, a Directing major and Kirk's gal pal, invited me to join the pair one afternoon for lunch at the Student, aka *Stupid*, Center. This soon became a recurring occurrence. And we've been buds ever since. . . . The rest, as they say, is H-I-S-T-O-R-Y.

"Not like that . . ." Kirk replies to my query regarding proper pasta preparation as if I'm the stupidest person born since my same-birthday buddy, Helen Keller. "And it's *vermicelli*, not spaghetti."

So now he's a culinary expert!

Just because his father owns his own sporting goods store while mine works as a produce manager at a major supermarket chain doesn't make the Baileys any fancier than the Paternos. Both our mothers are stay-at-home housekeeper / child-rearing types.

"Whatever." I give the remaining sticks a snap and drop them into the pot. "What do you know about Italian food? Ya dumb Pollack!"

Of course I'm just teasing. One might even call it flirting. This is when I realize that maybe I *have* had a bit more alcohol than I initially estimated. Never am I this blatantly obvious about my attraction to the man I've come to call my new best friend.

But I can't help it.

The way Kirk stands here in the kitchen of his off-campus apartment, aka "The Duplex," looking ever so handsome in his olive green and black-sleeved Oaktree jacket worn with dark mock turtleneck, matching slacks, and black leather shoes with silver buckles. (I couldn't feel more underdressed wearing the navy and gray snowflake sweater I've had since high school with my Girbaud jeans.) The way his blond bangs cascade ever so casually across his high forehead . . . The stubble on his cheeks and his crooked, dimpled chin . . . His straight, white teeth and bright blue eyes staring back at me.

It takes every bit of restraint in my being not to shove him up against the refrigerator and ram my tongue down his throat. But we're both aware he wouldn't like that. . . . *Would he?*

Once we get the cooking of the main course under control, we start in on the salads. Kirk takes care of cutting and washing the romaine, while I commence with chopping up the toppings: cherry tomatoes, red pepper, and . . .

"Where's the cucumber?" I know we bought one at Country Market, aka "Country *Markup*," when we did the shopping for this evening.

"Right here," I hear Kirk reply. When I look over at him, he's got the eight-inch gherkin in the palm of his hand, extending out from the crotch of his pants. "Come on, grab it!" He wags the fruit back and forth at me like he's taking a whiz.

"You wish you were that big," I say, totally busting on him. Of course I can't help but wonder how Kirk would actually measure up, once he's succeeded in making the thought cross my mind. "Now who's wasted?"

God, I hope I'm not blushing too badly!

"You ain't seen nothing yet."

Kirk finishes off his beverage, pours another. He reaches into the freezer, removes a plastic Tupperware tub filled with something red and frozen.

"What's that?"

"This would be the sauce."

He pops the top off and places the contents in the microwave at the far end of the counter next to the Mr. Coffee coffeemaker.

"At my house," I reveal, "we just open up a jar of Ragu and consider it jake."

"Not my mother," he says, rolling his eyes. "She makes everything from scratch. Cakes, pies, *golumpki*...

I shake my head at his sudden Eastern European accent. "Okay, you lost me."

"Stuffed cabbage," Kirk clarifies.

"Gross," I grumble, despite having never sampled anything remotely close to the dish he's describing. Growing up, if it couldn't come with mashed potatoes and canned corn on the side, my mother wouldn't cook it. "You really *are* Polish."

"I told you," he tells me. "Bailey isn't my real last name."

Apparently, back in the 1950s, Kirk's grandfather got fired from his job at Hudson Motors, so he went and reapplied—and got rehired—under a pseudonym. How the man milked Bailey from Szlachta, I have no idea. (Kirk seems to think it had something to do with his grandpa's liking Irish cream.) Regardless, Kirk's dad, who was already grown and married at the time of the surname switch, decided to follow suit, thus allowing Kirk all his life to pass as something other than *Polski*. Or is it *Polska?* As in *kielbasa*.

Beep!

The timer goes off, and Kirk extracts the container. He dips a wooden spoon into the not-yet-defrosted sauce, stirs, returns it for another two minutes.

"What are you doing?"

He holds the tomato-stained object mere inches from my mouth. "Have a taste." I let my lips part, sense the savory sweetness on my tongue. Kirk takes a try himself, not bothering to wash off the utensil beforehand. "Oh, no. . . . Now I've got your cooties."

"Shut up!" Giving him a gentle push, my hand lingers a moment, copping a feel of his bulging bicep.

"You like?" he inquires, eyebrow raised.

For a moment, I assume Kirk's referring to the mass of muscle beneath his sweater. Then I realize he must be talking about his mother's recipe.

"It's nice," I say, double entendre intended.

Our eyes meet.

He steps toward me.

Reaching out a hand, he brushes my lower lip with his thick thumb.

Not since the first love of my life, Joey Palladino, have I been so turned on by someone's digits. If I didn't know better, I'd think Kirk Bailey was going to kiss me right here and now. But we're both aware that can't possibly be the case. . . . *Can it?*

"You got some sauce," he says, wiping it away. Then he licks his own fat finger as if it's a lollipop, calling to mind thoughts of—

Beep!

Like that ridiculously popular TV show that I refuse to watch (despite how incredibly hot that Slater stud might be), I'm *Saved by the Bell.*

Ten minutes later, we're ready to sit down and dine. . . .

"We need some music," I decide before diving in.

"What do you wanna hear?" Kirk asks en route to the stereo system.

He's got one of those record/CD player/dual cassette deck combo deals, all stacked one on top of the other, inside a protective glass cabinet. On opposite sides of the room, two ginormous speakers sit propped up in the corners.

"I don't know," I say, contemplating his question. "Something Christmas-y."

Kirk peruses a tower of CDs almost as tall as I am. Or in my case, as *short*. At five-foot-seven, I've always been somewhat vertically challenged.

"You're in luck," he tells me, opening a jewel case and sliding a silver disc into the slot. A moment later, the room fills with the sound of somber piano playing.

"That's pretty. . . . What is it?"

My companion sits opposite me. "George Winston, *December*."

My face lights up. "I love George Winston!"

My friends and I used to listen to him back in high school (on cassette, of course). But this particular track doesn't sound familiar. There's a mellow, haunting quality to the tune that immediately brings a tear to my eye. I don't know why.

Maybe it's because I am indeed inebriated. Or maybe it's because it's the final day of class with only five more months to go until graduation. Soon I'll be surrounded by a bunch of people who barely know me, meaning my mom and dad, and my sister and brother, and the folks I work with at Farmer Jack's. Up here at MSU, for the most part, I'm finally able to be myself. Whenever I'm around my family, I can't talk freely about certain important facts: like how I've totally fallen in love with the *guy* sitting across the table from me.

"So how come you look like you're gonna cry?"

The sound of Kirk's baritone snaps me out of my melancholy-baby moment. Shaking off my sorrow, I raise my stemware. "Cheers."

"Here's lookin' at ya," says Kirk, returning my toast.

Dinner is delicious. I polish off two plates, my abdominals about to burst. Yet I can't help but reach for another slice of garlic bread. (Love that Cole's frozen in a bag!) Kirk warns me to save room. But I can't possibly ingest another morsel, I'm so stuffed.

"Not even tiramisu?" he says, tempting me with my favorite dessert.

"Seriously," I say. "I'm gonna throw up."

He begins clearing away our plates, quoting from what I've come to learn as being classic Monty Python: "Not even one thin wafer?"

Holding my splitting sides, I demand, "Don't!"

Back in high school, I would *never* have found this type of British humor to be hilarious. Only geeks like Zack Rakoff and Claire Moody watched movies like *Life of Brian* and *Monty Python and the Holy Grail.* But if Kirk Bailey enjoys it . . .

So many new pleasures have I come to take part in since making his acquaintance on the first day of this fall semester. In less than three months time, I've gone from being a Preppie, Birmingham wannabe to an all-black-wearing Alternative. Back in mid-September, if somebody had told me I'd be listening to Nine Inch Nails and Nitzer Ebb, I would've laughed in his face.

"Don't look now. . . ."

Of course I disobey the second I step through the doorway from the dining area. "Where'd you get the mistletoe?" I wonder.

"In the box with all the other Christmas crap my mom unloaded on me when I moved."

Said items include: an assortment of figurines circa 1960s, a handmade 2½ by 1½ by 1½ foot wooden crèche complete with plastic Mary, Joseph, Baby Jesus (in a manger), Three Wisemen, some sheep, a donkey, and the ubiquitous angels, and an authentic "Electrified" Village. These objects we've strategically placed around the apartment, adorning the tops of bookshelves, the TV, the coffee table, and all the windowsills—anywhere there's an available surface.

Truthfully, the room looks quite festive with the white lights delicately draped around the perimeter and the fully decorated, tinsel-less tree in the corner. (According to Mrs. Bailey, icicles are

O-U-T.) I can't believe all the work we've done just for one single night. Come tomorrow, nobody's going to be around to enjoy the Currier and Ives–inspired setting. If I had my way, I'd stay here the entire Christmas break. But my mother would kill me if I didn't come home for the holiday.

"You know what they say . . ." I say, harkening back to the holiday matchmaker hanging high over our heads.

"Huh?" says Kirk. Like he has no idea what I'm alluding to. Even though he's the one who brought it up!

Like I've said, maybe it's because I am indeed inebriated. Or maybe it's because it's the final day of class with only five more months to go until graduation. Soon John Robert Paterno and Kirk Edmond Bailey will descend upon the world. Who knows what could happen come May 21, 1992?

Throwing all caution to the wind, I lean in and kiss him.

Tongues touch.

Lips linger.

Pelvises press together.

He smells of Tuscany, spicy and sweet.

Suddenly, Kirk pulls away. "I can't do this. . . ."

Clinging to the present for as long as possible, I whisper, "Why not?"

Since the day we first met, there's been no denying the spark between us. I know Kirk senses it too. . . . How can he keep resisting?

"Brrr!"

Before Kirk's able to fabricate an excuse, the front door flies open. From around the corner comes the sound of a feminine shiver.

"In here!" he calls, going back to the dirty dishes, totally avoiding my gaze.

Always one to make an entrance, in walks my *least* favorite actress in the entire Department of Theatre, decked out in a white (what I hope is faux) fox fur. Snowflakes fall to the floor as she shakes out her mane of chestnut brown, wrapping her arms tight about her.

"My God!" she exclaims. "It's fuh-reezing outside!"

"It's mid-December," I say.

"Hello, Jack..." Raquel Loiseau regards me, clearly not amused to be breathing the same air as I. "What are *you* doing here?"

"He's helping me decorate for the party," Kirk replies tersely, coming to my defense.

I gesture to the holiday explosion surrounding us. "Welcome to Santa's Bordello!"

Kirk continues reading Raquel the riot act. "What are *you* doing here?"

"Duh!" To her, it couldn't be any more obvious. "I'm here to see my *boyfriend*."

Lovingly, she's referring to Mr Bailey.

Ah, yes!

Why do I always fall for the wrong guy?

Talk about the worst holiday party—ever. Well, the soirée itself is fine. Most of the usual suspects show: Wayne and Guy. Dave and Shelly. Jim and Michelle. Sadly, Maureen couldn't make it. She's already headed home to "Long-k Island." And Peggy, aka Ellen DeGeneres, I'm pretty sure went back to Bloomfield the day before. Or is it Bloomfield *Hills?* I can never remember where she grew up, exactly. Someplace fancy-schmancy. Being that she lives in the duplex next door, I find it hard to believe when Bobbie arrives fashionably late. But who am I to talk? My mother is always saying I'll be late to my own funeral. Me and my Aunt Sonia, whose tardy genes I've apparently inherited.

Then of course there's *Raquel.*

Was she ever surprised to see her boyfriend sitting down to a pre-party dinner with his *male* amigo! Sorry, not my problem. Kirk's the one who asked me to help him decorate when his girlfriend couldn't be bothered. In return, he offered to fix me a romantic meal. (Okay, maybe the "romantic" part I inferred.) Don't get me wrong, the trip to the salon did wonders for Miss

Loiseau. She looked totally amazing when she finally arrived and interrupted us. I only wish her timing didn't suck so bad.

Once the other guests get there and Kirk starts playing host, he acts as if I'm not even in attendance. Every time I enter a room, he disappears. Downstairs, when I step out onto the dance floor, Mr. Bailey decides to stop boogying in favor of playing DJ. Sure, I took him by surprise with the lip-lock in the kitchen and all. I didn't expect it to happen myself. I was drunk. I don't know what came over me.... Guess I got caught up in the mistletoe moment.

Maybe I've been wrong about Kirk all along.

Maybe he really *isn't* gay.

Or maybe he's just not interested in me.

Thankfully, I've got the Christmas break to put some time and much needed space between us. To quote Chicago from their 1982 classic, "Everybody needs a little time away...."

It Ain't Over 'Til It's Over

So many tears I've cried
So much pain inside . . .

—Lenny Kravitz

No matter how many times I return to "Hillbilly High," it always feels like the walls are closing in. Not because being back is a reminder of how much I couldn't wait to get the hell out and really start living my life. It's as if the hallowed halls have literally shrunk. I used to think the exact same thing about Longfellow and even Webb whenever I went for a visit. But when I was a student at both of those schools, I was a whole lot smaller myself. Of course everything would seem bigger! How I ever managed to drink from that tiny kindergarten room fountain and sit at those miniature desks, I will never know.

Now, only 3½ years after the fact, I can barely believe I ever spent any time roaming about this building. Or that I keep coming back. But I couldn't possibly miss my sister Jodi's senior year Christmas choir concert. Which is the only reason I've once again set foot inside this "Home of the Vikings" known as Hazel Park High School. Which is where I am now, sitting in the auditorium, waiting for the festivities to begin.

Personally, I wasn't a songbird back in my day. At least not while at HPHS. I did do some singing during elementary and junior high. In fact I was quite good, if I do say so myself. In fourth grade, our Vocal Music teacher invited me to join Chorus after hearing me sing soprano in his class. That same year we put on a big to-do where we sang the number one hits dating from 1955 ("Rock Around the Clock" by Bill Haley & The Comets) up until 1980 ("Rock With You" by Michael Jackson). Some of the songs were done as big group numbers featuring dances ("The Twist" by Chubby Checker, 1960, and "The Loco-Motion" by Little Eva, 1962). Others were assigned to smaller groups ("One Bad Apple" by The Osmonds, 1971—I sang lead as Donny—and "Stayin' Alive" by The Bee Gees).

But my biggest turn in the spotlight came with 1959's "Venus" by Frankie Avalon. Some little old lady actually stopped me after the show and told me my voice brought tears to her cataract-covered eyes when she heard it. Honestly, I didn't know most of these songs ("California Dreamin'" by The Mamas & The Papas, 1965, and "Bridge Over Troubled Water" by Simon & Garfunkel, 1970) before we performed them. But I couldn't be more grateful to Mr. Derrick Diedrick for exposing me to the world of popular music. . . . I wonder whatever happened to him?

In eighth grade, my favorite English teacher, *Ms.* Cinnamon "Do you mind if I smoke?" Lemieux, got swindled into taking over Choir after the original director decided to up and switch to Computers. Poor Cin (as my best friend forever, Bradley Dayton, and I like to call her)! All because she had minored in Music, she got stuck with the sorriest bunch of so-called singers. At first, I didn't even sign up to take the class. Brad did. But when he and Cinnamon realized there were only *six* boys, none of whom could carry a tune with a proverbial handle, they recruited me. I had to rearrange my entire school schedule just to fit it in. And, boy, was I ever sorry I did.

Not that I didn't enjoy a second helping of Lemieux Love. I just couldn't stand any of the guys who were in the group. Except Brad, of course. He and I, being Teacher's Pets, got away with practically everything. (Maybe that's why the other boys hated us so bad?) We spent more hours hanging out in the back office attempting to teach ourselves Journey's "Don't Stop Believin'" on the piano than we did rehearsing any of the tunes Cinnamon chose for our repertoire. These happened to be

"Flashdance... What a Feeling," from the film of the same name, and "Up Where We Belong," from *An Officer and a Gentleman*. To this day, I still haven't had the pleasure of seeing this particular Richard Gere masterpiece. Though I did enjoy his recent performance in *Pretty Woman* ("Hello, Daddy!"), which I saw up at The Berkley for a buck-fifty.

Over and over we sang these same two songs. (Well, Cin did talk me, Brad, and these three lowlife losers—who shall remain nameless—into performing Billy Joel's "For the Longest Time" at one of our concerts, without any real rehearsal whatsoever. As lead, I literally had to write the lyrics down on my hand so that I could remember them. Talk about being the laughingstock!) Cinnamon couldn't help the fact that she wasn't able to teach us anything else. Her means were meager, since she specialized in Bassoon.

But since this was Hazeltucky we were dealing with, the school board considered Ms. Lemieux more than qualified to take over as Vocal Music Director of Webb Junior High School. And Brad and I loved Cin to death, so we didn't mind her being an "Incompetent Buffoon" as our Band teacher, Mrs. Jessica "Friends hold you back" Clark Putnam, had dubbed her. Thank God for Cinnamon's sake, the next year she up and abandoned teaching altogether so she could follow some man down to Florida. Sadly, the relationship didn't last but six months. The school year after that, she was back teaching my brother Billy's second grade class at Longfellow.

"Good evening, ladies and gentlemen..." A manly bass booms over the sound system. I look up from my program to find a familiar face appearing onstage through the crack in the curtain. "My name is Harold Fish, and I'm the Director of Vocal Music here at Hazel Park High." Better known as "Call Me Hal" according to Brad, who was a member of the top choir called Chorale—no idea why! (Our mutual buddy, Max Wilson, and I used to always tease Brad about it being a "horse thing.") "We thank you for attending our annual holiday concert," Mr. Fish continues. After being under the bright lights for not even two seconds, he's already becoming a sweaty mess. Fortunately, Hal's got his trusty hand towel at his side to mop off his brow. "Without further ado, we wish you a Merry Christmas. . . ."

Like magic, the curtain parts, revealing a wintery wonderland: a group of high school girls decked out in holiday sweaters decorate an artificial tree. Others gather around, all snug and cozy, in front of a non-roaring fake fireplace. From the rafters, bits of white paper fall like snowflakes. My sister stands leaning against a pathetic grand piano (what can you expect from Hazeltucky?), ready to sing her little heart out. She looks super cute in her red and green plaid skirt with black turtleneck, matching tights, and permed shoulder-length bob haircut.

Immediately, I recognize the song they're destroying—I mean *singing*—as one of my particular faves: "Do They Know It's Christmas?" by Band Aid. Too bad that song didn't come out until ninth grade. Brad and I could have talked Ms. Lemieux into letting us sing it. Instead, we got something called "Jazz Gloria," a riff on "Gloria in Excelsis Deo," but with a Caribbean twist. It's no wonder I dropped out of Choir after that experience.

"Jackie Paterno!"

An hour and a half later, who do I run into in the lobby outside the auditorium? None other than the former love of my life, Joey Palladino. Talk about a Blast from the Past! Of course he looks as hot as ever. Same tall, dark, and handsome Joey who I first fell for how many years ago? Same black leather jacket hanging off those same broad shoulders. Same long, muscular legs filling out a pair of Bugle Boy jeans. Same sunshine smile, same cherry lips . . . Not to mention those chocolate eyes.

"What's up?" Joey asks, sounding as surprised to see me as I am him.

I explain my situation, how I'm home on break from Michigan State and here to see my sister's performance. Turns out Joey came to the concert with his family, as his brother also sings in Chorale. (I almost forgot Jodi and Tony used to go together when they were both in junior high.) Speaking of . . . Little Tony sure has grown up to be quite the good-looking young stud, I must say! I almost didn't recognize him as the six-foot-two hunk of Italian sausage singing and dancing about the stage in a white tuxedo shirt with teal cummerbund and matching bowtie.

Hubba hubba!

"I'm here till the twenty-seventh," Joey says, snapping me back to reality. "We should hang out sometime."

"Sure," I say, happy to make time for an old flame—I mean *friend*.

Hard to believe I last saw Joey on the football field at graduation: June 16, 1988. As Brad and I like to say, "We are getting sooo old!"

Speaking of...

Back at my parents' house, the accordion-fold door opens into what used to be my bedroom, and my best friend since seventh grade appears, all bundled up like he's ready to embark on a journey across the Arctic tundra—as opposed to going out to a gay bar.

"*Today!*"

"What's up?"

Standing at the full-length mirror, I've been futzing with my hair for almost half an hour. I don't know how Luke Perry manages to keep his bangs all swooped up the way he does. I use gel; I use hairspray.... I still don't look like the dude. Though most people compare me to Jason Priestley. Which is fine. He's cuter. Why can't anyone else remember him being on that series *Sister Kate* with Stephanie Beacham circa 1989?

"Let's go," Brad orders. "We gotta get to The Gas Station by eleven." By which he means the bar we're going to. Not an actual gas station.

"Why so early?" I wonder.

"Because... Everybody and their gay brother is home for Christmas break. If we don't find a spot in the lot, we're stuck parking on the street. And you know what that means...."

"We get shot?" I ask, going along with our recurring joke. Not that it *is* a joke. I can remember on more than one occasion Brad and I driving downtown and fearing for our lives as we literally ran from the car, accompanied by the word "Faggots!" being screamed our way. God, I love Detroit!

"Plus, I promised Miss Peter we'd get there ASAP so she doesn't have to sit all by herself."

"How is The Once-ler doing?"

I don't think I've seen Miss Peter since last Christmas vacation when she invited us over for a holiday party at her apartment in East Detroit. (I still can't believe they're trying to change the city's name to East*pointe* in order to disassociate themselves from Motown. We'll see if it takes.)

Brad rolls his eyes. "You know. . . . Still smokes like a chimney. Still drinks like a fish."

Immediately, I imagine middle-aged Miss Peter propped up on a bar stool, legs crossed, sipping one of many Captain Morgan and Diets. "Does she still wear espadrilles?"

"Only when the weather's just right."

Sticking a small silver hoop through my left lobe, I clasp it shut. Then I take note of Brad's aural nakedness. "Where's your earring?"

He tells me, "I took it out," sounding somewhat disappointed.

"You're kidding?" Distinctly, I recall the cold winter evening back in 1990 when Brad and I decided we couldn't possibly partake in the Erasure concert at Masonic Temple without first maiming ourselves in homage to homo front man, Andy Bell. Not sure why we felt it necessary to drag straight Max down with us. Other than the fact that he first introduced us to *Wonderland* during sophomore year at Hillbilly High.

"My mom didn't like it," Brad reveals. "She said it made me look gay."

"You are gay," I remind him.

"Yeah, but she doesn't know that," he says. "At least not officially."

This tidbit comes as a tad bit of a surprise. As long as I've known Laura Victor-Dayton-Victor, she's been nothing but supportive of her son and his so-called sexual orientation. One time, she even went with him to this gay bar called Gigi's where she witnessed him performing in a drag show as Alexis Winston from *Ice Castles*. I would have thought four years later, Brad wouldn't still be hiding in a closet. Though who I am to talk? I still haven't said a word to anyone in my family about my homosexuality. "What they don't know won't hurt them," I always say, quoting some sensible person, somewhere.

"All set?"

Making sure I've got everything: keys, wallet, condom—just in case I should get some "sump'n-sump'n"—I take one last look around. Hard to believe the spot we're standing in is the exact same space where Brad and I passed so much time together, back in the proverbial day. The minute I moved out, my father turned the place into his own personal rumpus room.

The bunk beds may be gone, and the knotty pine paneling stripped of its *Days of our Lives* paraphernalia, but if these walls could talk... Oh, the tangled tales they would tell! The nights spent lying in the dark, discussing which guys we'd think were cute—if we were *girls;* reading through the torn and tattered trashy gay romance, *Now Let's Talk About Music*; or the night we conducted a séance, desperate in our attempt to contact the dearly departed spirit of *Making of a Male Model* and *Cover Up* star, Jon-Erik Hexum.

R.I.P. J.E.H.

Gone... But never forgotten.

Finally

Meeting Mr. Right, the man of my dreams
The one and only true love or at least it seems . . .

—CeCe Peniston

We arrive at The Gas Station with not a moment to spare. My little Dodge Omni snatches up the last available space in the snowy parking lot. Which is really more like an alley behind the building. Not that I come down to Seven Mile and Woodward all that often, but whenever I do, I can't help but think back to that first night in 1986, when at the tender age of fifteen, I set foot in this exact same bar, courtesy of Brad and our lesbian friend, Luanne "Lou" Kowalski. Hopefully it won't be too awkward if we run into her here tonight. Lou and I went through a rough patch after I went out with her best friend, Alyssa, who apparently she was madly in love with at the time. Then the following year, I supposedly "stole" sophomore Diane Thompson away from her. To tell the truth, I sort of did. I still can't believe what a jerk I was to Luanne, all in the name of keeping my sexual identity a secret.

"*Lock it!*"

Brad whips his parka off and wedges it down on the floor of my backseat. I hate the fact that we have to walk from the car in the cold without jackets on. But better to freeze for a brief moment than pay a dollar for coat check. Thankfully, we've arrived early enough to avoid the impending snowstorm, and better yet, the crowd. There are all of three people ahead of us waiting to pay Jabba the Hut (and her horse teeth) their cover.

"Hi, Nancy . . ."

The woman working the door reaches for Brad's driver's license. The way she scrutinizes it, holding it up close to her Sally Jesse Raphael frames, one would think she's never set eyes on my best friend before. Considering Brad knows her by name, and he comes here *every* week, I don't see why she's being so particular. "Next!"

I fork over my ID along with my five bucks. Once we're safely inside, surrounded by the sounds of C+C Music Factory and the stale scent of cigarette smoke, I ponder, "What's *her* problem?"

"Don't mind Nancy," Brad says, bellying up to the bar. "She just found out her boyfriend Steven is a total closet case." He pulls out a few bills, holding them in plain view to try and attract the bartender's attention. "What's a boy gotta do to get some service in this dump?!"

At first I think Brad's just being a brat and that we won't get served with that attitude. Until the totally hot, totally shirtless guy in the Santa Claus hat turns around and is all ear-to-ear grin beneath his snowy white strap-on whiskers. "Ho, ho, ho . . ."

Brad bellows, "Who you calling a 'ho'?" sounding insulted. Though I can tell by the hint of sarcasm in his tone that he's just playing around. (I hope.)

"Well, if it isn't Chicken Little . . ."

Brad leans across the bar and gives the babe a kiss on the cheek. He tells him, "This is my best friend, Jack." Then to me he says, "This is Mike."

How the hell could I forget?

Mike is the older brother of our dearly departed friend from high school, Audrey Wojczek. Sadly, Audrey was killed in a car accident during our senior year. We had gone to kindergarten together at Longfellow. But then Audrey moved away to Minnesota, and when she came back to HP, she ended up at St. Mary's. In ninth grade, we reconnected at Webb and became super close. Up until I decided I'd prefer being popular, as opposed to spending time with my *true* friends. Unfortunately, when Audrey died, we were estranged. I still haven't gotten over losing her. Neither has Brad, who became like her best friend once they bonded in Drama Club, playing opposite each other as Will Parker and Ado Annie in what we liked to call *Okla*-homo*!*

"Nice to meet you," Mike says, offering me a firm and callused hand.

Obviously, he doesn't remember that we've already been introduced. Why should he? It's been five years. The first time I ever came to The Gas Station, Mike was positioned in the exact same place. I'll never forget the way he filled out his army fatigues or the way he looked sans shirt with his dyed-blue mohawk. Or the way he flirted, calling me a "cutie" and teasing me about being a (bar) virgin. I was a *real* virgin, too, at the time. Still am when it comes to actual *intercourse*. But I'm not ashamed to admit that I'm saving myself for Mr. Right. Though Mr. Right Now is starting to look awfully good! Mike's hair has grown back, and he's put on a few extra pounds. But for a guy who has got to be at least *thirty*, he's still hot.

Speaking of . . .

"Try to talk without moving your lips," I say to Brad out the side of my mouth, à la our favorite *Laverne & Shirley* episode. "That guy over there is totally checking us out." We've moved down into the area known as "The Pit" to look for Miss Peter, who is supposed to be waiting for us somewhere, and yet, she's nowhere to be found. Instead, there's this totally cute guy standing solo on the upper level who keeps focusing his attention in my and Brad's direction.

Brad turns to catch a glimpse of said stud. Then he squeals like a total girl. "Oh, my God . . . It's you!" Like long lost lovers reuniting on the sands of some beach, Brad and this guy begin running toward each other.

"Brad-licious!" the guy cries, literally picking up my best friend and twirling him around. They remind me of a sailor on shore leave and his girl. "I was hoping I'd see you here."

"When did you get in?" Brad asks, beaming.

"Plane landed at Metro around eight," informs the stranger. "Got to my parents in Fraser around nine. I was on my way down here by nine-thirty. . . . What's new with you?"

"Same shit, different day," Brad drones. "Still working at Big Boy's. Saving money for school. One of these days I'll get my degree."

"Where you gonna go?"

"I'm thinking about Central," says Brad, sounding unsure. "To study Elementary Education." Much like the existence of Brad's long lost pal, this is news to me.

"Good luck!" The guy grins. "The thought of you and all those kids . . ."

"I know, right?"

Watching Brad carry on like this with someone I've never seen before, I must admit, makes me a tad bit jealous. It's obvious that he and this dude are well acquainted. I'm assuming he's some bar friend. Though from their witty rapport, I'm wondering if there's more to this relationship to which I've not been made privy.

"I want you to meet my best friend. . . ." Brad draws me into their duet and makes the proper introductions. "Sean, this is Jack. . . . Jack, this is Sean."

Sean and I exchange pleasantries. As I'm shaking his hand, I take a moment to properly size him up. About twenty-five or six, I'd say, he's a few inches taller than me (who isn't?) with blondish brown hair, cut in a similar style to mine, complete with *Beverly Hills, 90210* sideburns. His left ear is pierced, also like mine. He's wearing a denim shirt and jeans, same as me. When it comes to taste in style, we could be twins. Though I've got on a vintage wool blazer I picked up at Value Village last time I was home. This guy Sean sports a pair of silver-tipped cowboy boots, while I'm wearing my Sears DieHard steel-toes.

Sean says, "So you're Jack? I've heard so much about you."

I reply, "All good, I hope," when I'm thinking, *Why haven't I heard a word about* you?

"We're supposed to be meeting Miss Peter," Brad interjects. "You know how she gets when she's kept waiting."

"Isn't she out past her bedtime?" Sean jokes. Then he adds, "Actually, I haven't seen her. And I've been here for a good hour."

"You're kidding?" Brad furrows his brow. "I'm gonna go call her house. Maybe she got pissed and left. It wouldn't be the first time." He leaves Sean and I alone to get better acquainted over cocktails.

"So where are you in town from?" I ask, after a momentary lull in the action. The new Cathy Dennis ("Touch Me") just began, and we both seem to be enjoying the beat.

"I live in LA," Sean informs me.

"Never been," I'm ashamed to admit. There once was a time when I saw myself attending UCLA. Then I woke up to reality and realized I could barely afford a state school in my own state. "How do you like it?"

"It's awesome." Sean sips his Seabreeze. "I moved out there almost four years ago."

"Any particular reason?"

I can't imagine packing up my things and moving across the country, far, far away from my family and friends. Though I am thinking about heading to New York City after graduation. Maybe because Manhattan is an island, it doesn't seem nearly as daunting. And it's only a five hundred–mile flight back to the Motor City.

"I couldn't stand the cold," Sean confesses. "And spending another day in *Detroit* would've totally depressed me."

We pass what feels like the next hour getting to know each other. Turns out, Sean and I have a lot more in common than just our fashion sense. When I ask him, "What's your favorite band?" I'm totally riveted by his response.

"I used to be a big New Waver. . . . You know, Depeche Mode, The Cure, Echo and the Bunnymen. Now I'm more into Alternative: Nine Inch Nails, Front 242, Nitzer Ebb."

My eyes light up as if the man's uttered the magic words. "You like Nitzer Ebb?"

"I *love* Nitzer Ebb!"

Noticing Sean pronounces it *Knit*-zer, I ask, "Is it Nitzer or Nitzer?" as in *Night*-zer.

"Who cares?" he answers casually. "They fucking rock." He drains the last drop of his drink. "I'm dry."

"What can I get you?" I offer, about to go for another round.

Sean seizes me by the arm. "Stay here.... Make the *girl* come to us."

I can't help but notice he's still got a hold of me by the time our waiter returns with our beverages.

"Don't you two make quite the couple!" compliments the prissy little British boy in biker shorts with the fakest blue eyes I've ever seen, a hand firmly planted against his spandex-covered hip. Though I can't tell if he's being facetious or not. "That'll be two-fifty for the Molson Ice, love, and three dollars for the cocktail."

I reach for my wallet.

Sean stops me with a firm hand held against mine. "I got this."

"Are you sure?" Never have I been one to overlook the kindness of strangers. Especially since I'm only working part-time, and I've still got one final semester of tuition to shell out.

"Please," Sean insists. "These same drinks in West Hollywood would cost triple." He slips the waiter a ten spot and coos, "Keep the change."

"Big spender!" our server cries, adjusting the strap of his off-the-shoulder tank. "You boys enjoy yourselves." And with that, he winks at us and sashays along on his Merry Christmas way.

"Get a load of *her*," I say, appalled at such blatant behavior coming from a homo.

How dare Miss Thing imply that my and Sean's sitting here over pleasant conversation should be construed as anything other than innocent?

"Pay no mind to Aryc," Sean advises me. "She's harmless." He raises his glass and clinks it against my beer bottle. "That's one good thing about Michigan . . . cheap alcohol." Then he adds, "Now if only I could find me a cheap *boy*." He smiles at me a moment, before taking another sip. "Cheers."

Is it just my imagination . . . or is this Sean guy totally flirting?

I think so!

Maybe I will be getting lucky tonight after all.

In Like with You

Another pack of cigarettes
Twenty grade A filtered regrets . . .

—The Judybats

Last night was a total bust.

As suspected, it seemed Miss Peter had gotten her panties in a twist upon being kept waiting and had fled home to seek comfort in a bottle of Captain Morgan. Of course Brad felt guilty, despite blaming *me* for our tardiness—some best friend! I wasn't the one who insisted we stop by three different party stores to pick up a pack of Marlboro Lights. Don't smoke the most popular brand of cigarettes and wonder why you can't find them anywhere. That's all I'm saying! But that feeling quickly dissipated when Brad ran into his high school flame, home for the holidays from Ann Arbor, where he's majoring in medicine at U of M, and took off.

"You guys wish me luck," he begged, before up and abandoning us. "I've always wanted to marry a doctor."

Sean remarked, "I know that guy," as we watched Brad being whisked away by the blond babe.

"You do?" I asked, more out of polite conversation than because I actually cared.

"Before I moved to LA," Sean explained, "Brad took me to a New Year's Eve party at some girl's house in Ferndale. . . ."

"Shelly Findlay?" I remembered being at the exact same soirée back in 1987-going-on-88 with my then-friend, Tom Fulton. But I couldn't recall running into either Brad or Sean there. Perhaps they had arrived after we headed back to my house, where I proceeded to "throw myself" at Tom, causing him to flee—and later call me a *fag*—before he stopped speaking to me altogether. . . . *Ah, memories!*

I still can't believe that jerk. After I took Tom with me to Ann Arbor to see the "Giver Goddess, Fashion Plate, Saint, Earth Mother, Hostess, and Geisha Girl," otherwise known as Judy Tenuta. The only reason I ever befriended him in the first place was because he was dating my best female friend, Betsy Sheffield, all during senior year. Okay, so Tom also happened to be hot, if you're into light brown hair that's kind of long and flippy in front, short around the sides, and wedged in the back. And bright blue eyes, totally perfect smile, square jaw—and dimples!

Clearly I was.

"Shelly, spelled S-H-E-L-L-E-E?" Sean asked. "She was a cheerleader, and she smoked Capri cigarettes. Yep, that's her! I met that guy—what's his name?—on my way in."

"Richie."

Sean scoffed. "You mean *Rich*. . . . Now I remember. He made a point of making sure I knew just how butch he was."

I rolled my eyes. "Whatever . . ."

As far as I'm concerned, *Richie* Tyler will always be "the faggy little seventh grader from Prep Band who plays flute and carries his books like a girl." Let's just say, he and I didn't exactly get along when we were in school together. Which is why I didn't rush right over to say hello. Truth be told, neither did he and Brad. In fact, Brad's the one who coined the aforementioned descriptive phrase. I still don't understand how they ever ended up together.

"Brad introduced *Rich* to me at the front door," Sean continued with his story. "But he never said anything about them being . . ." He paused to add obligatory air quotes. "Romantically involved."

"Don't worry," I told him. "I had no idea either." But that's because, like with Audrey, Brad and I weren't the best of buds during our senior year. Again, all because I preferred trying to become popular—and straight—over spending time with my *true* friends.

"Good for him!" Sean gushed. "That guy is a total hunk."

As much as I agreed, I wasn't about to admit that Richie, two years my junior, had gone from ugly duckling to gorgeous swan. Personally, I thought he and Brad were through a long time ago. Guess when you're drunk and horny, a familiar face is better than some random one night stand.

With that in mind . . .

Sean and I ended up chatting and drinking, and drinking and chatting (and drinking some more), until Mike the hot bartender finally bellowed, "Last call for alcohol!"

A bit bleary-eyed, Sean said, "One more for the road?" Then he shouted out to our British bitch of a waiter, "*Aryc* . . . Get your ass over here!"

Putting up a hand, I shook my head, the room starting to spin. "No more for me, thanks. I'm driving." My mind was fuzzy as I mentally calculated just how many beers I'd imbibed over the past 180 minutes. Usually, I average one per hour. Something told me I'd surpassed my limit on this particularly entertaining outing.

"So sit with me while I have another," said Sean, taking ahold of my arm and keeping me glued to my stool.

Ever the voice of reason, I replied, "You sure that's a good idea?" My new friend had consumed enough vodka, grapefruit, and cranberry to call to mind my grandmother and her booze breath. "How are you getting back to your parents'?"

Sean's smile stretched into a dopey grin. "You're taking me."

Guess that was decided.

What else could I do? Leave the guy responsible for getting himself home all on his own? Never mind the fact that he might kill himself. What about all the other drunk drivers out there on the roads at two o'clock in the morning? So long as I didn't have to be the one to bring him back down to Detroit the next day to pick up his car . . .

Unfortunately, this was only the beginning of my troubles.

As we drove east on 696, just beneath the bridge before Groesbeck, Sean came up with a brilliant idea: "Let's stop at National's!" Overhead, the castors of the Grand Trunk railway cars clickety-clacked their way northwestward.

"Coney Island?" I questioned, sounding like somebody's skeptical mother. Personally, I never understood what's so special about a hot dog smothered in chili sauce.

"Doesn't a Hani special sound delish right about now?" Sean allowed his body to fall across the space between my bucket seats, leaning his head against my shoulder. Thankfully, I don't drive a stick, or I wouldn't have been able to shift.

"Where is there a National's?" I wondered, watching the scenery go by.

I hadn't been out this way since the last time I hung out with Max at his dad's house in Roseville. Which reminded me, I needed to give Max a call and let him know that I was home for a visit so we could get together.

"On the corner of Gratiot and the service drive." Sean started giggling as he repeated the street's name slowly: "Graaa-shit."

Whoever came up with that pronunciation anyway? Why is G-R-A-T-I-O-T, "Gra-shit," and S-C-H-O-E-N-H-E-R-R, "Shaner"? And what about L-A-H-S-E-R? "Lasher." Only in Detroit!

"I thought you lived at Fifteen and Garfield."

"It's a few extra miles out of our way, so what?"

The clock on my dashboard glared back in cold, blue digital: 2:45.

"I'm sorry. . . . I told my mom I'd be home by two-thirty."

I know, I know!

Twenty-one years old and I'm still aiming to please my parents. But what can you do when you're sleeping under their roof? Another reason I hate coming home for a Hazeltucky Christmas.

Stopping in front of Sean's parents' house, momentarily I put the car in park. Two stories high with attached two-car garage, aluminum siding on top and brick on bottom, it totally reminded me of Betsy Sheffield's house over in The Courts. Who knew Fraser was this fancy?

I don't think I'd set foot in this particular suburb since senior year when we held our Prom at someplace called Vintage House. But that whole night has become a blur. I ended up going with Betsy, after Tom told her I "hit on" him and she dumped his sorry ass. (Wonder how she'd feel if she knew I'm really a homo and Tom was totally telling the truth?) Afterward, we went with Pam Klimaszewski and her boyfriend at the time, Stan Blume, to some hotel party on Van Dyke, then for late-night fried food fare at Vern Haney's. Which happens to be located on the corner of the exact same street where Kirk Bailey grew up in Center Line . . . How's that for *quelle coincidence?*

"Thanks again for the ride."

"No problem," I told Sean, adding, "How long are you in town for?"

"Too long." He heaved a heavy sigh. "I head back on the twenty-sixth." Then he cooed, casually, "We'll have to get together again."

"Sure," I said, not knowing what else to say.

Suddenly, the moment felt awkward. I really just wanted to kick him out of my car and "drive away, Daddy, drive away." (What movie is that from? *Poltergeist*, maybe. Near the end where they're trying to split before the house implodes.) Not because I didn't think he was a nice guy. Or I didn't enjoy spending the evening with him. But the second Sean reached out to give me a hug, I could tell what was coming next. . . .

Open mouth, insert tongue.

"I'm sorry," said Sean, when all was done. "I'm a little drunk."

"It's okay," I assured him. "I'm just . . ."

Actually, he's a very good kisser. His lips are nice and soft, and he does this awesome thing where he half bites/half sucks. Which under other circumstances would've totally got me going.

"You're not into me." Sean hung his head in shame, pouting like a puppy. "Too old, huh?"

"No!" I insisted. All my life I've only been attracted to older guys. That wasn't the problem. "I'm just kinda"—before I could stop to consider, the words spilled forth from my mouth, surprising even myself—"in love with someone else right now."

Sean nodded and smiled sincerely. "That's great. I hope everything works out for you. You're a really terrific guy, Jack."

Now if only I could get Kirk Bailey to believe that.

At this precise moment, he and Raquel are off in Toronto. While I was heading home to Hazel Park from East Lansing yesterday morning, the lovebirds hopped the train in Windsor for their long-planned pre-Christmas getaway. (Who goes to Canada in December? They don't call it the Great White North for nothing!) In my heart of hearts, I had secretly hoped that once Raquel discovered her boyfriend dining with me à la *Lady and the Tramp* style, she'd start to question Kirk's and my relationship, concluding that her honey's a big homo, thereby calling off the entire trip. Of course I'd offer to go along in her place, not wanting my pal Kirk to waste his money. Or the *Phantom of the Opera* tickets he's purchased.

No such luck!

Time to Make You Mine

I know what it's gonna be
Me and you, you and me . . .

—Lisa Stansfield

To help get my mind off worrying about what exactly Kirk and Raquel are doing together across the border, I'm going shopping . . . which I detest!

Back in junior high school, Brad and Max were forever dragging me to the mall. One of their moms would drive us up to Oakland and drop us off. We'd have lunch at Burger King or maybe Olga's Kitchen. Every once in a while we'd take in a movie. But we spent most of the time walking around from store to store—for hours! I couldn't stand it. Especially when I could've been home watching TV. Instead, I was forced to endure a Saturday afternoon of "scoping" cute girls (Max's idea) and dodging pushy sales people. (Merry-Go-Round was always the worst!) Thankfully, Brad and I could count on Max's getting sucked into Kay Bee Toys, allowing us the opportunity to sneak off to Opus II or Spencer's, where we'd browse the greeting card section looking at pictures of half-naked Chippendales. I still can't believe neither one of us considered the other might be a homo until we got to high school.

I always liked the idea of going on a "shopping spree." Taking my time; trying on a ton of different clothes; standing in front of the full-length mirrors, asking my friends' opinions as to how I fared in each original outfit: "Do these jeans make my butt look good?" But when it comes down to it, the years have taught me that I prefer to know *exactly* what I'm looking for and where I can go to find it. No fuss, no muss. In and out, I'm done.

This same principle applies to Christmas. Tell me *exactly* what you want me to give you, where they sell it, and I'll go out and get it. But I don't want to have to "shop around" and find something on my own accord. I'll never understand these people who get up at the butt-crack of dawn on the day after Thanksgiving and intentionally put themselves out there with all those insane shopaholics. The pushing and the shoving, the fighting and the bickering, just to save a few bucks on a "Betsy-Wetsy." Or whatever the latest toy craze happens to be this holiday season. Something called a "Game Boy" is what my thirteen-year-old brother Billy wants, I believe.

This is why I've learned to avoid the malls altogether. Especially with only four days until the Big One. I can't even imagine what the parking lots must look like! Of course there's nowhere to park here on Washington in Royal Oak either. Which is where I've decided to come and buy Kirk's present, at Repeat the Beat. Before we left for break, he casually mentioned how he keeps meaning to pick up the new Lisa Stansfield CD. I could've easily gotten it up at Harmony House in Hazel Park. But I always enjoy coming over to the Eleven Mile and Main area with its quaint little storefronts full of vintage clothing and other antiques.

The structure over by the railroad tracks is pretty full itself. I end up parking all the way on the top tier. Thankfully, my Omni fits snugly into a space marked "compact only." Down the staircase I descend, almost murdering myself when I slip on an unsalted step. The second I appear to be safely on solid ground, it starts snowing. Living in Michigan for over two decades, you'd think I'd be used to it now. But I'm not. And I loathe it. The last thing I want to do right now is put my hood up. Royal Oak is where the hip and trendy hang out. I can't be seen browsing for records with hat hair! God forbid I should run into somebody I know...

The cool thing about Repeat the Beat is that it's not a chain.

They have one other location in like Dearborn. It's just this tiny little, unpretentious store filled with more obscure and hard-to-find titles. Don't get me wrong, it's no Trax like in *Pretty in Pink.* There's no Annie Potts behind the register, stapling records to the rafters. But for Detroit, it's decent. Plus, there's this guy who works here, and he always flirts with me whenever I drop in. And—occasionally, he gives me a discount.

"Hey!" Sure enough, his eyes light up the second he sees me waltz through the door. "You home for the holidays?"

"Just got here yesterday."

I can't say I've ever dated an African-American man before. But I certainly wouldn't rule out the idea. I do think he's cute, with a little goatee on his chin and tiny braids wound tight all over. Though at this moment, they're hidden under the Santa Claus hat he's wearing perched atop his head, à la Mike the hot bartender from The Gas Station last night.

We exchange hands. His shake is firm, just as I remembered. Only this time, he holds onto my palm a little longer than per usual. "Cold out?" he asks, a twinkle in his eye.

Involuntarily, I shiver. "Freezing."

"Well, stay for a while and warm up," he insists. "If there's anything I can help you find, just holler."

"Will do."

Considering I don't really know anything about him other than his name—Roger—he seems like a nice guy. Honestly, I don't even know if he's gay for sure. But one of the first times I ever came into this store, probably a year ago, I was looking through the Alternative section for something I'd heard on *120 Minutes*. (The Railway Children, if I remember.) Roger came right over and started chatting me up, asking me what kind of music I was into, where I went to school, what I was studying. The kind of questions that no straight guy is going to ask another dude, because why the hell would he care? But still, there's that whole "is he or isn't he?" game that we gay guys play with each other.

Truth be told, this makes it more fun sometimes when you

don't know for sure where someone stands with his or her sexuality. Like you're living dangerously or something, waiting around to figure it out. It would be so much easier if we all just came out and got on with it already. . . . But these are the times we live in. So much for the "Gay '90s!"

Making my way over to the *S*'s, I find Lisa Stansfield's *Real Love* right away. Picking it up, I flip the CD over, checking out the tracks: "Change," "Symptoms of Loneliness and Heartache," "Soul Deep" . . . None of these titles do I recognize. But then again, I'd never even heard of her until I met Kirk Bailey. Guess she had a hit a couple years ago called "All Around the World" that I remembered hearing once Kirk played it for me. She also appeared on a special collection to benefit AIDS research called *Red Hot + Blue,* featuring the songs of Cole Porter sung by popular artists. Apparently, she's from the UK and is like twenty-five.

"That's a really great record. . . ."

Over my shoulder, Roger's bass booms in my ear. If he got any closer, we could be slow dancing. Not that I mind his body's close proximity to mine. It's just that whole personal space issue that no straight guy would dare violate sort of thing coming into play.

"You've heard it?" I ask, not sure why I'm surprised. The man works in a record store. It's his job to be familiar with the merchandise.

"Oh, yeah. . . . Stansfield's one of my *faves.*" (What straight dude would say this?)

Handing it over for Roger to hold at the register, I reply, "I'll take it." I don't bother going into the whole "It's for a friend" spiel. Wouldn't want to make the guy think I've got a boyfriend—which I *don't*—out of fear of jeopardizing my potential discount. Sometimes in these situations, the less said, the better.

I spend maybe another half hour just browsing. My mom wants the new Reba McEntire and / or Garth Brooks. Something tells me they won't have either here at RTB. And even if they did, I'd be too embarrassed to buy them.

"Think I'm all set," I tell Roger, making my way up to pay for my purchase.

"You're outta here already?" he asks, sounding disappointed to see me go. "How long you around for?"

"Till after New Year's," I answer.

"A nice long visit." He punches in the price at twenty percent less than originally marked. (*Yes!*) "You gonna be going out any while you're in town?"

Handing over my credit card, I answer, "I actually went out last night."

"Oh, yeah?" Roger places one of those carbon paper slips onto the machine, runs it back and forth, reminding me of being a kid and going shopping with my mom at JCPenney's on Thirteen Mile and Woodward. "Where do you like to hang?"

This is the moment we've both been waiting for.

"Usually we'll go to Menjo's or Backstreet.... How about you?"

Roger replies with a grin, "Menjo's, Backstreet, Nectarine Ballroom in Ann Arbor." Which is not-so-subtle code for "all the fag bars."

Finally, we're on the same page!

"Awesome," I say. "Maybe I'll see you around?"

"Yeah," he tells me. Then he takes a flyer from next to the cash register, jots something down on the back. "Gimme a call."

Damn that Kirk Bailey!

If I wasn't too busy being hung up on him, I could probably have myself some fun while I'm home. How come when you're totally available, nobody wants you? The minute you commit your heart to someone, that's when everybody else takes an interest. First Sean, now Roger... Who next?

"Jackie Paterno!" As I'm making my way out into the cold, I literally bump into the last person I expected to see this afternoon. "Twice in two days, huh?"

"Hey, Joey..." I explain how I'm doing some last minute Christmas shopping. Like with Roger, I leave out the part about who I'm purchasing a present for. Though with Joey, I should probably make it known that I've got my sights set on someone so he doesn't think I've held a torch for him these past three-plus years.

As I've mentioned, Joey Palladino was the very first love of my life. We met way back in Mrs. Fox's third grade at Longfellow. Hitting it off right away, we became best of friends, despite being super competitive. When we bowled on a league together, we'd try to outdo each other's score. On Track and Field Day, we'd battle it out to see who could run faster or jump higher. Both straight-A students, our classmates would wager bets between us when it came time for the annual Spelling Bee. Finally it got so bad, our fourth grade teacher, Mrs. Landers, decided to split us up. The following semester, Joey got sent to Mrs. Arnaud's class, and I went to Mr. Smith's. The year after that, Joey's family moved all the way out to Clarkston near Pine Knob. We kept in contact over the course of sixth grade, talking on the phone, and spending the weekends at each other's houses whenever we could.

By the time junior high rolled along, Joey and I had lost touch, and me and Brad soon became best friends after we first met in Varsity Band. (Actually, we met at lunch. Some girls were going through a Slam-Book, discussing which designer jeans they liked best: Calvins or Jordache? Brad walked right up, plopped his tray down on our table, and stated, "*Fuck them!* I like Sergio Valentes better 'cause they make your ass look hot.")

It wasn't until the fall of seventh grade when his grandpa died that I saw Joey again. I remember feeling awful seeing him sitting in the front row of the Ashley-Scott Funeral Home crying his eyes out. I remember wishing I could reach out and wrap my arms around him and make everything better.... But I couldn't. Because back then, I didn't understand exactly what I was feeling.

Then second semester of sophomore year, Joey walked through the door of Mrs. Carey's French class.

That's when I realized how much he meant to me.

At the time, I was dating Alyssa Resnick. Once she and I broke up, me and Joey started hanging out on a regular basis. On

Valentine's Day, he made me a heart-shaped card out of colored construction paper that read *Joseph et Jacques... Meilleurs Amis Toujours.* ("Best Friends Forever.") Joey claimed he gave it to me since he didn't have anybody else to be his Valentine. That afternoon, when we were working out in his grandma's garage, out of the blue I heard myself ask him, "What would you do if I kissed you right now?" To which Joey replied, "I don't know.... Probably kiss you back." But then *nothing* happened! I didn't kiss him, and he didn't kiss me. We just stood there like a couple of jerks. Then we did some bicep curls.

This sort of thing went on for a few more weeks. Joey would spend the night at my house on the weekends. We'd be lying in bed together on the foldout couch down in my parents' basement, and before we'd say good night I'd ask the exact same question: "What would you do if I kissed you right now?" "I don't know.... Probably kiss you back."

But again, *nothing* happened!

Until my mother found Joey's Valentine's Day card and assumed he and I were having a scan-ju-lous affair. He sure was quick to put the brakes on. Before I knew it, our friendship was *fini.* If Joey really had cared about me the way I hoped he did, why didn't he stick around?

"So when are we hanging out?" he says, all devilish grin. "How's tonight?"

Groaning I report, "I've already got plans." Regretfully, I told Bobbie I'd do something with her since her two best friends, Kirk and Raquel, were out of the country. But quickly I remember, "We could do something tomorrow." I'm working from 10 a.m. to 6:30 p.m., but after that I'm free.

Joey places a paw upon my shoulder, sending a thrill through my spine, warming me from head to foot. "It's a date."

Looking at him now with bits of melting snow in his hair, I feel actual butterflies in my belly. It's like time has stood still and we're right back in high school....

And I'm still totally enamored with Joey Palladino.

Kirk who?

Love Will Never Do (Without You)

Never did I have a doubt
Boy it's you I can't do without . . .

—Janet Jackson

When Bobbie Reynolds reported that she grew up in "some hick town" south of Ann Arbor, we immediately hit it off. Though said city of Milan, apparently, had never been bestowed with a nickname à la Hazeltucky, so naturally I took it upon myself to dub it Milanville.

We decide to meet downtown at the DIA where we go to see *La Gloire de Mon Père* (*My Father's Glory*), a French film they're showing at the DFT. All the years I've studied *le français*, I'd never even heard of Marcel Pagnol. *Mais le film est très magnifique*, and I'm adding the book upon which it's based to my last minute Christmas Wish List.

I love coming to see shows at the Institute of Arts. Sitting in the twelve hundred–seat auditorium with its ornate design and terra cotta tiles along the staircase (from someplace called Pewabic Pottery) always makes me feel as if I'm being "cultural." Like I've finally escaped my white trash roots, and I'm amounting to something.

The first time I had the pleasure was back in 1978 while a student in Mrs. Fox's third grade. All thirty-two of us piled into a big yellow bus and headed down to Detroit to take in a stage play based on the life of Harry Houdini. While I don't remember much about the production itself, I do recall one particular scene in which the great magician, born a Hungarian Jew, got help from his friends in choosing a new moniker: *"Houdini, Houdini, a name we have found. . . ."* Did I mention the actor playing H.H. was also quite cute? At least from what my eight-year-old memory remembers.

"Where did you want to go for dinner?" Bobbie asks as we cross the parking lot, gravel crunching beneath our feet. "I'll drive." We climb into her car, which looks exactly like mine—only hers is a Plymouth Horizon—and head south on Woodward toward downtown. "How about Xochimilco?"

"What's So-shi-mil-ko?" I say the name slowly, repeating it back the way Bobbie just mumbled it. Of course I assume it's a restaurant. But one I've never heard of before.

Her jaw just about drops. "You've never been to Xochimilco?!" You'd think I committed a carnal sin the way Bobbie slams on the brakes at the stoplight near some theatre called The Bonstelle where they're presenting a production of *Peter Pan*. "In Mexican Town?" she explains in the form of a question.

I shake my head. In fact, I had no idea there was even such a place as Mexican Town. Greektown, yes. My ex-girlfriend, Diane Thompson, and I used to hang out at Trapper's Alley during the brief time we were going together back in eleventh grade. I always enjoyed walking around, holding hands as we rode up and down the escalators, feeling like a *real* couple. By that, I mean a hetero one. . . . Now I'm wondering what it would be like to do that with Kirk. I bet his skin feels rough and manly, with those thick, fat fingers—

"Really?" Bobbie asks incredulously, interrupting my thoughts. "My parents used to take me there all the time, whenever we went shopping at Hudson's."

To me, this fact is more amazing than my not knowing about some south of the border food joint. "You went shopping in Detroit?"

Growing up, the only time we ever came downtown was when my uncle would take me and my cousins to the Renaissance Center and let us run around like banshees. I remember us being terrified of all the "black people" we'd see on our journey, ducking down in the backseat, making sure to keep the doors locked out of fear of being abducted. God forbid Uncle Jim should actually engage in a conversation with one. Which he did constantly. Going to Michigan State now, I can't even believe there was a time when I didn't know one single African-American, other than my high school French teacher, Mrs. Carey. ("*Bien . . . Bien!*")

We hop on I-75, down by the Fox Theatre, and head toward Toledo. I remember once reading on a Trivial Pursuit card that Detroit is the only place in the United States where you head south in order to get to Canada. (Now I'm thinking about Kirk and Raquel in Toronto, again. *Great!*) Sure enough, we round the bend, and there's the Ambassador Bridge. Years ago, when I was a kid, my parents took me and my brother and sister to Bob-lo Island. For some reason, my dad had it in his head that it would be easier / quicker / safer to drive to Amherstburg, Ontario, and board a ferry from over there. Truthfully, I didn't mind missing out on the whole Bob-lo Boat experience. Whenever we went on class trips in junior high, the boat ride was the worst part about the entire excursion. Though Brad and I would spend most of the hour-long ride following guys from other schools around—*discreetly*—deciding which ones we'd think were cute "if we were girls." And how can I forget the time during freshman year at Webb when Brad and I devised a fiendish plot to break into bully Craig Gershrowski's locker at the Carnation Dance, crack eggs into his fifty dollar Adidas high-tops, and steal his duffle bag and textbooks. Which we later took with us on our end-of-the-year Band trip to Bob-lo and threw off the Bob-lo boat, to be forever lost to the depths of the Detroit River. (And to think, I was a straight-A student, named "Student of the Year"!)

Bobbie pulls onto the exit ramp at Porter Street. The surrounding neighborhood looks a tad bit sketchy with its run-down houses and what I'm guessing are abandoned buildings. Perhaps she senses my apprehension, because Bobbie tells me, "Don't worry. It's totally safe."

Up near some street called Bagley, we park in a dirt lot on the side of a white building. Apparently, the restaurant's name roughly translates to "some place with flowers," according to the sign above the front door. Personally, I've never been a big fan of Mexican food. Growing up, every once in a while my cousin Rhonda and I would stop by the Taco Bell at the end of her block and grab ourselves a little snack, after spending hours up at the House of Beer playing Pac-man. Being Mr. Finicky, I didn't really care for anything on the menu, so I'd always order the exact same thing: a taco with just meat and cheese. I have no idea what the hell I'm going to eat now.

As soon as we enter, we're greeted by the scent of refried beans and the sound of José Feliciano's "Feliz Navidad" (I happen to know all the words, thanks again to Mrs. Fox, who hailed from Spanish Harlem), followed by a boisterous, "Good evening, my friends . . . Welcome!"

Through a doorway leading to the dining area, a middle-aged man appears, addressing us like a Mexican Mr. Roarke from *Fantasy Island*. Only in his drab polyester suit and tie, with mousy hair parted on the side and combed across from left to right, looking like it's been pasted to his head with a serious amount of product, he's not nearly as handsome as Ricardo Montalban. Don't get me wrong, he's the friendliest host I've ever encountered in a *hacienda*. Which makes me wonder if he's the manager. Or maybe even the owner.

Bobbie sings out, "*Hola!*" Followed by some other select words of Spanish that I don't *habla* with the exception of *por favor*. If it wasn't taught to me on *Sesame Street,* I can't comprehend it. My guess is she's asked about a table for two, because our host cops a couple menus from the stand and leads us to one in some far-off side room all decked out for the upcoming holiday. I can't say I've ever seen a Rudolph the Red-Nosed Reindeer piñata before, but at this moment, there's one hanging from the ceiling directly above me. (What I'd *really* like to see is the Hermie the Dentist model. . . . Or is it Her*bie?*)

And the poinsettias! One is planted on each table, and another dozen or so decorate every other available surface. Whenever I see one, it reminds me of being nine years old, when my mother actually took us to church, before we officially became heathens.

At Campbell Memorial Methodist in Ferndale, they used to line the altar with them. After the holiday season, my mother would always rescue one and bring it home. "Don't eat the leaves," she'd tell us kids. "They're poisonous." As if that was the first thing we'd think of the second she placed the potted plant on the end table in our living room, next to the terrarium she got from my Grandma Freeman's funeral two years prior.

"Here are tonight's specials, and they are most excellent." After Bobbie and I have situated ourselves, our host tells us this tidbit. "Can I bring something to drink for the lovely couple?"

Bobbie blushes. "Yes, please... But we're just friends."

Señor Roarke beams, looking like he's the Hispanic Dolly Gallagher Levi. "And may I ask why?" He turns to me. "Such a beautiful young lady... Why are you not snatching her up before some other *hombre* gets his hands on her?"

Um... How do you say homosexual *in Español?*

Speaking of...

We order a carafe of margaritas. While we're awaiting their arrival, I decide to broach what some may call a *delicate* subject....

"Kirk's not gay, is he?"

Without skipping a beat, Bobbie replies, "Why do you ask?"

In the past, I wouldn't have been so forthcoming with my answer. I'd hem and haw and beat around the bush, totally avoiding the question. But being that I've only known BJ, as I sometimes call her (her real name's Bobbie Jo, but she *hates* it), since September, so our history isn't as solid, I feel I've got nothing to lose. "Well, because I am," I confess, "in case you didn't realize. And I thought maybe he might be too."

The fact that Bobbie doesn't even bat an eye when I reveal my "deep, dark secret" reminds me how far things have come since I first came out to Brad back in 1986. Those years of thinking that if I told anyone I'm a homo, they'd totally hate me appear to finally be behind us.... Welcome to the 1990s!

"What makes you say that?" Bobbie asks. She dips a *tortilla* into some *salsa fresca*, mmm-ing like she's having an orgasm. "You gotta try that."

I do, and it's not nearly as tasty as a jar of Tostitos. But I say nothing, nodding politely. "I don't know," I tell her, playing it safe. "Based on some things that have happened between him and me." Or is it *he and I?* Already, I'm feeling a little tipsy.

Bobbie raises an eyebrow, eagerly. "Ooh! What sort of things?"

Contemplating whether I should tell her what went down on Thursday, pre-holiday party, I go with, "You know . . . The hugs hello and good-bye. The fact that he loves Morrissey." I know there are plenty of straight guys who fall into this category. But back in the day, Brad and I would always gauge which side a man butters his bread on based on his affection for The Smiths. Now that I think of it, I'm not sure where we came up with that compass.

"A lot of the guys in the Theatre Department are gay," Bobbie reveals. "I mean, they're not out of the closest. But everybody knows they are. Which is probably why I assumed Kirk was too. But then sophomore year, I directed him and Raquel in a scene from *Streetcar*. . . . They've been together ever since. As far as I know, they're totally happy."

"They are?" I ask, hoping to stir up a bit of hesitancy on her part.

"Let's just say," Bobbie says, "Kirk and Raquel's bedroom wall is next to mine."

Her insinuation makes me shudder. The thought of Kirk actually having sex with a *girl* is one I can't stomach. Especially Raquel Loiseau. She totally doesn't deserve the dude, the way she flirts with every single man she meets—myself included. The first day in Theatre Lab, the second I walked in the door, she was all like, "And who are *you?*" I'll admit it was nice having an attractive woman notice me after spending my high school years only getting looks from girls who I'll politely describe as being "big-boned." But I can't count how many times I've seen Raquel blatantly seduce her way in or out of a situation, and Kirk doesn't even realize what's going on.

What do I have to do to make him realize *I'm* the one he's meant to be with?

Valerie Loves Me

And she could have that anything she ever wanted
But she can't have me . . .

—Material Issue

The only good thing about working at Farmer Jack's on a Sunday is that I get paid time and a half. Eight dollars and fifty-six cents, multiplied by 1.5, means I'm raking in a cool twelve eighty-four an hour. Not bad considering I started out five years ago at three-fifty. Of course that's back when I was a lowly bagger. Being a cashier is the only way to go. Except for at this time of year. Between the complaining customers, lined up from the registers all the way over to frozen foods, and the infernally incessant holiday Muzak being pumped through the PA, it takes about all I got in me not to grab a bread knife from the "Hearth Oven" bakery and slit my wrists. Which is where I am now, hanging out with my best work pal, helping her finish her closing duties so we can get the hell out of here for the night.

"You sure you don't want one?" Before Saran-wrapping a bunch of day-old crullers and marking them down to the bargain price of twenty-nine cents, Val offers me a sample.

From my position wiping down the stainless steel counter with Windex, I proudly resist. "Thanks, but no thanks."

Val tosses the paper tray of what might as well be a box of fat slathered in lard onto the wire baking rack next to a brick of Italian bread. She moves onto the next batch. "How come?"

"I'm not hungry." Nanette in the deli saved me some Stouffer's mac'n'cheese for my break, my absolute fave, and I couldn't even eat it all. With only three days until Christmas, all I've been doing is pigging out on cookies, candy, and everything but fruitcake!

Val furrows her brow and purses her lips, regarding me with a glance reminiscent of the one Audrey used to throw my way whenever I said something she didn't approve of. This I often referred to as her "Don't Even" look. As in "Don't even tell me you're on a diet." Which is what Val says to me next.

"I wouldn't call it that," I clarify. More like, I'm watching what I eat. And this doesn't include indulging in donuts. Especially if I plan on getting naked with a certain someone sometime soon. Which I do. Now if I could only figure out how to make that happen.

"Suit yourself." Val pushes the bread rack aside, next to the industrial-sized oven in which all of these lovely goods were baked. "All set," she tells me, taking off her smock. Wadding it into a ball she groans, "I don't think I'll ever look good in *orange*." Then she asks, "Would you hand me one of them bags?"

"Paper or plastic?" I say, ever the smart-ass. Seriously, I don't think I've asked a customer this question in all my years of working in a supermarket. Talk about stereotypical!

On our way out, we stop by the beer and wine section to pick up the six-pack Val paid for earlier in the evening. "Let me make sure I got my receipt," she says, digging into her purse. "God forbid I should get fired."

Outside, the lot is a blanket of white, the streetlights shining down, the snow sparkling like stars fallen from the sky. Being that we're both parked alongside the building, I offer to give Val a hand with cleaning off her Camaro while it warms up. As my reward, she agrees to share her High Life.

"That's okay," I say. It's one thing sitting in someone's car after work, drinking beer on a warm summer's evening. But in the middle of December . . .

Val practically pleads. "Come on! It's your first day back. We should celebrate."

Given the fact that I'm still working at the same place since junior year of high school, I see no reason for revelry. Granted, I'm only ever here during the summer and on Christmas and Easter breaks. Which is how I keep my sanity—and seniority. Which is something I apparently want to maintain according to my father who's been a Farmer Jack's employee since before I was born. I don't know how he's managed to do the same thing day after day after day for the past twenty-two years and not lose his mind. Most of the full-timers are in the exact same boat. Don't get me wrong, they're a nice bunch of people, and I like them all a lot. But I can't see myself ringing up other people's food for the rest of my days.

"It's Sunday night," I say, struggling for an excuse. "*In Living Color* and *Herman's Head* are on." These happen to be two of my current favorites, along with *Northern Exposure*, *Murphy Brown*, and *Dinosaurs* ("Not the mamma!"). Though this isn't the *real* reason I need to rush home. Tonight's my big date with Joey Palladino.

"Thanks a lot!" Val snaps, totally sarcastic. "I haven't seen you since September. You wanna blow me off for some stupid TV shows?"

"Guess I can have one beer," I decide since Val's a good friend and I only get to see her a couple times a year. We've known each other since high school. She went to Royal Oak, a year ahead of me. I started working at "The Jack" (as Max Wilson tends to call it) in August 1986, and Val followed sometime in either October or November. Besides, how can I resist when I'm being offered free alcohol? "Just let me call my mom and tell her I'll be home late. . . ." And to let Joey know, if he calls, that we're still on.

Fishing into the pocket of my khakis, I find a quarter, drop it into the coin slot of the pay phone in the vestibule. (Jane, our head cashier, calls it the "vesti-view." I don't have the heart to correct her. Sort of like when my junior high English teacher, Miss Shelton, referred to parentheses as "paren-*fe*-ses.")

After a few rings, my father answers. "Hey, Dad . . . It's me." Not sure why I always feel uncomfortable talking to him. Maybe because I've always known that he's always known his son is a homosexual? Don't get me wrong, I love my dad. I just wish we could be closer.

There was the time when I was ten, and I joined Little League. Dad would take me out back, and he'd send me over into our neighbor's yard so we could toss the ball back and forth across the fence. Surprisingly, I had a pretty decent arm. Didn't throw the least bit like a girl as far as I can remember. (My hitting, on the other hand, we won't talk about! Struck out *every* single time at bat. Except for the one occasion during our season opener against Hazel Park Bowl. With bases loaded, I stepped up to the plate.... only to have my future friend-turned-enemy, Tom Fulton, nail me with the ball—right in the back. My first and only RBI.) But for whatever reason, Dad and I would barely say a word to each other the entire time we were playing catch. Maybe because I was afraid if I talked too much, he'd hear the sound of my voice and it would give my gayness away?

"What's up?"

"Is Mom there?" Not sure why I feel the need to tell my mother what I'm doing. I could just as easily let my father know the reason I've called. But Mom's always been the go-to gal for permission getting. Not that I need to *ask* if I can stay out. I'm officially an adult, after all.

"Just a second," my dad tells me. "She's getting ready to watch *Life Goes On*."

Can't say I've ever seen it. But everybody tells me that my sister Jodi looks like the sister on the show. I hear it's a good program. Not sure why I never watch it. Maybe I'll check it out over the break. Who am I kidding? All I'm going to be doing is working in order to save up money to make up for the fact that I don't work when I'm up at Michigan State. No time for any more distractions in my life—including Kirk Bailey. Bad enough, I've been thinking about him the entire day. Earlier when I was ringing up some old lady's order, I almost took off her double coupons *twice!*

"Don't bug her," I decide. "Let her know I'll be home in a little while. I'm hanging out with Val."

Taking me by surprise, my dad wants to know, "Who's Val?" Rarely does he make any inquiries into my personal life. Normally, he allows me to go about my business, turning a blind eye. One time during my senior year of high school, I went to this "popular" party and came home totally wasted. Literally, I fell through the front door. There's my dad, sitting on the couch watching *Matlock*. Didn't bat an eye. Now he's grilling me about my girl friends? And by that I mean friends who are *girls*.

"She's just someone I work with," I say, hoping he won't ask any more.

He doesn't, stating, "Don't stay out too late."

Considering it's only six forty-five, I assure him, "I won't." And then I almost forget the main reason I phoned, I'm so flummoxed. "If Joey Palladino calls, tell him I'll be ready to go by eight o'clock."

"Will do," says Dad, again thankfully minding his own beeswax.

Back at the "Bitchin' Camaro" . . .

The motor's running when I return. Val's got the heat cranked. When I climb inside, before I can unzip my coat, she's offering me a cold one. "Everything all set? Your mommy said you can stay out and play?"

Like I've said, I've known Val for years, and we've become pretty close. Which is why I don't take offense to her teasing. This is how Val's always treated me. If she *wasn't* being a bitch, that's when I'd start to worry.

"So what's new?" I say, settling back in my seat and sipping my less-than-stellar-tasting beverage. Maybe college has spoiled me. Rarely do I drink anything other than Corona with lime anymore.

"Same shit, different day," drones Val. We sit for a moment, staring ahead at the cars passing by on Campbell Road. Across the way, there's a house all done up with holiday decorations.

Which reminds me: I want to go looking at Christmas lights sometime this week. Then she asks, "How's Michigan State?"

"Another five months and I'm out of there," I answer.

"Then what?"

"Good question."

To that, we toast.

What the hell *am* I going to do after I graduate? Part of me really does want to go to New York and pursue a career as a playwright. It's the whole reason I wound up in Theatre Lab this past semester. Ever since I decided I want to be a writer, I always imagined I'd end up working for a newspaper. Or maybe a magazine. But then I thought about what I really enjoy, and the answer was: watching TV. If I can get my career going as a playwright, maybe some day I can make the switch to writing for television.

Though moving to New York means I'll have to leave my family. But being away at Michigan State for the past three and a half years, it's like I already have. And given the fact that they *really* don't know me (read: that I'm gay), I think it would be much easier to live my life the way that I want to (read: being gay) without having them lurking around. Not that I think they'd care if they ever found out. Back in high school, when I fell head over heels for Joey and my mom found his VD card, she wrote me a letter telling me she knew I was gay and that, growing up, so was her uncle. At the time, I was only fifteen years old, so she didn't exactly condone my behavior—not that me and Joey were actually *involved* or anything. (I wish!) For whatever reason, I get the feeling that if I sat my mom down and told her all about Kirk and how much he means to me, she'd totally accept it one hundred percent. One of these days, when I finally have a reason, I know I'll do it.

"So are you seeing someone special?" Out of the blue, Val asks me this. Can't say I saw that one coming!

Unlike with Bobbie, who I just up and spilled the beans to about being gay, I'm still reluctant about making it known to my good friend Val, who I've known a heck of a lot longer. (Why is that?) Part of the reason has to do with the fact that we work together. Again, don't get me wrong, they're a nice bunch of folks here at Farmer Jack's. But they're also *heterosexual.* They're not college-educated individuals, and I'm not sure how open-minded they'd be about having a gay guy in their midst. The women, maybe . . . But the men?

One time back in the summer of '87 when we went on strike, I remember this guy from Produce making fun of me when we were out walking the picket line. And he's this weaselly little dude. Imagine what the burly Night Crew workers would say! Plus, they've all known me since I was sixteen years old. How awkward would it be now for me to come right out and come out? ("By the way, I know we've been working together forever. . . . but I never told you, I'm a fag.") Better to just keep quiet. Come the end of next summer, I'll be moving onward and upward. No one needs to know the ugly truth about my being a blatant liar. What good is it going to do?

But since Val asked, I confess, "There is someone I sort of like." All day I've been dying to tell somebody what's been going on with me and Kirk. But like I've said, I doubt if anybody I work with would appreciate my love for another boy, let alone approve of it.

"Hold that thought. . . ." Val tosses her empty into the mess she calls a back seat and cracks open another. Seriously, if I kept my car in this condition, my father would kill me. From the looks of it, she must've had Arby's for lunch. Or at least at some point in the recent past. That, and Chicken Shack. And Rally's. "Okay, ready," she reveals. Followed by, "What's her name?"

At this moment, I realize I have two options: Number one is to finally come clean with Val about who I am, as they say, "deep down inside." Number two is to continue along the same path we've been traveling since the beginning, with her thinking I'm normal (read: not gay). Obviously, my mind is made up when I hear myself declare, "Kir . . . sty."

I do realize that I just got through lamenting how I've been lying to all my work friends since the day I met them. The second reason as to why I haven't told anyone here in the grocery biz about my (homo)sexuality—least of all Val—is because from day one, I'm pretty certain that Val's had a crush on me. Especially since the weekend before I first moved up to East Lansing for freshman year, Max threw me a party at his dad's house in Roseville, and Val came by with her best friend, Tina, and pretty much told me so.

As parties go when you're eighteen years old, we all got a little wasted. At one point, Val and I ended up alone together in Max's room, making out on his water bed. Val was crying about my leaving, and I was crying because she was crying—and because I was crocked! She kept telling me over and over how much she's always liked me. But how she could never figure out why I didn't like her back. I kept wanting to explain: It wasn't that I didn't like her. . . . I *couldn't* like her. At least not the way she deserves to be liked by a boy.

"Kirsty?" Val totally makes a face, obviously disapproving of the love of my life's (made-up) moniker. "And what does Kirsty do?"

Hating myself for continuing with the charade, I say, "She goes to Michigan State. She's an actress. . . ."

Val rolls her eyes. "Just what you need, a drama queen . . ."

"She's originally from Center Line," I say. "Class of '87."

"I thought you didn't like older women." Val interrupts with another dig at why I never went out with her, I'm sure.

"And she's got a boyfriend," I add, downing my beer. "So it's totally beside the point if I like her or not." Like a manly man, I crush the can with my palm and pitch it over my shoulder.

"Watch it!" Val warns. "You think my back seat's a dumpster?" She grins to let me know she's just joking and offers me another Miller. Then she orders, "Forget Kirsty . . . If she can't see what a great guy you are, she must be blind."

We clink cans and drink. Having not eaten anything substantial since five o'clock, I'm starting to get a little tipsy. Which is probably why I can't seem to let go of this thing with Kirk—I mean *Kirsty.*

"The thing is," I say, hoping I'm not totally slurring my words. "If she's got a boyfriend. Which she does—Ralph . . ."

Ralph?

Nobody's name is Ralph! Except for Ralph Malph on *Happy Days*. But it was the first *R* name I could come up with. Guess I really must be wasted.

"Then what the hell," I continue, "is Kirsty doing inviting me over for dinner when Ralph's not home and letting me kiss her under the mistletoe?"

"Sounds like maybe Kirsty likes you after all," Val surmises, after I conclude my story. "I wouldn't let some guy kiss me if I didn't want him to." Then she says, "You know what you have to do, don't you?"

Right now, I can barely form a sentence. How could I possibly come to a conclusion of any kind? "No. . . . What?"

"If you really like this girl," Val replies, "you have to find out how she really feels about *you*. . . . Ralph or no Ralph."

As much as I understand this advice in my heart, my head feels too fuzzy to wrap my brain around it. On top of the fact that Ralph's name is really *Raquel*. That woman is a force to be reckoned with. She's played Lady Macbeth for Pete's sake! There is no way she's going to give her man up to another guy. Not without a fight.

But I love Kirk Bailey, and I want him to be mine.

That's it!

As soon as he gets back from Toronto tomorrow, I'm calling up Kirk and asking him out. Once and for all, I need to know where he stands. . . .

And if we have a future together.

Wicked Game

What a wicked game you play
To make me feel this way . . .

—Chris Isaak

My so-called date with Joey begins with him picking me up at my parents'. Though he doesn't come to the door. He waits outside in his car—thanks to our scan-ju-lous past, I'm sure. I think Joey's afraid to see my mom after what went down with him and me and her and that letter all those years ago. I doubt she'd say anything about it to Joey if she saw him. My mom's not that kind of woman. She would never blatantly embarrass somebody to their face. Truth be told, she's probably as uncomfortable about the whole incident as me and Joey. Though she's never brought it up again, I can tell she hasn't totally forgotten about it.

"Tell Joey I said Merry Christmas," Mom says, as I'm heading back out the front door. Luckily, he was running a little late. I barely had time to get home from my beer drinking with Val, take a quick shower, and rinse the booze taste out of my mouth.

"I will."

According to Channel 2 *Eyewitness News*, it's like twenty degrees outside. Funny how in summer, the thought of forty seems like freezing. What I wouldn't give right now for it to be that warm. Thankfully, Joey's got the heat on high. The inside of his car is all hot and toasty as I settle into my seat.

"Jackie P!" he exclaims. "What's shakin'?"

Watching him tap his leather-gloved hands to the beat of Heavy D's "Now That We Found Love," I can't believe we ever got along back in the day. Me, I was totally into bands like Depeche Mode and New Order. Joey was all about Run-DMC and the Beastie Boys. I'll never forget after Joey and I "broke up," we had this all-school variety show. Joey got up and performed this rap routine, wearing a jogging suit and these tacky gold chains around his neck. And he break-danced! As much as it tortured me to watch him onstage in the HPHS auditorium "busting on the mic," I couldn't help but think he looked totally hot.

"What happened to the Fiero?" Realizing Joey's gotten himself a new car since I saw him last, I have to wonder. This one, believe it or not, is a Probe. Whoever came up with that name needs to be neutered.

"I got that thing for my sixteenth birthday," he reminds me. "My dad decided it was time for a trade in."

Must be nice having a rich father with a guilt complex over divorcing your mom and abandoning you. Of course I don't say this out loud. Going to school at Michigan State, I've come to make friends with a lot of kids from the wealthier suburbs. At this point, I've gotten used to being a poor boy from Hazeltucky. Maybe someday when I'm a rich and famous writer, I'll look back and wonder how I ever managed to resign myself to this fact.

"Where did you want to go?" We never really did decide what we'd be doing this evening other than "hanging out."

"Have you been to see Santa yet?"

I give him a look to see if he's being serious or not. With Joey Palladino, it's always hard to tell. "Um . . . No."

"Then that's what we're doing first."

"You really wanna brave the mall?" I ask, imagining it must be jam-packed during this extended-hour shopping season.

"How you gonna get anything for Christmas," Joey says, "if you don't tell the big guy what you want?"

I can't even remember the last time I paid a visit to old Kriss Kringle; back in high school, probably, when I was friends with Ava Reese and Carrie Johnson, and Audrey was still alive. Junior year, they dragged me, Max, and Brad with them out to Lakeside, and the six of us all piled onto poor St. Nick's knee. Let's just say he wasn't feeling particularly jolly at that point. Like trick-or-treating on Halloween, it's one thing when you're still a kid to participate in this pastime. I can't imagine the old man playing Mr. Claus is going to appreciate bouncing two college-aged boys upon his lap.... Though who knows? Maybe he will!

We hop onto I-75 and head north to Fourteen Mile. On the way, Joey and I play a quick game of "What Have You Been Doing Since We Graduated High School?" I start. Went to Michigan State in the fall of '88 where I'm majoring in English with an emphasis on Creative Writing. During the summers and on breaks (like the one we're on now), I come home to Hazeltucky and stay with my parents so I can work at Farmer Jack's and save money. In the spring, I'm either moving to New York City to pursue a career in playwriting or to Los Angeles to try and break into TV. Worse case scenario: I'll publish a novel.

"And that's all she wrote," I conclude, "when it comes to my exciting life."

"Do you have a boyfriend?"

Even though Joey knows I'm gay, based on what went down with us, the fact that he has the balls to come right out and ask me this question sort of takes me by surprise. Sure, it's been the elephant in the room since we ran into each other the other day. But I kind of hoped we wouldn't have to address it. Now that he's put it out there, looks like I have no other choice.

"At the moment," I say, "I do *not.*"

Joey nods and smiles. "Well that's good."

What's that supposed to mean?

Shifting the focus onto Mr. Palladino and away from yours truly, I inquire, "How about you?"

"Do I have a boyfriend?" he says. "Not anymore."

While that's not what I was asking, I'll take the tidbit as Joey's confession that he, too, plays for the pink team. I kind of figured that would be the case. Though I still can't figure out why he dated my ex-girlfriend, Diane Thompson, all through junior and senior years if he wasn't straight. Brad claims Joey did it to get back at me for not returning his affections. Even if that were true, why would Joey waste two years of his life going with a girl if he wasn't into her?

"Where did you end up going to college?" I ask, switching to a less touchy subject.

"I'm up at Central," Joey says. He puts on his blinker and moves over into the right lane, preparing to make our exit. "Getting my degree in Business Administration. My dad says he'll get me a job at Kmart's—if I ever finish." World headquarters. Not one of the regular old stores.

The way Joey says this leads me to believe he's not enjoying his studies. I can't imagine the pressure he must be under to follow in his father's footsteps. Thankfully, my parents have always been supportive of me and my dreams. As long as I'm paying for my own education, I'm allowed to study exactly what I want.

As expected, the Oakland Mall parking lot is full to the max. Row after row we drive up and down, eventually finding an empty spot all the way in back, out near the movie theatre marquee.

"Have you seen *For the Boys*?" Joey asks, as we bundle up in preparation for the trek across the frozen tundra.

"Is that with Bette Midler?" I say, tying my faux-cashmere scarf tight about my neck. "Not yet."

"You're kidding me?" he says. "I've seen it five times. . . . Maybe when we're done with Santa, we can go and check it out?"

"Sure," I say, surprised at Joey's adoration for the Divine Miss M. Sure, I enjoyed her in *Big Business*. But that one I went to see mainly because of Lily Tomlin. After all these years, I've still not seen *The Rose*. Or *Beaches*. Brad keeps threatening to stop being my best friend until I do.

Despite the hustle and the bustle, I do enjoy the mall when it's all decorated for the holiday season. Ever since I've gotten older, I never seem to sense that "Christmas feeling" anymore. When you're a kid, there's this magic in the air that starts round about the day after Thanksgiving and goes on for the next month or so. I remember being in kindergarten and making these chains out of red and green construction paper. There'd be like twenty-five of them all looped together with a white one on the very end. Every morning when you woke up, you'd tear one off, counting down the days until Santa's arrival. By the time you got to December twenty-fourth, you felt like you were going to die from anticipation. Forget about getting any sleep that night!

When my brother and I still shared a room, we'd lie together in bed—me on the top bunk, Billy on the bottom—and we'd listen to this Alvin and the Chipmunks Christmas tape ("It's caroling, Clyde") on our dual-cassette player. Even though I was like fourteen years old and my belief in Santa Claus had been dashed a long time before, the fact that Billy was super excited about him *finally* coming to town got me totally geeked too.

The line to see Santa is a mile long. Not even exaggerating. It starts all the way up at his castle and extends down and around past The Sharper Image and Suncoast Video.

"Are you sure you wanna wait?" I ask Joey. The longer we stand here, the more embarrassed I feel about being surrounded by all these little kiddies and their parents. Don't they realize it's a Sunday night? They should all be home getting ready to watch *Married With Children*.

"Come on!" Joey says. "I wanna get our picture taken together."

Forty-five minutes later, we arrive at the front of the line....

Santa's all "Ho ho ho... Have you been a good boy?" to both me and Joey. I can't even believe the old dude is going along with it. (I do a double take, just to make sure the guy doesn't got a hard-on.) He's like, "And what would *you* like for Christmas?"

I answer. "Um... I could use some new socks. Maybe some underwear. Hanes or Fruit of the Loom." Had I known I'd be under this pressure, I would've made a list. "Contact lens solution... Clearasil soap... Some Dep." All the basic beauty necessities that I hate wasting money on for myself.

Santa chuckles warmly, turning his attention to my comrade in arms. "And what about *you*, young man?"

"Me?" Joey replies. "I want a new boyfriend."

Say cheese!

The pop of a Polaroid flashes in our faces, and I just about shit a brick. Not only can't I believe Joey Palladino had the audacity to go there with Santa Claus . . . He stole my bit.

Next we go to the movies.

As we get in line at the ticket booth, Joey's brown eyes fill with light. "*Beauty and the Beast!*"

"Would you rather see that one instead?" I say, wondering if he really wants to pay five dollars to see a kiddie flick. Me, I've always been a fan of animated movies, my all-time faves being *Charlotte's Web* and *The Fox and the Hound.*

"Can we, please?" Joey asks, sounding like a six-year-old. Funny, I don't remember him ever being quite this (dare I say?) *gay* back when I knew him before.

We buy our *billets*, along with an industrial-sized bucket of popcorn and a pop. Taking our seats in theatre three, I'm surprised to see the number of childless adults in the auditorium with us. Of course Joey and I are the only two guys sitting together. Thankfully, we're just in time for the previews, which include *JFK, Prince of Tides* with Barbra Streisand, and something that looks sort of cool called *Until the End of the World.*

Finally, the show begins. But not before Joey and I have almost completely finished our snacks. "Save some for me," he says, reaching a hand into the bucket.

Is it just my imagination . . . or did Joey's fingers just brush up against mine—and linger?

"What should we do now?"

Around eleven thirty, the movie lets out. I have to say, I truly enjoyed it. But I've been an Ashman/Menken fan since their earliest collaboration, *Little Shop of Horrors*. How tragic is it that Howard passed away this past March from AIDS-related complications? And to think, he was only forty years old. . . . I hear that before he died, he and Alan put together an *Aladdin* musical for Disney that comes out next Thanksgiving starring fellow Michigander, Robin Williams. That should be fun.

For me, the best part of *B & B*—other than Gaston's being a total babe—has to be the waltzing "Tale as old as time..." scene. Gotta love old Angela *Murder, She Wrote* Lansbury as Mrs. Potts! Not only does Belle look fabulous in that gold chiffon number... The animation itself—incredible! The marble pillars, the floor, the chandelier—it all appears so three-dimensional. Sitting beside Joey in the darkened auditorium, the entire sequence took my breath away. Though I can't help but think, *We'll condone bestiality... but* not *the love between two men?*

On our way back to Joey's car, I figure the evening has just about ended. Seems like he's not ready to say good night...

"I should probably get home," I say. "I told my mom I wouldn't be out too late."

"What did you do that for?" Joey scolds, playfully. "I was thinking we could go down to Menjo's."

"I guess...." Though I didn't really dress for the bar, it might be fun. I'm sure the place will be packed full of cute boys home from college. Just like me and Joey.

"Awesome!" Out of nowhere, Joey reaches down, scoops up a ball of dirty ice, and pelts me in the face with it.

"Watch it!" I cry. Not only does it hurt—that shit is cold. "I said I'd go."

"What's-a-matter?" Joey says, putting on his tough guy act. "Can't take it?"

Back and forth we start beaning each other. Closing my eyes, I don't so much aim as I just let the snowballs fly. Like I've said before, for a gay guy, I've got a pretty good arm. And Joey was always the athletic type, so we're pretty well matched in this battle. Down behind a bank I dive, popping my head up like a periscope. Nowhere do I see Mr. Palladino when *BAM!* He gets me from behind. Not only does Joey hit me full force—the next thing I know, he's taking a flying leap through the air and landing on top of me.

"You give?" His groin presses into my backside. With his left arm, Joey pins me to the ground while his right takes ahold of the back of my head. "Somebody's gonna get a white wash!"

With all my might I manage to flip myself over. Joey's still on top of me, his face mere inches from mine. He really is a beautiful man with his olive skin and prominent Italian schnoz. Obviously, he's been trying to make it clear to me all night that he's interested in being more than just *mon ami*. It would be so easy to allow whatever is happening to happen.

Wouldn't it?

Chocolate eyes peer down at me as Joey licks his cherry lips. "Had enough?"

My chest heaves up and down as I struggle to catch my breath. "I give."

But Joey doesn't take this as my surrender. Instead, he uses my own game against me. "What would you do if I kissed you right now?" he says, grinning his sunshine smile.

"I don't know," I respond, playing my part. "Probably kiss you back."

And with that, Joey Palladino's full lips press firmly against mine.

I've Been Thinking about You

We must have been stone crazy
When we thought we were just friends . . .

—Londonbeat

As anticipated, Menjo's is packed!

First off, the line for valet spills out from the front lot and onto Six Mile, aka McNichols. There must be at least a dozen cars all vying for a spot. Per usual, nobody wants to risk their lives parking on the street. Being that it's already after midnight, I thought most people would've gotten down here by now. Or moved on to another location. But this is Detroit we're talking about. Not only is there a shortage of gay bars, the ones that do exist only do business depending on the particular night of the week. Ever since I officially started coming out—of the closet and to the clubs—Sunday nights have always belonged to Menjo's. . . . I wonder who exactly established this tradition and when?

"We don't have to wait," I inform Joey. After a good fifteen minutes of inhaling fumes from the Ford Tempo in front of us, I'm ready to call it quits.

"Shut up!" he says. "We drove all this way. . . ."

Again, I can't help but worry what my mom's going to think when I don't come home immediately following the movie. I'll be so glad when I get back to Michigan State. As much as I love my mother, I do *not* miss having my comings and goings carefully monitored.

Freshman year when I first moved into Shaw Hall, it was like, "*Woo hoo!*" Me and my roommate at the time went to some kegger at some frat house with some kid he knew from Port Huron. We got totally trashed off our asses and didn't come back to the dorm until four in the morning. Of course I had a 9:00 a.m. class five hours later. Totally sucked! But I couldn't believe how cool it felt rolling in at all hours, all like, "Yeah, I'm wasted.... So what?"

Eventually, the line starts moving, and we make it inside the bar right before 1:00 a.m. Unfortunately, this only gives us an hour. But it's not like I'm looking to get drunk or pick anybody up. I'm with Joey. I still can't believe it: Joey Palladino and Jack Paterno, out together at a G-bar. What would our Hillbilly High classmates think if they ever found out? Probably not a whole lot!

"What are you drinking?" Joey demands over the blaring beat of Black Box. (At least this time it's not Christmas music blasting in my ears. If I hear one more rendition of "Carol of the Bells" or worse yet, "Grandma Got Run Over by a Reindeer," I'm going to ralph!) Taking the lead—and my hand—Joey pulls me along through the crowd, past the piano near the front bar, and into the room on the opposite side. Thankfully, the lesbians aren't playing pool tonight. Not because I've got anything against them, there's just not enough room right now for a game of eight ball. I swear this place is *never* this crowded except on Christmas break. Whenever Brad and I come down here during the summer when I'm home, it's busy. But not like this.

"I'm really not that thirsty," I decide.

Again Joey orders, "Shut up! We came all this way.... You're having a drink."

"Fine," I say, giving in. "I'll have a Sloe Gin Fizz." Don't ask me where that came from. Call it a throwback to my youth, when all Brad and I ever drank were sissy drinks like Strawberry Hill and Fuzzy Navels.

Joey uses his hotness to flirt his way to the front. He orders our cocktails. We carry them back to the open area over by the dance floor where, like the rest of the place, it's wall-to-wall bodies, bumping and grinding against one other. Fortunately, we left our coats in the car. It's like a sauna in here, and I'm way too overdressed in this turtleneck sweater.

"Do you see somewhere to sit?" I shout. Don't know why I bother; there isn't a vacant seat to be secured.

"Let's stand over here," says Joey.

I follow him to a darkened corner over by the DJ booth. He raises his beer bottle to my plastic cup, and we clink. Then Joey presses me up against the wall and leans in for a smooch. Looks like we're picking up where we left off back at the old shopping mall snowbank.

A firm hand grips my shoulder. Soon after, I figure out it doesn't belong to my new boyfriend—if that's indeed what we're calling Joey. I haven't made up my mind. Fearing that some perv is trying to trap us into a three-way (there's a time and place for everything, and this isn't it!), I open my eyes, turn my head, and who do I see standing beside me?

"Kirk?"

As in *Bailey*.

"What's up?" he says, oh so nonchalantly. Like I didn't just catch him hanging out at an establishment for homosexuals. (Or he caught me. Still . . .)

"I thought you were in Toronto." If memory serves, he and Raquel weren't scheduled to return from their trip until tomorrow morning. Believe me, I've been counting the minutes.

"We got back early," Kirk slurs, adding, "Not my idea."

From his tone when he says this, coupled with the fact that he looks as if he's been knocking back the booze for quite some time, I can only conclude that there must be trouble in paradise. Now I want details!

"Hi, I'm Joey. . . ."

How could I forget my manners?

My date extends his arm, and he and Kirk take hands. I can't tell if Joey senses something going on between me and Mr. Bailey. Considering technically there's *not,* it shouldn't be a problem. Though it sure does seem like Joey's sizing up the competition, the way he gives Kirk the once-over, looking him up and down.

After the introductions, I invite Kirk to join us. "That's okay," he declines. "I'm here with Bobbie. She wanted to go dancing and invited me to tag along."

While this makes total sense, I know for a fact that there are plenty of other (read: straight) clubs in the city of Detroit. Why did Bobbie and Kirk happen to choose this particular party pad for their Sunday evening outing? Because the music is good?

I think not!

"Where is she?" I wonder, more to make conversation than because I want to say hello. We did just see each other last night at dinner. (Note to self: Refried beans do not agree with my stomach. That's all I'm going to say!)

"Waiting in line for the bathroom," Kirk answers. "I told her good luck!"

Yes, finding a place to pee can be a real chore for any girl in a gay bar. So long as she doesn't mind discovering that the stall she selects is occupied by two dudes doing God only knows what... And if I know Bobbie, she won't. She'll most likely get a kick out of it.

"I love this song!" Joey lets out a squeal at the sound of the new Stereo MC's. "Wanna dance?"

"You go," I tell him. "I'm gonna stay here and catch up with Kirk."

Joey walks away in a huff. Even though I can tell he's pissed, I don't care. I need to get the skinny on what brought Kirk back from his trip so soon.... And what he's *really* doing down here at this so-called den of sin.

Luckily, a seat opens up, and I lead Kirk over to it. Helping him along, he leans his arm on my shoulder to steady himself as he slides into it. I hate seeing him this way, all drunk and disorderly and unable to handle himself. I wish we were somewhere by ourselves right now, and not in this sardine can, where I could care for him.

"So Toronto was a bust?" Getting a whiff of Kirk's cologne as I lean in close to talk into his ear makes me realize just how much I've missed that smell—and the man sporting it.

"Pretty much." He sips his Heineken. "All me and Raquel did was fight the entire time." Kirk makes a sour face like he's had enough, slams the bottle down on the ledge behind us. It almost tips over and spills onto the drag queen duo seated to our right. Thank God it doesn't. I don't think I could handle finding myself in the midst of a bar fight tonight.

"I'm sorry," I say. Though secretly I'm thinking, *Sa-weet!* But I'm not about to utter this aloud. Not when Kirk seems so down in the dumps. Of course now I need to know *everything.* "Don't tell me.... Your *Phantom* seats weren't good enough?"

He ignores my smart-ass remark. "Everything started out fine. We had a nice dinner at the Old Spaghetti Factory. The show was good. Afterward, we went for drinks, then back to the hotel...."

"Feel free to skip this part," I plead. The last image I need in my mind is Kirk and Raquel, postcoital.

"Pretty soon," he says, "she starts talking about what happens after we graduate and we get *married*."

Everyone's always assumed that this was part of the plan since K & R have been a happy couple for over two years now. They're like the Tom Cruise and Nicole Kidman of the Theatre Department, destined to be together forever. Only without the scary Scientology aspect.

"Sounds like you don't want that," I say, trying to be sensitive.

Kirk says, "Maybe some day... But not now." He pauses a moment to reflect on some profound thought. "This isn't the 1950s. Who the hell gets married when they're twenty-two years old?"

I remind Kirk that my dad was seventeen and my mom fourteen when they were wed back on January 3, 1970. But that's because they got themselves "in trouble" and had no other alternative. Other than abortion. Or pawning me off on my aunt and uncle. I can't imagine Raquel Loiseau doing anything that would involve bloating her body or running the risk of stretch marks.

"Besides," I interject. "What's the point in dating someone long-term if it's not going anywhere?"

"Yeah, but . . ." Kirk gives this some thought. "Why are we both getting our degrees in Acting if we're not gonna be actors?"

"I thought you wanted to go to New York." On more than one occasion we've discussed this option for him. In fact, Kirk's the one who put the idea of moving to the Big Apple into my head in the first place.

"I do," he sighs. "And Raquel knows this. Suddenly, she's all about staying in Michigan."

Other than Meadow Brook and The Attic, there aren't any professional theatre opportunities in Metro Detroit. It's not like you can audition for any of the touring shows that come through the Fisher. They're all cast out of NYC, according to Kirk.

"What's she going to do here?"

"I don't know!" Kirk shakes his head in exasperation. "She says she wants to get in with one of the local agencies and start doing commercials or industrials. Either Affiliated or the Talent Shop, maybe Productions Plus."

Not knowing the first thing about the whole biz, I ask, "Is there a lot of that kind of work available?"

"Not really . . . There's always the Auto Show," he says with some spite. "Who wants to stand around all day talking about cars?"

"So what are you going to do?" I have to wonder.

At this point, Kirk Bailey drops the bomb on me. . . .

"Nothing," he says with a shrug. "We broke up."

Oh my f-ing God!

Finally, some good news.

But really, what can I say?

Other than, "I'm sorry to hear that."

"No, you're not!" Kirk snaps. "You don't even like Raquel. Why should you care?"

He's got a good point. Though has my—I won't say hatred—*dislike* of Ms. Loiseau been that transparent? It's not even that I don't like her. I just don't believe she deserves a beau like Kirk Bailey.

The way I do.

With total sincerity I answer, "Because I like *you*."

Kirk turns his attention toward Joey dancing up a storm in the dark, gyrating himself between the hips of two total hunks. "What about your boyfriend?"

There's no denying Joey's dazzling. Since the day I first laid eyes on him, I've made that claim. But after all these years, I've come to this conclusion: Joey Palladino is *not* the Man of my Dreams....

That honor belongs to Kirk Bailey.

"He's not my boyfriend."

"How come? He's totally hot...."

"How would you know?" I ask. "You're not gay."

Kirk turns to me, tears swelling in his eyes. "I'm not?"

Thinking back on all the pressure I've felt along this familiar road to accepting my sexuality, I wouldn't wish this moment of realization on anyone. Least of all Kirk. But we all go through it. Every single one of us gay men—and women. We grow up thinking we're "the only one." That we're all so unique. No one else can possibly understand what we're struggling with. The kind of suffering we fear causing our family and friends by revealing our secret selves... No one else can possibly understand what it feels like to be such a bitter disappointment.

I'm sure this is exactly what Kirk is thinking because I've felt the exact same way too.

Unable to resist any longer, I reach out and wrap my arms around him, rubbing his broad back. Softly I whisper into his ear, "It doesn't matter if you are or you aren't.... I'll always be here for you."

And with that, we share our second kiss.

Years from now, after Kirk and I have been together for fifteen, twenty years, living in New York City somewhere, still pursuing our dreams, I hope we'll reflect on this night as a defining moment in our past. There's a part of me that knows full well I should let him go. That I shouldn't ruin his life by fighting for whatever this is we've got going on. That I should encourage him to go back to Raquel, ask her to marry him, and allow him to live "happily ever after." Yet, what kind of person would I be if I did that? If I let him go on living a lie.

Come on!

Haven't we all seen enough made-for-TV movies to know this never works?

As my high school World Literature teacher, Miss Horchik, once told my best friend, Brad (quoting the late, great William Shakespeare)...

"To thine own self be true."

Apparently, this is also Joey Palladino's motto. I don't know if he witnessed my make out session or what.... But when two o'clock comes, my date—and my ride back to Hazeltucky—has gone AWOL. Guess he got pissed and went home. Or maybe he's off somewhere having a *ménage* right now. Thankfully I figure this out *before* Kirk and Bobbie hit the road, and Kirk offers to drive me to my parents'.

"It's not like it's out of my way," he says, opening my door like a true gentleman.

On our way up Woodward, we say nothing of what went down between us at the bar. In fact, we barely speak a word at all. Which is the true sign of a real relationship: the ability to just be present in each other's presence.

"What are your plans for tomorrow?" I ask, correcting myself, "I mean *today*."

"Not sure," Kirk answers. "I might stop by the store and help my dad with some work in the morning.... What are you doing?"

"Nothing until the evening."

Unfortunately, I'll be slaving away at The Jack from 5:00 to 11:00 p.m. December 23rd is no doubt the biggest day of the year in the grocery biz. All those last minute shoppers scouring the aisles in search of Durkee's fried onions to top off their green bean casseroles and wondering why the hell we're all out of Hormel ham. ("Gee, I don't know. . . . Because tomorrow is Christmas Eve, maybe!")

Pulling up in front of my folks' house, Kirk asks, "Wanna have lunch?"

"You mean like go on a *date?*" I say, unable to resist using the word.

Anticipating some smart-ass reply, I'm quite taken aback to hear Mr. Bailey answer, "Yes. . . . Like go on a date." Of course then he gives me exactly what I expected: "But I ain't paying!"

Followed by another kiss.

The Promise of a New Day

One step closer
To make love complete . . .

—Paula Abdul

My first Christmas memory isn't one that I remember, per se. It surfaces from a series of shots snapped round about the Year of our Lord 1972. At the time, the Paterno family consisted of me and my parents, Jack and Dianne. (Yes, like the John Cougar song. Only Mom spells her name with two *N*'s.) Living in a tiny, two-bedroom house on McDowell in Ferndale, this was in fact a step up from our first humble abode on Hampden in Madison Heights, where I'm told I shared a double bed with my folks, despite having yet to outgrow my own crib. Eventually, we made the move to nearby Hazel Park, and my sister, my brother, and I would all one day obtain our own sleeping spaces. There I resided until September 1988, when I left for college at Michigan State.

In the first photo, taken on the last Christmas of the first Nixon administration, a two-year-old me sits atop a white Humpty Dumpty toy box beside my seventeen-year-old mother. On my head rests a red fireman's hat, a plastic toy engine parked at my stocking feet. Mom dons a pink nightgown and matching fuzzy slippers, her hair flipped up à la *That Girl*, her spectacles, horned-rimmed. Grinning ear-to-ear for my father behind the Instamatic, we both bear a resemblance to Disney's famous Cheshire.

The second shot, snapped on the same snowy morning, reveals my same-age cousin, Rhonda, sandwiched between our grandpa and grandma, George, aka "Guff," and Helen Freeman, who inhabited the corner house across the street. Granny, as we called her, wears her hair in a graying football helmet coif. Grandpa Guff's bald head reflects the camera's flash like a cue ball. Thumb in mouth, Cousin Rhonda stares blankly, a deer-in-the-headlights expression frozen on her cherub face, as if no one had informed her of the impending Kodak moment.

The final image, shot four years later in the Hazeltucky house, shows me as a six-year-old sporting my Spiderman "footie" pajamas, mugging for the camera, holding high that particular Christmas's most prized possession: a pair of twelve-inch plastic *dolls*. But these were no ordinary run of the mill Barbies. Or even the uber-butch "okay for boys to play with" G.I. Joe. This duo was none other than the ultimate brother-sister act of the mid-1970s: Donny & Marie, who came complete with cardboard TV studio set and plastic 45 rpm record you could play on your portable Fisher-Price record player while you danced Mr. and Miss Osmond about the soundstage in their purple and pink designer costumes. While I can't recall the exact expression on Santa's Helper's face when I dropped my Donny & Marie dolls request on him earlier that holiday season, I'm sure it fell somewhere along the line of: "We've got a gay one on our lap here."

In the background of the aforementioned photo, Uncle Roy can be seen reclining in the corner comfy chair assembling the tiny plastic TV camera that came with Donny & Marie's television studio. After sticking all the stickers on all the pieces, right where they belonged, Uncle Roy and I put that plastic 45 rpm record on my portable Fisher-Price record player, and we put on our very own *Donny & Marie Show*. Of course I manned control over Marie, manipulating her "little bit country" body across our green shag carpeting. Not because I wanted to *be* Marie Osmond. I didn't. I mean, if I were Marie Osmond, I couldn't possibly have a crush on my own brother, now could I?

These are the thoughts preoccupying me as I zone out on our couch, the colored lights a-twinkling and a-blinking on the artificial Christmas tree my mother's set up in the usual spot in front of our living room picture window. This year, however, Mom went out and treated us to a new model that she bought up at Arbor's ("Only $9.99!"). Affectionately, she's christened it "Scrawny Pine." Seriously, I thought the tissue paper wreaths Brad and I made when we were in ninth grade and trying to save money for Spring Break were pathetic. This thing makes the so-called spruce from *A Charlie Brown Christmas* look like the one in New York City's Rockefeller Center. It's not even so much that it's small as it is short. So much so, my mom's got it propped up on a box that she's draped with some Christmas-y cloth she found God only knows where. Still the angel atop doesn't come anywhere close to touching the ceiling.

Honk!

A car pulls up in our driveway. Doing my best to peek out the window without toppling the tree, I hold up a finger, giving the "be right out" signal to the person behind the wheel. As I grab my coat off the rack behind the front door and slip it on, I take note of the stockings Mom's tacked up the way she does every holiday season. As per usual, there's one for each member of our family: MOM, DAD, JACK, JODI, and BILLY. Though this December, it seems we've gained the addition of my seventeen-year-old sister's boyfriend, DAN. Guess Mom figured they've been going together since ninth grade and will probably end up married someday, why not stick a red felt sock up with the guy's name on it? Talk about unfair . . . How I've longed to see *my* significant other's name in glitter someday! (Maybe next year?)

"I'm leaving!"

Mom doesn't hear me over Johnny Mathis singing about those sleigh bells jingling and ring-ting-tingling. She's too busy in the kitchen slicing up some "homemade" Pillsbury sugar cookies. For some reason, Johnny Mathis always reminds me of my grandma, God rest her soul. Not that I knew Helen very well; she died when I was seven. But according to Mom, he was always one of her favorites. Him and Liberace. Granny also liked Bing Crosby and Engelbert Humperdinck, so she wasn't exclusively partial to the homosexuals. Though there was also Tab Hunter, aka Mr. Stuart the "Reproduction" teacher from *Grease 2.*

Down the front stairs I fly, floating on Cloud Nine. Partly because the steps need shoveling and I almost slipped, partly because of the person I'm about to see the second I open the passenger door of the idling Chevy Cavalier.

"Hey, Kirk . . . What's up?"

Not even five seconds after I've hopped into his car and we're on our way, Kirk pops a cassette into the tape deck. A piano starts playing, followed by a young man's baritone singing a beautiful ballad about how love changes everything.

"What is this?" I wonder.

"It's the new Andrew Lloyd Webber," Kirk answers. "*Aspects of Love.*"

According to the program I discover sandwiched between the bucket seats, the show, based on a novel by someone named David Garnett, focuses on the romances between an actress, Rose, her adoring fan, Alex, his cousin, Jenny, his uncle, George, and George's mistress, Giulietta. The production originated in London in 1989 starring Ann Crumb and Michael Ball, and opened on Broadway a year later. Unfortunately, it closed last March after receiving not-so-rave reviews, according to Kirk.

Perhaps this is why I've never heard of it. Though I'm not a big Musical Theatre fan, so who I am to talk? Other than the classics I've seen on cable (*The Music Man, The Sound of Music, Hello, Dolly!*), I never really got into the whole singing and dancing thing. But when I first started hanging out with Kirk at the beginning of the semester, he introduced me to *Les Misérables*, and I just fell in love with it. Maybe it's because I've studied *le français*, so I was already familiar with the source material. The whole Jean Valjean imprisoned for stealing a loaf of bread, then he becomes mayor of the town and adopts poor dead Fantine's daughter, Cosette, who grows up and falls in love with Marius, the student, who risks his life fighting on the barricade . . . And that Éponine! "On My Own" has got to be one of the most heartbreaking songs ever written. Believe me, up until recently I totally understood how that girl feels, pretending he's beside her.

"Raquel and I saw it in Toronto on Saturday night," confesses Kirk, referring to *Aspects of Love*. Judging from the sound of his voice, the memory isn't a pleasant one. And not because he thought the show sucked.

Not sure if I should continue along this line of conversation, I sit quietly in my seat, staring out the window, listening to the melody. Apparently love changes *everything:* hands, faces, earth, sky. The way you live and die. It makes the summer fly. Or the night seem like a lifetime. It'll turn your world around and bring you both glory and shame. But above all, love will never let you be the same.

Don't I know it!

Sitting here in Kirk's car, listening to this sappy song and smelling his special scent, I think I'm going to lose it.

"You okay over there?" he asks, hearing me try my best to stifle my sniffles. "You got awfully quiet all of a sudden."

"I'm fine," I reply.

What could be more perfect than going on a lunch date with the man I love? Especially when he takes hold of my hand and doesn't let go until we've arrived safe and sound at our destination.

Over at ye olde parking structure, Kirk takes a ticket and we begin the search for a spot. Much like my last visit to Royal Oak, the lot is full up, so we find ourselves all the way on the tippy-top.

"Let's take the stairs," Kirk suggests.

Thinking back to how I almost killed myself on the slippery steps, I start to say, "Be careful . . ."

Too late!

Kirk's foot slides across an icy patch, and he falls—smack dab into my open arms. He allows himself to be held, our faces mere inches apart. Then we lock lips for the third time in less than twelve hours.

And on our way we go!

A hop, skip, and a jump, and we're over on Fourth Street outside the Metro Music Café.

"Is this cool?" Kirk asks, as we enter the Hard Rock knockoff. *Last Christmas* by Wham! plays quietly in the background. (Only *two* more days of this holiday music!)

"Sure," I say. "I love this place."

Truthfully, I've only been here once before. The summer after I finished my freshman year at State, a few of my just-graduated friends met up for dinner one evening. We were supposed to be seeing Rick Astley at Pine Knob. But the show had been cancelled, and we got together anyway. The part I'll always remember about that night was when the waitress asked me what I wanted to drink with my burger. At the time, I had just turned nineteen, so I told her I'd happily have a Coke. All my friends had ordered Coronas, and the waitress took it upon herself to decide that I needed something stronger. To my surprise, she brought me my own beer without bothering to ask for ID. This I bring up as being odd since I barely appear to be *sixteen*.

"Oh, look . . ."

Kirk points out the piece of musical memorabilia hanging on the wall next to where we've seated ourselves: a guitar signed by Joey Ramone.

"Cool," I say, before confessing, "I actually don't know much about them."

"You're kidding?" he says in shock. "You've never seen *Rock 'n' Roll High School?*"

Vaguely, I recall a wasted night almost a decade ago in my parents' basement with me, Max, and Brad staying up until all hours, watching a bunch of bad movies on "Skinemax." My personal fave had to be *H.O.T.S.* Not because I was into the half naked co-eds running around in their wet T-shirts. I just thought the title totally ridiculous. ("Help Out The Seals," indeed!) Then I remember: "Didn't The Ramones sing the theme song to *Pet Sematary*?" The only book by Stephen King I've attempted to read, after seeing the film three times. Surprisingly, I didn't find it to be that well written for someone so successful a scribe.

Kirk says, "As a matter of fact, they did."

A lull falls over the table. I don't know about Kirk, but I keep thinking about our being alone in that stairwell together just a few moments ago. Holding him in my arms; feeling his body pressing heavily against mine; taking all of his weight. Less than a week ago, when we shared our first kiss, I thought that was it, a once in a lifetime opportunity, come and gone, never to occur again. Now here we are, beginning what I hope becomes a lifelong partnership. If only we could seal the deal!

Last night when Kirk dropped me off, it took every bit of restraint I have in my body to hold myself back. Had we been up at State, I would've totally dragged him inside and totally had my way with him. Another downside of our both spending the holidays at our parents' houses. I don't know if we can wait until we get back to East Lansing to stay the night together. If only we had someplace we could go. . . .

"Are you ready?"

Our waitress comes over to take our order. We both choose the chicken sandwich. I ask for a Molson Ice. Kirk opts for a Labatt's Blue. Nothing like getting your buzz on in the middle of a Monday afternoon. Of course I can't get too crazy. I do have to be at work soon. Just wait until I tell Val the news: "Kirsty" and "Ralph" are no more.

Outside, a gentle snow has started to fall. Hard to believe tomorrow is actually Christmas Eve. Again, I'll spend the daytime hours at Farmer Jack's. Hopefully, it won't be too busy. But I'm sure it will. Thankfully the store closes at seven. Then it's home to make a quick change, and off to my grandfather's for our annual Paterno family party. Growing up, I always envied my cousin Rhonda, who would bring her steady boyfriend to all our family gatherings. The only time I ever took anyone along was sophomore year when I dated Alyssa. And even then, I introduced her as my "sometimes" girlfriend. Don't know what the hell I was thinking!

Surely it's too early to consider asking Kirk to come with. Besides, he's got his own festivities to frequent. But maybe in the late evening, after the fact, we can sneak away somewhere. I've always enjoyed attending midnight mass, and being that Kirk is Catholic, this would supply us with an excuse to see each other.... I'll have to remember to bring it up.

Our waitress returns with our beverages. Before she heads back to the kitchen, she grins, giving us a look that says, "Aren't you a cute couple?"

And for once, I can officially agree....

We are!

Right Here, Right Now

I was alive and I waited, waited
I was alive and I waited for this . . .

—Jesus Jones

To quote Blair Warner from *The Facts of Life*: "I've just had another one of my brilliant ideas." Don't ask me why I didn't think of it sooner. Tonight, after I'm freed from The Farmer, Kirk and I will finally consummate our love.

As anticipated, *le supermarché* is a madhouse of aisle-to-aisle shoppers. But I'm so excited about this evening, I can't even be bothered to complain. As soon as I get the H-E-double hockey sticks out of this place, to my parents' house I will go, pack my bag, and get the H-E-double hockey sticks out of there. (Last night, I caught a rerun of *The Golden Girls*, and picked up that phrase from Rose Nylund. God, I love Betty White and hope she's around for a good long while!)

All I have to do is get through six simple hours.

To accomplish this feat, every thirty minutes I stop by the produce department and pop a Starlight mint into my mouth. The sugar buzz keeps me bopping around the store's perimeter, putting back what we in the grocery biz like to call "under stock." As of 7:00 p.m., we've got eight buggies parked over by register nine, full of items customers decided they didn't care to purchase. On a normal night, we get like two, three tops, so this trivial chore is going to take extra time. But again, I won't complain. Because I am young and in love—and about to get laid!

"Somebody's in a good mood. . . ."

Val catches me singing to myself while restocking day-old Danish on the shelves outside the Hearth Oven. But she's wrong. . . .

"I'm in a *great* mood," I correct, before giving her all the gory details of the budding romance between "Kirsty" and Jack.

"Congratulations!"

Even though she says this with total enthusiasm, Val seems a tad bit disappointed. Not that I assume she's still carrying a torch for yours truly. But there's a definite glint in her eye that says she doesn't want to see me with another girl. Thankfully she won't have to! Someday I'll come clean with her, I promise. At the present moment, I haven't got time to start baring my soul.

"Jack . . . take your break."

Around eight o'clock, the head cashier on duty, Therese, utters my three favorite Farmer Jack's–related words. She's a perky little blonde around thirty, with whom I've worked since the beginning of my career in the commercial food industry. Immediately, I make my way into the vestibule to partake of the pay phone. It's been four hours since I last spoke to Kirk, and I already miss him. Plus I'm getting antsy about our big outing tonight.

"I'll pick you up around eleven thirty," I inform him. "Don't forget to bring your sleeping clothes."

"What exactly are we doing?" he wonders.

"I told you," I tell him, "that's for me to know, and you to find out."

Ever the Machiavelli, on our way back from Metro Music Café earlier this afternoon, I came up with a plot as to how Kirk and I can finally spend some much-needed one-on-one time together. I kept thinking how awesome it would be if he and I had someplace we could go and be alone. By which I mean *intimate.* If only we knew someone with their own house or apartment. Someone who could loan it to us for even just an hour. Or preferably, the entire night. And then I remembered. . . .

Shortly after we graduated high school, thanks to his deadbeat dad, Brad's poor mom ended up forfeiting the home he grew up in over on Wanda in Ferndale. Back in the 1950s, the house itself used to be a small grocery store. Once Brad's father bought the building, he converted it into a residential dwelling, dubbing it "Dayton's Depot." We had some good times in that house, me and Brad, swinging on the chandeliers that hung from the twenty-foot ceilings in the front room. (Just kidding! Though we always said we were going to, we never actually made an attempt. Laura Victor-Dayton-Victor would've killed us.) Unfortunately, on the salary she made working at Detroit Osteopathic Hospital, Laura wasn't able to keep up with the bills, on top of feeding Brad and his three sisters.

Even after her eldest daughter, Janelle, found herself in "a family way" and moved out to get married, and only son Bradley spent all his time busting his butt waiting tables at Big Boy's, there were still his younger siblings to look after. Which is why Laura later accepted the proposal of a man named Albert, allowing "Dayton's Depot" to fall by the wayside, and moved herself, Nina, and Brittany in with her new husband. Sadly, the marriage ended prematurely, and Laura and the girls are now living over in Madison Heights. As for Brad, he's been renting a room in the upstairs of a house belonging to his father off Van Dyke, over in Warren.... Directly across the street from Kirk's father's pro shop, B & B Sporting Goods, coincidentally enough.

Which is exactly where we are now, me and Mr. Bailey.

"What are we doing here?" The second we spot the Shopper's Market on the corner of Maxwell and pull up across the street, Kirk starts giving me the third degree.

"Spending the night," I say, cutting the engine and turning off the lights. "Now be quiet and come on."

Lifting the hatch on the back of my Omni, I reach inside and grab our overnight bags. Save for the glow of the streetlight and one left-on Christmas tree twinkling in the window of the house across the way, the road is dark and deserted.... It's also freezing! Which is why Kirk and I scurry up to the side door where I desperately dig through my coat pocket in search of the key Brad dropped off earlier when I was still at work. Which promptly I locate—and immediately let fall to the frozen tundra.

"Careful!" Kirk cries, as if I meant to commit such a stupid folly.

"I got gloves on," I remind him. "It slipped right out of my fingers."

Down on the hard ground I go, digging around for the tiny piece of silver attached to the tacky plastic ring proclaiming, *Niagara Falls Is for Lovers*. If it weren't for the fact that we trip the motion sensor hanging high above our heads, I don't think we'd ever find the stupid thing. But thank God we finally do, buried deep within a bank of snow.

Wouldn't you know? The stupid lock must be frozen because now the stupid key won't fit inside. No matter which direction I try—teeth up or down—it's no use. Knowing Brad, he probably gave me the wrong key; that's how absentminded he is.

"Stick it in!" Teeth chattering away, Kirk hisses in my ear as he snuggles up close behind me for warmth.

As ticked off as I am, how can I resist seizing the opportunity to be obnoxious? "That comes later."

Though I can't help but wonder (without getting too graphic), what exactly is going to happen once Kirk and I—to steal a phrase from one of Aunt Sonia's favorite country songs—get "behind closed doors"? And to borrow from Detroit's own Miss Aretha Franklin, who's gonna be zooming who? Guess that's one thing we'll have to figure out... If we can ever break into this stupid building!

Giving it the old heave-ho, I finally manage to force the door open, and into the damp and dark entryway we disappear. I believe there's a light switch somewhere. But I'm not about to turn it on at this time of night. As far as I know, Brad's dad is home and asleep in bed. The last thing I want to do is wake up the man. ("Good evening, Mr. Dayton... Remember me, Jack Paterno? Bradley's best friend since seventh grade. This is my *boy*friend, Kirk Bailey. We're here to get it on in your son's bedroom.")

"Now what?" Having never been here before, Kirk has no idea where we're heading.

"Up the stairs," I instruct, "and all the way down. The door at the end of the hall."

I do find it a tad bit odd that Brad's *renting* a room in his own father's home. But the way his dad has set up the place, it is more like an apartment. Brad's got his own separate entrance, along with private bedroom and bathroom. Where Kirk has just stopped off while I forge ahead to what I'm calling our "love den" and will commence getting things ready.

Inside the room, I don't dare turn on the lamp. Again, God forbid Mr. Dayton should for some reason notice there's someone upstairs. As far as he's concerned, Brad's over spending the night at Max's dad's. I have to say, I've got the greatest friend in the whole wide world. Who else would give up sleeping in the comfort of their own bed, just so his best pal could get lucky? Thankfully Brad understands just how much Kirk means to me. After my incessant rambling about the guy every time I call or have come home for the past three months, how could he not?

Either Mr. Dayton really is a deadbeat or he's taking a lesson from my father when it comes to being a tightwad because Brad's bedroom is colder than a witch's tit! The last thing I'm going to want to do is take off my clothes. Looks like Kirk and I will have to rely on our love to keep us warm. Not to mention our body heat. Also the candles that I've brought along and light one by one, strategically placing them around the abode.

Don't that look pur-ty!

Reaching into my bag, I remove the bottle of white zinfandel purchased before picking up Kirk, pop the sucker open, and pour two paper cups full. All we need now is some romantic music. The question is: what does Brad have in his cassette collection? Much to my surprise, I come upon the perfect selection . . . by none other than Mr. George Winston. From this day forward, whenever I hear these eight opening chords, my memory will transport me back to this most special of evenings.

December 23, 1991.

"Oh, my God!" Kirk shivers the second he crosses the threshold. Glancing about the room, he seems rather surprised to see what I've done with our humble surroundings.

"Ta-dah!"

He reaches out, takes me in his frozen-stiff arms, tickling me with frigid fingers.

"Don't do that!" I cry, arctic chills running up and down my spine.

Struggling to free myself from his glacial grasp, Kirk reels me back in. "So what are we doing here?" he says softly as we nuzzle noses.

"I told you," I tease. "We're spending the night . . . *alone*."

"But it's so cold."

"Allow me to warm you up."

Our lips meet, and we share a tender kiss. This action turns more aggressive as tongues entwine, hearts begin beating faster, and hands start doing their thing. Clothes fall into a heap on the floor beside the bed. Which we barely manage to pull back the covers on before collapsing into it. Luckily Brad assured me he'd supply us with fresh sheets. . . . Who knows the mess we're about to make?

Looking over at the lit face of the clock atop the dresser, I take a mental note of the time: ten past midnight.

"Merry Christmas Eve," I whisper in Kirk's ear, accompanied by a gentle love bite on the lobe.

"Merry Christmas Eve."

His weight crushes me. But I could care less. I've spent the last how many months longing to feel him this close. Now here we are, two bodies becoming one, like in every love story I've ever seen in the movies and on TV: from *The Blue Lagoon* to *Ice Castles* to *Somewhere in Time*. Only we're not a pair of cousins stranded on a deserted island, or a champion figure skater and her hockey player boyfriend, or a playwright and the woman he traveled sixty-eight years to find.

We're just a couple of college-aged guys who want nothing more than to be together. . . .

For what I hope is the first of *many* Christmases to come.

Missed Connections

Michael Salvatore

Christmas Eve. Those two words should have filled Theo with joy; they should have decked his halls and filled his head with visions of muscular, leotard-clad sugar plum fairies from an all-male touring company of *The Nutcracker* like they had since he was a little boy, but this year all they did was make him feel glum. No matter how hard he tried, he just couldn't muster up any Christmas spirit; it simply wasn't the holiday he had wished for.

Up until a few months ago he had been planning on doing something radical this year, something he had never done before, something he never thought he'd be brave enough to do: He had decided not to spend Christmas with his family. Instead, he was going to spend it at home with Neil and a small circle of friends. This year was going to be the year of the all-gay Christmas. But Neil had other plans.

Neil was Theo's partner, and it was a partnership Theo was convinced would last until death do they parted. But Theo, like so many homos who just want to be happy, ignored his unhappy reality and the oh-so-many clues that Neil dropped along the way during their tenure together, to convince himself that their relationship would last forever. As it turned out, their relationship, like an all-male touring company of *The Nutcracker*, lacked staying power.

First, he disregarded the fact that *partner*—the word Neil chose to describe how he was connected to Theo—is simply an empty, unemotional word that means more stable than a boyfriend, but not as permanent as a husband. It's the perfect word for those who want to live in limbo.

Second, even though they had cohabitated for several years in the Commonwealth of Massachusetts and could, therefore, enter into a legally binding marriage contract, Neil considered a same-sex marriage certificate contraband from Breederland and refused to partake in their age-old institution until, as he would often quote—The president of the United States of Gaymerica affords homosexuals the same right to marry as any other Homo sapiens. It was rhetoric that worked, and Theo believed his partner was political. The truth, however, was that Neil's rhetoric didn't stem from a political belief, but a biological one; he just didn't believe one homo should be legally bound to experience old age with only one other homo, whether that homo be sexual or sapien.

Finally, the third, and probably most damaging clue was that Neil had a lifetime subscription to Grindr. He was always logged on, at home, at work, in bed. Why should a man who is in an allegedly monogamous relationship need to have an app that gives him the ability to rendezvous randomly with the near and the non-ogamous? It's a question Theo only asked once while they were lying together in bed watching an *I Love Lucy* rerun. While two-thumb typing to some potentially two-timing guy who was currently a little over two hundred feet away, Neil replied, "I just like to know there are other gays nearby; it makes me feel connected to our community."

While Ricky demanded Lucy 'splain how she had spent roughly half their community assets on a wild shopping spree, Theo sat less than two inches from his partner and didn't make any demands of his own. He didn't ask any more questions; he didn't demand that Neil 'splain why he didn't just join a political activist group to remain connected to the gay community or ask if he communed more frequently with the assholes on Grindr than with his. He didn't want to know the truth, so he did what he always did when he thought the truth could make him unhappy; he remained quiet. And as a result he remained in limbo.

Until of course Neil came home one day and called off their partnership, forcing him out of limbo and into reality. A few days later Theo called off their Christmas party. He hated to do it; he and his friends had been so thrilled knowing they were going to have a very homo and very local holiday and not have to hop on a plane to visit family to be part of *their* celebration, how nice it was going to be to have a gay gala they could call their own. But as disappointing as it was, it was an easy decision to make. Being the only single man sitting around his family's table would be depressing enough, but being the only single man at a gathering of paired-up gays would make Theo want to play the role of George Bailey in the remake of *It's a Wonderful Life*. Though in this version he would insist there be no happy ending, no restitution; no bell would ring, and prissy Clarence would have to get his wings by saving some other loser from committing suicide. Theo would be swan diving off the bridge to his death.

And that's why Theo found himself spending the start of Christmas Eve where he didn't want to be, in an airport waiting for a connecting flight to bring him to his parents' home in Phoenix, Arizona, to spend Christmas in the sand. Like Jesus. But unlike Jesus he wasn't in a forgiving mood, and he resented having to leave his own home, take a cab to Logan Airport, catch one flight to St. Louis, and wait for another to bring him to his final destination. He resented having to spend all the extra money to fly west, money that he didn't want to spend now that he was no longer splitting rent on his luxury-priced, but definitely unluxurious one-bedroom apartment in Boston's gay South End. He resented the fact that his parents hadn't even asked why he and Neil had broken up—they either assumed since he was gay it was an inevitability that their coupling would ultimately dissolve or it was because they had never really come to terms with the inevitability of their son's sexual persuasion. And most of all he resented Neil more than ever for turning back the clock and turning him back into what he never thought he'd be again—a single gay man forced to spend the holiday with his family because he didn't have a family of his own.

Of course some friends had pitivited him to celebrate Christmas with their families on the East Coast so he wouldn't have to travel as far, but he knew he couldn't accept; he couldn't be that mean-spirited and tell his mother that he would be spending the holiday with someone else's mother. Even though he made the choice out of guilt and not love, the guilt would still be too overwhelming. No, after thinking it over he realized he had no alternative, so he reluctantly agreed to do what he and Neil had agreed several months ago that they wouldn't do and booked a flight. Now, standing in a line at Lambert-St. Louis International Airport waiting to pass through the security gate, he regretted his decision. He was as miserable and unmerry as the wise man who unwisely agreed to bring Mary's newborn the gift of myrrh. It smelled almost as bad as resentment.

Twenty minutes later he was still waiting in line, still unmerry, still trying to push the smell of myrrh and resentment from his nostrils. With his carry-on bag snugly stuffed between his stocking feet, Theo cradled his loafers in the crook of his arm and flipped through the pages of a magazine in search of a celebrity who had been dumped, had stumbled into rehab, or had been photographed in the grocery store without make-up and looking like an ordinary person, anything to make himself feel better about his plight. His ploy backfired, and he was soon about to feel worse. He forgot that he had tried to get rid of his parents' Christmas card by stuffing it into the pages of the magazine.

No matter how many times Theo looked at the card he felt the same way: it wasn't right. Yes, it had a full-figured Santa Claus on the cover dressed in his de rigueur red pantsuit with fluffy white trim and wearing pseudo-masochistic black riding boots, yes he was standing in front of a two-story house decorated with two-hundred sparkling lights in two-dozen different and defiantly clashing colors, and yes, he was holding onto the rein that held onto a harness that was wrapped around the neck of one of his nine aviatrix reindeer. But even with all those iconographic graphical elements, Theo still felt the card looked as false and as fake as a Christmas tree that used the Star of David as its topper. It was all because of the damned cactus.

The red-clad Santa in the card wasn't captured frolicking in the middle of some winter wonderland; he was depicted in the middle of some sort of Death Valley–esque desert with his pudgy arm draped around a plump cactus. When did Martha Stewart decide that cacti should replace poinsettias as traditional holiday foliage? Theo did not recall the woman's ever saying that. Silently, he reread the riddle on the front of the card: "How are Santa Claus and a cactus the same?" Then, mechanically he opened the card and silently reread the ridiculous punch line once more—"Because they're both surrounded by little pricks."

The answer to the riddle was enhanced by the image of Santa Claus, dressed in the same gay apparel as on the front of the card, but now donning an undeniably un-gay expression. Santa was seething. He resembled a Caucasian Grinch before the epiphany, and he stood towering above a throng of naughty-looking elves, one of whom actually wore a red thong, revealed a bit too much elf-ass, and held onto the cactus like he was an expert North Pole-dancer. 'Tis the season to be inappropriate. But what made the card even more distasteful was his father's personal inscription.

Underneath the half-naked dancing elf, his father had written, "Looks like your mother entertaining the Rotary Club last Saturday night!" Oh comfort, oh joy. Ever since Theo's parents had retired and moved to an adult community complex in Phoenix, Arizona, from a suburb in northern New Jersey, his father had become one of those elders who has forgotten all about decorum, all about tradition, all about basic holiday principles; he'd turned into a senior citizen with seasonal dementia. Everyone knows that Santa Claus resides above the Arctic Circle, not south of the border. Everyone knows that he should only have his arm around

Mrs. Claus or a frost-colored snowman and not a cactus. And everyone knows that elves should never, ever appear half-naked or as sexually active little people. Or be compared to someone's mother. Only the faithful should come, not a parent.

Disgusted, Theo folded the card and stuffed it back into the fold of the magazine, right in between a photo of two other sexually active little people, the Olson twins, then shoved the glossy rag into his bag. Even though the card was out of sight, he still felt out of sorts. Maybe it was because he had no sense of humor; Neil had accused him of that before. Or maybe it was because he was a prude and didn't want to entertain the concept that his parents could have an entertaining sex life. Or maybe it was simply because he was jealous of his parents' relationship, with or without the entertaining sex life.

Whoa Nellie! Could he really be jealous of his parents' happiness and close connection especially during this season of unending joy simply because Neil had made sure that his joy came to an end? Theo thought for a moment, he pondered, and then decided 'why not'? They had what he was supposed to have, dammit, what he had thought he had until Neil dumped him, a string of memorable holidays that strung together would create a collection of holiday memories. But instead he had gotten a Labor Day that was work, a Halloween that wasn't happy, a Thanksgiving that was far from thankful, all disappointments because of Neil's disappointing decision. Now here he was on the threshold of what should be the most joyous two weeks of the year—Christmas Eve, Christmas Day, and then the granddaddy of all celebrations, New Year's Eve—feeling miserable, lonely, and definitely not filled with holiday cheer. How pathetic that the last enjoyable holiday he had spent was Ramadan. If he couldn't take his jealous, angry wrath out on Neil, his parents, like Mary, would be the perfect surrogates.

Startled, Theo almost dropped his loafers. Not because of his oafish, blasphemous thought, but because it appeared that by blasphemously invoking the name of the Blessed Mother, a blessed event was about to occur. Theo was next in line, and anxiety had shifted to excitement because the security guards were changing shifts. Gone was the burly Burl Ives clone and taking his place was a handsome, rugged-looking, forty-something man who looked like he could star as the widowed father wishing for a romantic miracle in a Lifetime TV Christmas Special. Solid as a fruitcake with probably the same IQ. Traveling was starting to get better.

The last time Theo flew was almost a year ago, before the bigwigs who created the national guidelines for airport security got together and decided that, thanks to unveiled threats from unscrupulous and probably unsanitary groups in, near, or connected to the Middle East, precautions needed to be upgraded to ensure the safety of American citizens who traveled by airplane. Passengers now had to allow themselves to be photographed by mutant digital cameras that took pictures that were a cross between X-rays and pornography; every item underneath the top layer of clothing, every piece of flesh, firm or flabby, every strand of hair, curly or straight, every orifice, clenched or relaxed, would be photographed and then viewed, inspected, and possibly ogled by an unidentified airport security worker sitting in a dark room that Theo imagined smelled like cigarette smoke and bleach. And if that wasn't disconcerting enough there was the pat down.

Those who refused to be photographed, lest the pictures of their love handles and other physical imperfections be catalogued for all eternity in a file labeled "Unphotogenic And / Or Simply Ugly American Travelers," could choose to be manhandled by a stranger. This hands-on procedure was about one degree less invasive than a full cavity search, the only upshot being that there was no lingering photographic evidence to agonize the innocent. Sometimes, however, passengers didn't have a choice; sometimes they were picked at random to undergo this alternative security measure or, if like today, the super-duper, very expensive ultra X-ray machine was on the fritz. Today every traveler was going to receive a complimentary and extreme pat down. The skies were no longer friendly, but the welcoming party had just gotten a whole lot more sociable. And thanks to the shift change a whole lot more attractive as well.

As a thirty-six-year-old gay man, even one who was just coming out of a three-year relationship, Theo knew what it felt like to be manhandled by a strange man. But such indelicate indiscretions had only taken place in the privacy of his or the stranger's apartment or, on occasion, in the darkness of the backroom of a bar, not in the fluorescent-lit, open space of an airport surrounded by people of the heterosexual persuasion, half of them women and many of them children. It was a scenario that should have made him feel incredibly uncomfortable, but Theo was desperate. The only person he had had sex with since Neil left was himself, and the past few outings had proven unsatisfactory; in fact the last time he was intimate with himself he faked an orgasm. And he didn't even notice. Like the orphan on Christmas morning, he would take whatever gift he could get and incredibly, upon closer inspection, the gift of the new security guard was even better looking than he originally thought.

Second in line, Theo had a perfect view of the man who, shortly, would once again make him feel like a man. He saw that the guard had dark brown eyes as sharp as his dark brown buzz cut, skin as smooth as his ironed uniform, and perfect posture that made the most of his five-foot-eight-inch frame. From this vantage point he looked less like a Lifetime headliner and more like a cross between Tom of Finland and Tom Cruise, which meant he looked nothing like fair-haired Neil, which meant he suited Theo just fine.

Prior to the regime change, Theo had dreaded having to go through security with Burl Ives as the checkpoint guard. He knew it was a necessity, he knew there was no way out of it, but he kept trying to come up with some excuse so he could bypass the inevitable and avoid having to be felt up by the man who up until a few moments ago was feeling up every other man in line. But now with Mr. Finland-Cruise at the helm, he couldn't wait for his turn to be manhandled, felt up, and touched in any way humanly possible. Just as he finished tossing his belongings into the bin on the conveyer belt, things got even better.

"Next."

Only one word and yet the security guard's Southern accent was unmistakable. Simultaneously rough and soft, equal parts command and invitation, the voice was so enticing Theo momentarily forgot that he was standing at the cross section of Blue Hair Avenue and Crying Kid Lane in Heteroland and thought he had fallen down the rabbit hole into some X-rated fantasy. He tried to smile, fully aware that his smile looked more like a smirk, and felt his arousal grow a few inches in length, as finally he was going to experience some Christmas joy. Maybe the trip would be worth it after all.

Taking a step closer to the gentleman who was about to show him some southern hospitality, Theo opened his mouth to introduce himself, but the security guard spoke first, this time sprinkling his Southern accent with some no-nonsense, but even more arousal-inducing Midwestern attitude.

"Raise your arms, please."

Holy stocking stuffer! The trip was being salvaged by the second because here was a man who knew how to give orders. Neil had always been a bit too passive in bed. Theo dealt with it, but he preferred guys who easily took on the more dominant role in their relationship, especially if they were a few inches shorter than he was. Obviously, Theo was a bit more desperate than he had realized and involuntarily he took the X-rated fantasy a step further.

"Yes, sir," Theo responded. It wasn't a completely inappropriate response except that Theo employed a tone that a) made it sound as if he too was from the South, which wasn't true, and b) made it seem that the man was a *prison* guard instead of an airport security guard or possibly even a plantation owner, which was most definitely not true. To his credit, the security guard didn't acknowledge Theo's tonal faux pas except for a two-second glare aimed directly at Theo's smiling green eyes, which could have been interpreted as a come-on or a come-off-it. Before he had a chance to decide which it was, the guard got to work.

As latex-clad fingers scampered across the tops of Theo's arms, then underneath, he tried to flex his outstretched arms as much as possible to show the guard, who he now mentally referred to as simply Mr. Tom, that he hit the gym several times a week. Moving on, Mr. Tom pressed against Theo's chest, back, and stomach until he was satisfied that Theo wasn't concealing any weapons of mass destruction on the upper half of his body. Now it was time to move below deck.

Theo couldn't conceal a sigh when Mr. Tom slipped his fingers inside the waistband of his slim-fit Levi's jeans. If Mr. Tom heard him he made no indication; he was deeply focused on his work, and it was clear that Mr. Tom wasn't a multitasker. Using Theo's belly button as the starting point, Mr. Tom rotated a finger to the left until it reached the apex of his ass and then another to the right. Immediately, Theo felt the area around his crotch grow tighter. He couldn't help himself; he was stressed, depressed, and repressed, and here was a hunky man in uniform kneeling in front of him mere inches from his crotch with his hands down his pants. If it hadn't been for the projectile vomiting of the pregnant woman standing in line a few passengers behind him, he would, without a doubt, have projected his own fluid.

Interestingly, Theo had never heard or seen projectile vomiting before. The one and only time he saw *The Exorcist* was on television, and that scene was cut out to maintain non-cable broadcast purity, and yet the moment it happened he knew what had occurred. He also knew that the woman had eaten cornflakes for breakfast. The smell was sour, the sound was gross, but Theo was grateful—his erection was gone.

While Mr. Tom continued to press against Theo's Levi's from inseam to ankle, front and back, his female counterpart ran to the aid of the vomiting pregnant woman. Theo kept thinking about the mother-to-be experiencing mid-afternoon morning sickness and stayed flaccid even while Mr. Tom ran his hands over the soles of his feet as if Theo was Ralph Lauren's exclusive foot model and Mr. Tom was a shoe designer in search of the perfect arch. Yes, the woman had ruined his fantasy, but he had gotten a little carried away so it was with only the mildest disappointment that Theo accepted Mr. Tom's dismissal when he barked, "Next."

Five minutes later, his feet that were so-recently caressed were encased once again in brown leather driving moccasins not made by Ralph Lauren and straddling the sides of his carry-on duffel bag, also brown leather and also not made by Ralph Lauren. He looked around at the other travelers and saw that most of them were in groups, friends chatting, mothers holding babies, couples holding hands, he hated them all. How quickly the bliss from the dream sequence starring Mr. Tom had faded, no more heated fantasy, back to reality.

Theo grabbed another magazine from his bag, this one featuring high-priced furniture instead of high-priced celebrities. He couldn't afford any of the designer merchandise artfully spread out on page after page, but just looking at the accoutrements made him feel sophisticated and urbane while breathing in the unsophisticated and possibly baneful Midwestern ambience. However, the feeling of superiority was short-lived. No matter how hard he tried to occupy his mind he couldn't get over how annoyed he was to be sitting in the lounge area of Gate 27 waiting for Flight 422 to depart Lambert-St. Louis International Airport for Phoenix, Arizona, the new hometown of Mr. and Mrs. Theodore Franklin, Sr., his parents. They had lived their whole lives in Fairfield, New Jersey, and were planning on living there for the remainder until his mother's twin sister, Clare, was diagnosed with acute asthma and needed to move to a dry climate in order to breathe. Theo's mother, Alice, needed to be near Clare in order to breathe, so she and her husband made the trek from the suburbs to the desert.

Absentmindedly, Theo stroked the armrest of his chair, stopping abruptly when he realized that it not only looked, but also felt very much like the earth in Phoenix—faded by the sun and hostile to the touch. God, how he loathed Arizona! The state made no sense to him, miles and miles of sand and not an ocean in sight. Plus, every month of the year you had to walk around with a bottle of water and wear a sun hat to ward off dehydration and melanoma. You might be able to breathe easy there, but you couldn't live. You couldn't even keep time there, as the state ignored the time-honored concept of Daylight Savings Time, refusing to spring forward and fall back. It was an obstinate, stupid state, and as much as he loved his Aunt Clare and wished her a long life devoid of respiratory ailments, he resented having to fly from his adopted home state of Massachusetts to his parents' adopted home state of Arizona just to see them for the holidays.

Theo took several deep breaths, each one a little slower like his analyst had taught him in order to push out the negativity and only allow positive thoughts to inhabit his bloodstream. Out with evil Arizona, in with good old Christmas dinner. Out with the blazing hot sun and cactus trees decorated with twinkling lights, in with watching *The Year Without a Santa Claus*, his favorite Rankin/Bass Christmas Special for the thirtieth time. Out with all the annoying, repetitive small talk he was going to have to engage in with his relatives, in with embracing being a single gay man during the holidays. What?! No. Take another breath. Out with being a single gay man during the holidays, in with a horrific—though not fatal—accident befalling his ex-partner Neil as he and his latest boy toy, Pockmarked Peter, drove to Vermont to spend their very first Christmas as a couple with Peter's pockmarked parents in their little pockmarked cottage on a pockmarked village at the base of some ugly, pockmarked mountain! He was making so much noise breathing in and out and in and out that he almost didn't hear his name.

"Teddy?"

Out with dwelling on the past, in with celebrating the future. Even if the future wasn't worth celebrating just yet.

"Teddy? Is that you?"

Looking up from his magazine with visions of a horrendous—though it must be noted again, *non-fatal* car accident—still dancing in his head, Theo felt like he was looking into the harsh Phoenix sun; he couldn't make out who was standing in front of him and why that unseen person was addressing him with a name he hadn't responded to in well over a decade.

"Teddy! It's me, Rob."

Suddenly it was as if a mass of clouds swept in from the east and softened the harsh, ugly Phoenix sun so Theo could see who was standing before him. Seeing was one thing, believing was another. It was him, it was indeed Rob, but it couldn't be, it was impossible, there was absolutely no way that Rob was in the airport standing in front of him. It was a hallucination, that was it! A byproduct of the last few months of emotional turmoil, the angst of having to travel during the holidays, the Mr. Tom interlude interrupted by the projectile vomit, the collection of all those feelings had snowballed into an avalanche that now threatened to bury Theo alive right there in the airport. He was having difficulty breathing, but he knew that the only way to convince himself that he was hallucinating was to reply to the mirage; when the mirage failed to respond, he would know his mind was just playing tricks on him and he wasn't being visited by the ghost of Christmas Past.

Squinting up at the vision, Theo asked cautiously, "Rob?"

And then the ghost of Christmas Past spoke again. In a thick, New Jersey accent that Theo knew all too well, "Dude! This is freakin' unbelievable!"

It was no hallucination, it was Rob.

"Dude! I knew it was you!" Rob exclaimed, squealing like a man from New Jersey who has no idea that squealing is something that only tween girls should do in public.

Before Theo could fully comprehend what was going on, Rob grabbed his hand in a firm handshake and yanked him up out of his seat, causing his magazine to fall to the floor. He didn't even notice; he was mesmerized. Smiling warmly, Rob threw his left arm around him in a hug that was even more welcoming and pressed Theo close to his chest. Just as Theo thought he would faint from the warmth of the physical connection, Rob pulled back and rested his palms on Theo's shoulders. The silence crackled as both men took each other in and was only broken when Rob spoke. "Seriously dude, I can't believe it's you."

Neither can I, Theo thought, *after all this time, in the most random of places. For years I imagined what it would be like to see you again, to say all the things to you that I never got a chance to say.*

"Dude, say something!" Rob said again in that same squeaky voice, slapping both of Theo's shoulders lightly as if to jumpstart his dialogue.

"Merry Christmas," was all that Theo could manage.

Rob threw his hands up and laughed. "Well yeah, you too, but after all this time that's all you can come up with?" he replied. "Come on, Teddy, you can do better than that."

"My name's not Teddy." And in today's performance the role of the bitchy queen will be played by Theodore Franklin, Jr. "Sorry I didn't mean it like that," Theo stammered. "It's just that I haven't, you know, been called that since . . ."

"High school," Rob said, finishing his sentence.

That wasn't what Theo had wanted to say, but he didn't think he should make another bitchy comment so soon after his first one. "Exactly."

Shrugging his shoulders, Rob said, "Sorry, I forgot you're, uh, Theo now, right?"

Theo nodded, too surprised that Rob actually knew that piece of information to reply verbally.

"Whatever you call yourself, dude, I'm always gonna think of you as Teddy Roosevelt Franklin."

And whenever I think of you that's who I am. After a few seconds Theo realized that he was actually standing in front of someone he hadn't seen in years, someone he never thought he'd see again, and all he was doing was staring at him blankly. It was time to speak and in full sentences. "Thanks to my history buff of a father."

"You remember what I always said?" Rob finished his question by repeatedly jabbing a finger into Theo's chest.

I remember most everything you ever said to me. "About what?"

"Your name!" Rob replied, a bit shocked that Theo couldn't read his mind. "It's a good thing your last name wasn't Cleveland, your father would've called you Grover."

Yes, Theo remembered that; he also remembered exactly when it occurred, in ninth grade during American history class. But Rob had never said it; he wrote it on a note and passed it to him, he risked getting into trouble just to share a joke with him.

"Of course I remember that!" Theo exclaimed. "It made being Theodore Roosevelt Franklin, Jr., a lot easier to bear."

When Rob smiled, Theo noticed for the first time that there were some crinkles around his blue eyes. The eyes themselves were still youthful, still projected a boyish spirit. The surrounding frame, however, had aged a bit, not much, just enough so that there were some cracks, some wear, nothing substantial, just evidence that the shell wasn't invulnerable, that it had to work a bit harder to maintain its youthful resilience. Theo knew what that felt like.

"So, um, sit down," Theo said. It was the most obvious thing to say and yet the most difficult. It was also exactly what Rob had been waiting to hear.

"Thanks."

With the expert skill of a frequent flyer, Rob picked up his tote bag stuffed with Christmas presents and his overcoat in one hand and with the other gripped the handle of his suitcase, spun it around, and timed it perfectly so he sat on the yellow chair at the same time that he compressed the handle back into its slot. He tossed his coat onto his suitcase, placed the tote bag next to it, and leaned back into the chair with the same casual ease Theo remembered. Rob never looked like he exerted himself; everything he did, whether it was make the final basket of a championship basketball game, answer every multiple choice question correctly on a pop quiz, or just sit down, he did effortlessly. It was a gift, and as Theo watched him cross his ankles and fold his hands in his lap it was clear that it was a gift he still possessed.

"I don't think you've aged a day since the last time I saw you,"

Rob said, the skin around his blue eyes crinkling even more than before.

Theo didn't respond immediately. He wondered if Rob really was thinking about the last time they were together. He glanced down at Rob's lap and noticed the wedding band wedged in between his clasped hands; he was still married, though Theo had learned from experience that nuptial vows couldn't always prevent a man from remembering things his wife would probably want him to forget. Theo looked closer, saw Rob's fingers were different, still thick and blunt, but the nails were smooth, even, each one identical to the next as if they had been perfectly manicured. *Stop staring, Theo, say something.* "You either," Theo said. "You look great."

And it was true. Rob looked a bit older, but even under the harsh lights of the airport lounge he was unmistakably handsome. Except for the few wrinkles around his eyes, his skin was smooth, his nose just as long and important looking as the day they took their graduation pictures, and his lips just as full and curvy as Theo recalled. The flecks of gray hair above his sideburns were completely outnumbered by a head of hair that was otherwise dark brown, and even though he wore his straight hair parted on the left and swooped over like he had when they were kids, adult bangs actually worked on Rob's face; they looked like they belonged there, softly touching his forehead, skimming over his eyebrows, and weren't just a desperate attempt to reclaim his youth. Effortless.

His easy beauty spilled out onto his clothes too. Theo had spent more money than he cared to admit on his own wardrobe, so he knew without touching the fabric that Rob's suit was made of an expensive, lightweight wool and impeccably tailored. Even in this relaxed position, the navy blue material fit perfectly around his shoulders and down his arms, the cuffs rising just enough to reveal a powder blue cuff link, designed to look like some kind of intricate sailor's knot, the color perfectly matching the thin blue stripe of his yellow shirt, a shade of yellow much more appealing than the harsh hue of the chair that he sat in. And then there were the trousers.

My oh my. From ankle to waist the material was smooth despite Rob's languid pose; the suit was a perfect fit around his calves, his thighs, his lap, not too tight, not too loose. Rob was like a gym-fit Goldilocks, the fabric falling across the dips and curves of his muscles perfectly, not hiding or enhancing what lay beneath, just presenting it as it was, not that it mattered—Theo knew what was there. Then Theo realized that Rob knew that Theo knew what lay there too and suddenly his stare made him self-conscious.

In an instant he was transported back to high school gym class, and he was desperately trying to keep his eyes forward, focus on his locker in front of him as he undressed, not steal a glance left or right to optically salivate over a glimpse of a classmate in his underwear or better yet at that perfect moment when all he's wearing is his jock and he's bent over reaching for his gym shorts, but he can't find them because they're buried in the back of his locker underneath some books, so he has to bend over even further and his ass rises just a bit more to reveal the dark hairs that are beginning to spread across the small of his back and in between the crack of his ass like little curly flowers with an aroma that's both pungent and pretty. That was exactly how Theo felt gazing at Rob's crotch. "And your suit looks great too," Theo stuttered, his eyes finally rising to meet Rob's eyes. "Brooks Brothers?"

Rob smiled, the wrinkles around his eyes deepening. "You can still do that! It's like you're this retail psychic or something."

Shrugging his shoulders, Theo actually felt his ears grow warm and knew they were turning red. "Just a knack."

"Freakin' sixth sense is what it is," Rob declared, lengthening his arms, so his clasped hands traveled away from his lap and toward the insides of his thighs. "You should write a book about it and go on *Oprah*, get all rich and famous."

"What makes you think I'm not already rich and famous?"

Theo's spontaneous quip made Rob do that thing with his face that he always did, ever since they were kids and he was greatly amused. He raised his shoulders so his head looked like it had been lowered a few inches, at the same time his eyebrows shot up, his chin dropped, and his lips formed a little 'o'. They referred to it as Robface, and it always made Theo laugh, like it did now. "And I see that you can still do that thing with your face."

Feigning innocence, Rob asked, "What thing?"

"You know what I'm talking about," Theo said. "Robface!"

Of course the second Theo mentioned the expression by its formal name, Rob's face became a blank mask, his voice for some reason British. "Teddy, I haven't the foggiest notion what you're blabbering on about." A perfectly timed second later and Robface emerged, making Theo laugh harder than he had in weeks, making him laugh so hard he didn't care that he was making little sounds, snorts through his nose, making his face scrunch up to advertise every line and wrinkle. Vanity had been replaced by nostalgia.

"You laugh just like my daughter does when I do that face," Rob announced.

Theo stiffened involuntarily, his hand clutching the rough yellow cloth of the chair, not because Rob had compared his laugh to a little girl's, but because he ruined the privacy of their moment by bringing in an outsider. Robface was theirs, it was something between the two of them and wasn't supposed to be shared or enjoyed by another, regardless if that third party was bound to one of them by blood. "Right," Theo said, affording the word three syllables. "I heard you had a daughter."

Rob pushed himself up in his chair; now that the conversation had abruptly shifted to talking about his children, it was time he sat like an adult. "Yeah, a son too."

"Yup," Theo replied. "I heard about that too." Feeling the need to move, Theo crossed his leg like a less seductive and more appropriately dressed Sharon Stone. He then felt the need to speak, thinking his last comment might have been construed as a bit rude. "Him, I mean, you know, your son."

In contrast, Rob felt no need to adjust his position. However, he was curious about what Theo had said. "So are you keeping tabs on me?"

If Theo had been standing on the patio at 28 Degrees, his favorite bar back home in Boston, he would, without question, have known that Rob was flirting with him, but here without a Blue Moon in his hand sitting in an airport in Conservative Country, USA, he wasn't sure. Theo uncrossed his legs and brushed away an imaginary thread from his jeans to buy himself some time so he could think of an appropriate and hopefully equally ambiguous response, but the only thing he could think of was that he didn't have anything appropriate or ambiguous to say. So he simply spoke the truth. "My mother fills me in on all the Fairfield gossip."

"Even now that she's living in Phoenix?"

Oh how quickly the tables turn, Theo thought. *Now who's been keeping tabs on whom?* Chalk it up to maturity or just that he was still off kilter from being ambushed in the airport, but once again Theo opted for honesty over wit. "She talks to her lady friends from church every day, and she still subscribes to the *Home News,*" Theo explained. "She may live two time zones away, but she still has her finger on the pulse of what's happening in Jersey."

Rob leaned forward, his clasped hands dangling in between his knees. "Is she feeling okay? My mother said she moved there 'cause of her health."

Theo forced himself not to sink back into his chair despite the fact that Rob leaned in closer, his clean-shaved face about a foot away from his. His tie swayed a bit, and Theo saw that what he had thought were white flowers against a navy backdrop were actually rows of snowflakes, identical in their geometry. Suddenly Theo realized how completely underdressed he was in comparison to Rob's business attire. His jeans, dark brown V-neck sweater, and matching driving mocs were suitable for travel, but not for such an important impromptu reunion. "She's fine," Theo replied. "My aunt's the sick one."

Forcing himself to inject a tone of concern into his voice,

Theo relayed the details of his Aunt Clare's respiratory ailments, his mother's extreme devotion to and dependence upon her twin, and the remedy for both their diseases being relocation to the Land of the Neverending Sun. Despite Theo's attempt to sound serious and relieved that a solution had been found, Rob knew Theo too well; he instinctively understood that Theo would have preferred his family stayed put and found a distributer who sold inhalers wholesale. "I think it's a conspiracy," Rob declared.

"No, I don't think so. I always got along with my Aunt Clare."

Clearly, Rob's instincts were better than Theo's. "Noooo, Teddy," Rob said, swinging his hand in front of Theo's face, the nonviolent version of a slap to the side of the head. It was what Rob always did when Theo exasperated him, when Theo didn't follow the flow of the conversation. This time was a bit different: When Rob swung his hand, Theo caught a whiff of cologne that rose off his wrist and swirled in front of Theo's nostrils. The scent lingered there until Theo had no choice but to breathe; he inhaled and was surprised to smell something sweet, like vanilla and something denser, something he couldn't identify, but that he liked much more than the cologne Rob used to wear when they were in high school. Back then he drenched himself in something that smelled like the final dying embers of burning wood, heavy and charcoaley and forcibly masculine; this softer smell was much more appealing. "I mean between doctors and real estate agents."

Theo still had no idea what Rob was talking about, and he couldn't blame it on the olfactory interruption. "I'm sorry, what are you talking about? What conspiracy?"

Jabbing a perfectly manicured finger in the air for emphasis, Rob went on to explain that he thought doctors and real estate agents had concocted an idea to convince wealthy older people to sell their homes and move to Phoenix as a solution to their asthmatic conditions. "I bet you dollars to doughnuts," Rob continued, "that when a doctor prescribes a move to the Sunshine State he gets a kickback from a local realtor."

Pursing his lips to keep them from erupting into a smile, Theo was happy to hear that Rob still had some outlandish ideas. He might look and dress like a responsible adult, but very close to the surface was the goofball Theo remembered so fondly. "Whilst I find your theory possibly plausible," Theo began, adopting the same British accent Rob had previously, "I have a few problems with it."

Ready, willing, if not completely able to defend his beliefs, Rob sat back, shrugged his shoulders, and crossed his arms. "Bring it on, Franklin."

Keeping a straight face, Theo continued, "First of all, Colangelo, why am I going to bet you a dollar if I'm only getting a doughnut in return?"

Rob nodded. "Point taken."

"And second of all, *Florida* is the Sunshine State, Arizona is the *Grand Canyon* State."

"The *Grand Canyon* State?" Rob asked. "Really?"

It was Theo's turn to nod his head. "Yes."

Again, Rob looked at Theo with a blank expression, but this time it wasn't as a cover-up, it was honest. "Seriously?"

"Yes! When my parents first moved there they kept sending me all this information, all these brochures about the stupid state, hoping I'd follow them and move out there too," Theo answered. "Completely ignoring the fact that I had built a life for myself on the East Coast and deliberately chose to live in Boston to be close to them in New Jersey and not move to San Francisco or Los Angeles or some other place that I would really have loved to have moved to, plus the fact that I was living with Neil."

Theo stopped short. Thus far they had avoided any mention of sexual orientation whether consciously or not, and it wasn't like Theo was hiding his homosexuality from Rob—in fact Rob was probably the first person on the planet who knew he was gay. It was just that he didn't want to bring it up in conversation so abruptly or in connection with the N-word, which was how Theo usually referred to Neil out loud. It was fortuitous then that Rob wasn't really listening to Theo's tirade; he was still trying to comprehend his last comment. "Honestly, the Grand Canyon is in Arizona?"

Now it was Theo's turn to adopt a blank expression, "Seriously?"

"I'm still no good at geography," Rob confessed. As Rob laughed at himself, at his own inability to retain basic grammar school knowledge, Theo grew uncomfortable. He was still in the past: he was twenty-one and fifteen and ten all at the same time; he was frightened and hopeful and confused and the only constant in his life was Rob, the man who now was sitting next to him, inexplicably grown up while Theo was still floundering in childhood, adolescence, young adulthood. The imbalance was disconcerting, it was making Theo remember things that he hadn't in a very long time, from when he was twenty-one and fifteen and ten and Rob was his constant companion. But that had ended, suddenly and brutally, and Theo needed to remember that most of all.

When Theo returned to the present he heard Rob still talking through his laughter, something about how his daughter didn't want him to help her with her homework because whenever he did she always got the answers wrong. Theo wished he could picture Rob sitting next to his little girl, a girl who hopefully had inherited his pretty blue eyes and soft brown hair, his arm around her protectively, proudly, watching her make sense out of fractions, not having the faintest idea of how to help her divide one-fourth into one-sixteenth, but he couldn't. When he tried to imagine Rob as a parent, as the patriarch of some family, all he saw was himself sitting at a table alone, no children, no math homework, just an empty table. It made his chest tighten, his stomach go numb.

On and on and on Rob rambled about his kids and homework and soccer practice or was it softball. Theo was trying not to listen. It wasn't that he didn't care, it wasn't that he was anti-family, he just didn't want to think of Rob as a family man just yet—he wanted to keep him as his possession, his rediscovery, his creation for a little while longer. He would get his wish.

"Ladies and gentlemen due to a very overcrowded departure schedule today and some inclement weather in the Rockies, Flight 422 from St. Louis to Phoenix has been delayed," said the upbeat, feminine Midwestern voice over the loudspeaker. "Our current departure time is 6:15."

Amid the groans and thrown magazines, Rob smiled. "Dude, this gives us more time, my flight doesn't leave until six," he announced. "Let's have a drink."

Theo could feel a slight tingling sensation in his stomach, feeling was starting to return, the air in his chest was flowing freer, always good to be able to breathe. He glanced at his watch; it was 3:58, a bit early, but since he was still on East Coast time, his biological clock was at well after five, so why not have a drink? Theo could think of a lot of good reasons why he shouldn't, but he heard himself agree. "Sounds good to me," Theo said, "dude."

Once again Rob displayed an effortless ability to laugh at himself. "I know, I know, I totally overuse that word." Rob tossed his coat over his arm and then grabbed the tote bag chock full of gifts with one hand and disengaged the handle of his carry-on suitcase with the other in one fluid, multitasking movement. Leading the way, he turned to the right to speak over his shoulder, causing his bangs to bounce gently. "Gotta hold on to your youth any way you can, I guess."

Walking behind Rob's confident stride, Theo almost stumbled. *Hold on to your youth,* he thought. *What if you never let go of it?*

"Teddy, are you okay?"

Sprawled on the sheet of ice, Teddy thought for a moment. "Yeah, I fell."

Rob tilted his head to the side. "I can see that ya doofus, are you hurt?"

Teddy wasn't sure just how much he should admit to his friend. "Um, well, not really."

Standing over Teddy, Rob peered down, mittens on his hips, to assess the damage Teddy had done to himself. "Ya leg's kinda bent funny," Rob declared. "Can you move it?"

Determined not to show Rob how much pain he was in from slipping on the stupid ice, Teddy shouted, "Of course I can move it!"

"Well then do it!" Rob shouted back. "Lemmee see."

Slowly, Teddy straightened his leg, but before he could unbend it completely, he let out a yelp, "Ow!"

"I knew you were hurt!" Rob exclaimed, kneeling on the ice to get a closer look at Teddy's leg.

"So what do you want? A medal?" Teddy yelled.

"Oh shut up and stop being a show off," Rob said. "It's no big deal that you fell."

No big deal for you, Teddy thought. *You never fall.*

Gently, Rob straightened out Teddy's leg the rest of the way, his eyes never leaving Teddy's face so he could tell if he was hurting him any further. "Ya got blood on your knee," Rob said. "I'm gonna see how bad the cut is."

Nodding, Teddy whispered, "Okay."

Nine-year-old fingers expertly rolled up Teddy's pant leg, inch by inch, so pinkish-colored flesh was exposed. Rob was thoughtful, careful to lift the cloth high over Teddy's knee so as not to aggravate the wound. When Teddy's knee was fully revealed, Rob said reassuringly, "Oh it doesn't look too bad."

"Really?" Teddy asked, expecting much worse.

Shaking his head, Rob diagnosed the situation. "Blood's already dried up, just a little cut."

Teddy's calm turned to panic when Rob started to run off. "Where're you going?!"

"Just to get some snow, ya doof!" Jumping over a tree stump, Rob scooped up some fresh snow and carried it back over to Teddy. He knelt beside him. "I need to clean out the wound."

Teddy wasn't sure this was a good idea. "With snow?"

Looking around them, Rob answered, "You want me to use a rock instead?"

"No! I don't want you to use a rock instead!"

"Good, then shut up and let me do my job!"

"Fine! Go ahead."

Just before Rob placed the pack of snow onto Teddy's knee, he turned to him and said, "This might be a little cold, but it's gonna make it feel better."

Nodding his consent, Teddy closed his eyes before Rob placed the snow on his knee. For the first few seconds the snow stung, cold shivers ran up and down his leg, and his knee felt like it was being pricked by tiny needles, but then the weird sensations went away and just like Rob said, he felt better. "Ya okay?" Rob asked.

"Yeah," Teddy replied, his voice filled with amazement. "It doesn't hurt at all anymore."

Rob brushed away the mixture of snow and dried blood from Teddy's knee. "That's 'cause I know what I'm doing."

Still in awe, Teddy said, "You should be a doctor instead of one of those guys who make video games."

Rob scrunched up his face. "Nah, video games are a lot more fun."

Teddy felt Rob hold his calf a bit more firmly as he brushed the last bits of snow off of his knee, but even after the last bits were gone Rob didn't let go, he kept one hand on Teddy's calf and the other on his knee. Teddy watched the smoke unfurl from Rob's mouth as he breathed; he watched it inflate like a balloon and then rise, swirl, disappear. He began to breathe in rhythm with Rob, so their breaths could unfurl at the same time, connect, rise, and become one before disappearing into the air. It was like magic.

"My mom always kisses my knee when I scrape it," Rob said, his eyes still staring at Teddy's cut.

Teddy held his breath, longer, longer, until he had to let it go. He watched it swirl and rise by itself. It looked lonely without Rob's breath wrapped around it; Teddy didn't like the way it looked. "Mine too."

Once again the boys breathed at the same time, their breaths rushing toward each other, latching onto each other's mist so they could journey into the unknown together. "I could..." Rob started.

"Sure," Teddy whispered.

"That is if you want me to." Rob looked up and saw that Teddy was looking right at him, "It might make it feel even better."

It would make it feel even better; Teddy didn't know how he knew it, but he was certain, it would make his knee feel wonderful. "It might."

"So . . . should I?"

No breath escaped for a few moments. The space between them was filled only with expectation and wonder and silence until Teddy spoke. "Yes."

His command transformed into a breath that skimmed Rob's head, making it look for a second like he had a halo. When it vanished, Rob bent his head and placed his lips on Teddy's knee, trembling slightly, amazed by their courage. Teddy couldn't see Rob's lips touch his flesh, but he could feel them, softly buzzing like a hummingbird's tail. He focused on the zigzaggy lines of Rob's crocheted hat, for some reason he started to count the lines, but only got up to eleven before he heard the ground thump.

On the other side of the playground the high school marching band was practicing for the annual Christmas parade. Next week they would march through the streets of Fairfield bringing the joyful sounds of the season to the townsfolk, but today the sounds of joy only reached two little boys. Teddy softly sang along, "Hark the herald angels sing, glory to the newborn king." He didn't hear Rob's voice, but Teddy understood that he wasn't singing alone. He felt Rob's lips flicker against his bruised knee and realized that he was mouthing the words to the carol along with him. It was just more proof that they were and always would be connected.

Theo lost sight of Rob, he couldn't find him anywhere. Maybe he had been right from the start, maybe it was a hallucination, just an elaborate daydream. But then he heard his voice, loud, distinctive, cutting right through the din of the crowd. "Get the table in the corner, they're leaving," Rob instructed. Theo nodded, more thankful that he wasn't losing his mind than that they had found an empty table. "I'll buy the first round," Rob offered. "What do you want?"

"Uh, just a beer," Theo said. "Blue Moon if they have it."

As Theo started to make his way to the back of the Cloud 9 lounge, Rob extended his arm and Theo took his coat and shopping bag; it was a perfectly executed handoff, as if they were members of a relay team or a couple in a long-term relationship, words weren't necessary, only instinct. Theo squeezed in between chairs and patrons to get to the table before it was scooped up by another inconvenienced traveler and, as he laid Rob's coat over the back of the chair, another whiff of that sweet vanilla scent wafted up and smacked him in the face, so unexpected, so refreshing. He placed the shopping bag down next to the chair gently like it was some treasure, which since it was filled with Christmas presents it kind of was, and finally sat down in the chair that faced the bar.

He draped his own coat over the back of his chair and then placed his duffel bag on the ground to his right. After a moment he switched it to his left so it would be out of the aisle and heard himself murmur out loud, "What the hell am I doing?" The rest of his conversation with himself was silent.

This is ridiculous! I should be furious with him, I shouldn't be having a drink with him. That comment came from the right, emotional side of Theo's brain. The left, more logical side, responded, *Then why are you acting as if you're on a date? Like he's your boyfriend and the two of you just went to see a movie starring Hugh Jackman's chest and decided to get a drink before heading home?* Theo didn't have any response, logical or emotional; he didn't know why he was sitting here, tucked away in an airport bar, listening to Mariah Carey sing about her solitary Christmas wish, waiting for Rob Colangelo to bring him a drink. It was like the past fifteen years had never happened, like they had been wiped away with a chalky eraser leaving behind a mere dusty reminder that something had happened, something different had taken place, something that didn't really matter because this is how it was supposed to be.

Uncomfortable, Theo adjusted himself in his seat and caught his reflection in a mirror that hung on the wall beside him. He thought he still looked pretty good. No bags or puffiness under his eyes, smooth skin thanks to an overindulgence in facial products and the occasional microdermabrasion, hair still golden brown, cut short in a trendy, yet classic hairstyle, and of course he had good bone structure. High cheekbones, more rounded than pointy, and a slender, longish face, which he had always felt was the ideal counterpart to Rob's more blunt, square-edged, masculine features.

This time when Theo's chest tightened, he felt his eyes well up too. He shut them tight and tried to shut off his mind, but was unsuccessful; there were too many memories with and without Rob, too many years in which he was the star and too many years in which he had been replaced. Breathing deeply, Theo fought to maintain control of his body if not his mind; he reminded himself it was Christmas Eve, it was really no big deal, everybody gets emotional on this night. Well, maybe not Jews, they probably don't get emotional, to them it's an unimportant evening. *Oh to be Jewish and unemotional,* Theo thought. *Oh wait, is that a slur? Sorry about that.* Theo wasn't overly religious, but still he was of Irish Catholic heritage and didn't think it proper to think borderline racist thoughts on the holiest day of the Christian calendar.

"It's official, I'm losing my mind."

Luckily the bar was noisy and Rob was concentrating on not spilling their drinks so Theo's comment went unheard. Rob's outstretched palm contained two tumblers filled with ice and an amber-colored liquid. "What happened to my beer?"

"You can't toast the holidays with a beer," Rob scoffed. Theo took the glasses and placed them on the table. Rob shook his wet hand and a small drop of liquid, water, maybe alcohol, fell onto Theo's knuckle; he didn't wipe it away, but let it glide toward his thumb. When Rob turned to sit and maneuver his carry-on suitcase underneath the table, Theo flicked his tongue in the crevice between his thumb and forefinger and tasted the unmistakable sting of Scotch.

Raising his glass, Rob held it in midair until Theo matched him. He hesitated for a moment and then said, "To old friends." Rob clinked his tumbler into Theo's, a not-entirely-gentle clink that caused some of the alcohol to tumble over the side of the glass. His lips a weird combination of a smirk and a smile, Rob licked the edge of his glass before taking a swig of Scotch. Self-conscious, Theo couldn't lick the glass or take a swig, his was more of a sip, still he felt enough of the warm, harsh liquid ripple over his tongue before plummeting down his throat to add to the tingling sensation that had erupted in his stomach.

After Rob swallowed he leaned back and smiled. "Merry Christmas, dude."

Shaking his head, Theo laughed. "Right back at ya . . . dude."

Raising his glass to his lips, the amber liquid swirling like a mini-whirlpool, Rob said, "So tell me about this Neil guy."

Stunned, Theo couldn't believe that Rob had been listening when Theo brought up Neil's name before and had kept silent about it all this time. He was also stunned because he wasn't used to hearing the N-word uttered by someone so nonchalantly. All his friends knew that if they were going to ask about Neil, they had to wait for the right moment, they had to allow the conversation to move organically from casual to serious, build up to a point where personal questions were acceptable, not just sit down and start off with a controversial topic. It was like meeting a gynecologist and asking right off if he'd ever performed an abortion or asking an interior designer if he'd ever shopped at Sears, completely unacceptable. It didn't matter that Rob didn't know the rules; he should know better.

This time when Theo took a sip of Scotch it more closely resembled a swig, and he felt not only his stomach, but his whole body grow warm. Was he unnerved talking about Neil in front of Rob or just uneasy addressing the whole homosexual thing? He was unsure; the only thing he was sure about was that he wanted to change the subject. And perhaps since it was the season of granting wishes, his wish was granted. Tired of watching newscasters report about the lack of clement weather, the bartender flipped through channels on the TV that rested precariously over the bar, pausing when he got to a station that was airing a football game. Theo had no idea what teams were playing, if it was a live game or a rebroadcast, but it interested Rob enough for him to turn around and stare at the TV intently for a few seconds as if he was watching something really interesting like *Project Runway* or a rerun of *All About Eve.*

"I can't believe the Raiders might actually make the playoffs!" Rob exclaimed, "They came back from one of the worst seasons ever."

For a second Theo almost wanted Rob to talk about Neil again. "You make the Raiders sound almost as exciting as Michelle Kwan."

"Who?" Rob asked.

Unbelievable! "Oh come on!" Theo screeched. "First you don't know where the Grand Canyon is and now you're going to tell me you don't know Michelle Kwan."

Rob thought hard for a moment. "Oh she's that gymnast who lost at the Olympics right?"

Close enough. "Figure skater," Theo explained. "Most decorated non-gold medal-winning skater in the history of the sport." Rob was about to say something, but Theo cut him off. "And, yes, figure skating is most definitely a sport."

Laughing, Rob said, "No, I was going to say sorry about the interruption, I was asking about Neil."

Back to that again. Theo had no choice: If he wanted to avoid discussing Neil he was going to have to be direct. "No longer interesting," Theo mumbled, gripping his glass so tightly his fingers were almost as red as his ears. "What I really want to know is what you're doing here on Christmas Eve?"

It was not the most graceful segue, and Theo was pretty certain Rob could figure out that he had stumbled onto tender territory that Theo didn't want to enter, but Rob didn't press the issue, he simply answered Theo's question. "Last minute business trip in Chicago, the only way I could get home tonight was to catch a flight here."

Another swig, another question. "What kind of business? My mother's spies, the desperate and *old* housewives of New Jersey, failed to obtain that piece of information."

There was that smile again. "Ever hear of CompuRation?"

Theo's brow furrowed. "I can honestly say I have not."

"It's a software company, pretty big in the industry," Rob explained. "But if you don't know the tech field intimately, there's no reason you should have heard of it."

Theo's brow unfurrowed and his green eyes grew wider. No, he had never heard of CompuRation, but once again the past came flooding into the present. "Oh my God, Rob, that's great!" Theo squealed. "You're living your dream."

Head tilt, shoulder shrug, Rob opened his mouth to speak, but no words emerged.

"You were always playing video games, made me waste hours playing them too," Theo said. "Those stupid Mario Brothers, and the one, you know, the one with the, uh, gangstas in the ghetto."

Confused, Rob merely repeated the words in question form, "Gangstas in the ghetto?"

Theo was so excited he didn't even realize he was patting Rob's hand with his fingers to coax his memory. "You know, the one where the kids steal the cars, rough up some hookers, shoot some cops."

"Grand Theft Auto?"

Slamming his palm on the table, Theo shouted, "That's the one! That game was fun! I know it got a bad rap for being a little violent, but so was Bugs Bunny. I distinctly remember an episode where Bugs retaliated against some policemen that ended in bloodshed." Theo only stopped talking because he took another sip of Scotch. Rob could tell by the quick way he drank that he wasn't finished talking so he remained silent. "I can't believe you're actually creating your own video games, that's what you always wanted to do."

Theo was so lost in his own reverie that he didn't notice Rob's smile grow wider while his eyes remained the same. They stared out blankly, looking at Theo's glowing face, but seeing something else, something that was no longer attainable, something that was lost forever. "Sorry to disappoint you, but I don't do anything quite like that," Rob began. "CompuRation is a mainstream migration company." When Theo looked at him blankly, he continued, "And once again if you aren't immersed in the tech field there isn't any reason why you should know what that means."

Before Theo could ask any more obligatory questions and feign excitement over Rob's career, Rob explained that mainstream migration was simply the transference of computer servers, the bulky pieces of hardware that run all of a company's computers and maintain every piece of information they generate, onto software. Rob admitted that it wasn't as exciting as creating video games, but it was essential.

"No, it sounds really, really interesting," Theo said, then suggested, "kind of like technological downsizing."

"Yes, exactly," Rob said, grateful that his friend understood not everything from childhood could be dragged into the adult world. "And what do you do back in Boston?"

"I'm in marketing, VP actually for a company that makes menus."

"Menus?"

"Yup, just like this one," Theo said, yanking a small laminated card from its aluminum clip that had been resting on the table. "See all the unique names for these drinks and the fun descriptions and of course the absence of prices?" Rob nodded. "All created by a company like mine."

Examining the menu, Rob looked at Theo dubiously. "There are really companies devoted to just making menus?"

With an equally dubious expression, Theo replied, "This coming from the man who migrates hardware?"

Laughing, Rob threw up his hands. "Ya got me." Rob stopped

laughing and was genuine when he spoke. "I wasn't making fun, I just never thought there was a science behind making menus. I thought they just appeared, you know?"

Theo understood completely. "A few years ago I was working as an assistant at an advertising company, very glamorous, but very cutthroat, and I realized it wasn't for me."

"And menu marketing is?"

"Well I didn't even know such a thing existed until I went on the interview," Theo admitted. "But the pay was good, and they were willing to give me a title that was all nouns, no adjectives, no 'Assistant to' somebody, so I took it. That was eight years ago."

Rob looked like he wanted to say something, but remained motionless, his hands clasped around his glass, staring at Theo more intently than he had since they first bumped into each other. Karen Carpenter was now singing Merry Christmas to her darling, and Theo wasn't sure whether to take this as irony or encouragement. Before he could make a decision, Rob spoke. "I never pictured you taking the safe route."

That's definitely not how you talk to your darling. "Well I'm not sure if I'd call menu marketing stable, you know, in this economy."

Shaking his head, but still staring at Theo intently, Rob clarified his statement. "No, eight years. I don't know, that just seems like a long time for someone like you to be in one job."

"Someone like me?" Theo asked, unsure what point Rob was trying to make. "What's that supposed to mean?"

"Well you're not a family man," Rob said. "So I just figured you'd jump around from job to job a lot more. I know that's what I'd do if I were you."

Well you're not me, Rob, so please keep your hypocritical comments to yourself. Theo wasn't sure what he was feeling, but he knew it wasn't pleasant. He did know, however, that it was time for another drink. "Round two's on me."

* * *

"Thanks."

Before Theo's ass hit the chair Rob was apologizing. "I'm sorry, dude, I didn't mean to upset you."

"You didn't upset me," Theo lied.

"Yes, I did, and I'm sorry," Rob said, directly looking at Theo's face, his eyes not darting to the side, his body not squirming in his seat; it was the most heartfelt apology he had ever received. And so he accepted it.

"No harm, no foul," Theo said, taking a sip of the Scotch that he was actually getting used to. "Whatever that means."

"It's just that you're single, no kids. . . ."

Oh enough with skirting the issue. "You can say it, Rob," Theo announced a bit louder than he had anticipated. "We both know it, I'm gay."

"Well yeah . . ." Rob said.

"No, not well yeah, it's who and what I am," Theo said in the same tone of voice, but before he got even louder he took another sip of the increasingly delightful Scotch. When he continued, he was speaking at a normal decibel. "Yes, I'm gay, but that doesn't mean I don't have any responsibilities and can flit around from job to job just because I feel like it."

"No, no, I didn't mean that," Rob implored.

Now some group that sounded like the musical version of the gangstas in the ghetto from the Grand Theft Auto video game series was singing "The Twelve Days of Christmas." Every time they got to the lyric "four calling birds" the word *calling* was bleeped out. If the song had come at an earlier point in the conversation, Theo and Rob might have tried to figure out what the bleeped out substitute was; now they ignored the urban reinterpretation of the classic song as Rob tried to interpret his comment as something other than a classic insult. He failed.

"I did, I did mean it," Rob confessed. "I'm sorry. It's just that, well, all the gay guys I know do jump from job to job and live pretty irresponsible lives."

"According to whom?"

"What do you mean?"

"They live irresponsible lives according to whom?" Theo clarified. "You?"

"Not just me, no," Rob stuttered.

"You and all the other heterosexuals who like to judge?"

Just like he used to do when he was in high school, Rob bent his head in search of the answer, but this time instead of searching in the cracks of his desk, he scoured the smudges and the imperfections of the table. And just like back in high school when he came up empty and couldn't find an answer he relied on his charm to get out of a sticky situation. "Dude listen . . ."

"Stop calling me dude," Theo demanded. "My name is Theo." He stared at Rob, unblinking and unapologetic and was prepared to maintain his focus until Rob spoke. He only had to wait a few awkward seconds.

"I'm sorry, Theo, I really am." Rob waited for him to respond, joke, forgive, but all he did was nod his head; that would have to be enough. "Can we rewind? Go back to the beginning and start over?"

If only Rob, if only that were a real choice I'd grab it in an instant. "I don't feel like being a skinny ten-year-old in the school yard with no friends."

"Du . . . Theo, you had lots of friends."

"Only when you were around."

"That isn't true! Everybody loved being around you, you were like the funniest guy in class."

"When I knew that you'd be there to laugh at whatever lame joke I said."

Rob's eyes drifted away for a second, backwards, Theo didn't know exactly where, but he was sure it was toward the past to some classroom or lunchroom when Theo had said something silly or maybe witty, something that would thwart the inevitable cruel comment, something that would work as a shield. When Rob laughed, Theo joined in—they didn't know if they were laughing at the same exact memory, but it didn't matter, they were linked again, they were two boys, friends who relied upon each other. "If it hadn't been for you I don't think I would've survived high school."

The declaration made Theo choke on his drink. "You cannot be serious."

"Dead serious, I hated high school."

Theo leaned forward, inching toward the edge of his seat, and he felt his knees touch Rob's underneath the table. He was so surprised by Rob's comment that the physical connection didn't even register in his mind. "That can't be true, even I didn't hate high school! And God knows I had way more reasons to hate it than you did."

Their knees pressed harder against each other as Rob leaned in even closer. "You remember how popular I was?"

"Yes."

"And kind of a jock?"

"Kind of?"

"None of that came naturally to me," Rob confessed. "There was a lot of pressure on me to maintain my status."

Theo leaned back in his chair, not because he grew self-conscious over their tangible connection, but because of the incongruity of the intangible memory. "That makes no sense! You loved being popular, Rob; it totally came easy for you."

"The only time I felt at ease was when I was with you!"

Silence floated over the table like snowflakes at dawn, more welcome than disruptive. Both men allowed Rob's comment to drift over them and settle before feeling the need to respond. Since the words were Rob's he felt more of a need to speak. "The very first time I met you, in second grade, you made me laugh. Miss Donnelly asked me to name the capital of Alaska, and I had no idea what it was. You were sitting next to me, and I heard you whisper something to me."

It was as if Theo was transported in time along with Rob: He saw himself as an eight-year-old sitting next to him in their second grade classroom, as clearly as he saw himself sitting next to him now. "I gave you the correct answer."

"Yes, you did, but since I didn't know what the answer was, I thought you were saying 'Jew know?' so I whispered back, 'No, I don't know,' which only made you whisper the answer louder. Miss Donnelly asked me again, and you whispered 'Jew know?' again even louder, so I yelled back all annoyed 'cause I thought you were making fun of me, 'No, I do not know the answer, Teddy!' Which made Miss Donnelly respond . . ."

"If you had cleaned out your ears this morning, Mr. Colangelo, you would have heard Teddy say *Juneau*," Theo interrupted, "which if you had studied your state capitals you would know is the correct answer."

Caught up in the memory, Rob clutched Theo's hand. "Yes! The entire class howled, and once Miss Donnelly joined in, I think I laughed the loudest."

Theo wasn't laughing along with Rob, he was holding onto his hand, marveling at how soft it still felt, how familiar and yet how different, never did he think he'd hold his hand again. He was back in his basement, in the little room next to the laundry where he convinced his parents to let him have an old loveseat and a portable thirteen-inch TV so he could have his own retreat, privacy, where he and Rob could hang out, talk without worrying that they'd be overheard, and sometimes hold hands like they were doing now. He was amazed then and he was amazed now that Rob didn't pull away; he let Theo's fingers glide over his knuckles like he used to, he let them slide over his now-smooth fingernails, wondering if Theo remembered how uneven they were when he used to bite them habitually. Theo would've let his fingers trace the veins on the back of Rob's hand, but he stopped when he touched his wedding band. "Sorry," Theo whispered.

"No need to be," Rob said, meaning his words.

Theo held his own two hands together, pressing them against each other hard, and then put them underneath the table. He rubbed them for a moment, but the sensation was nothing like when he touched Rob; it paled in comparison and only reminded him how lonely he was without that touch, without any touch actually. There was no holding back now, might as well feel even lonelier. "I guess now's a good time to tell me all about your wife."

It was the first time Theo noticed Rob look really uncomfortable. He breathed deeply as his shoulders stiffened; he held the air in his lungs for a few seconds, perhaps trying to suspend reality or perhaps trying to decide what to say. He fidgeted with his wedding band and looked away. It was clear he didn't want to mention the woman he had chosen to spend his life with, but he knew that Theo needed to hear about her. It was just that part of Rob wished he didn't have to mention anything that had happened after the last time they were together. "I thought you might ask about her."

Rob's voice was almost apologetic, which was sweet, but it still didn't change things. Rob was married and Theo was not and both of them knew it. "Well, Rob, come on," Theo said. "It's not like you're exactly a closeted heterosexual."

Quickly and without thinking Rob replied, "I'm not a closeted homosexual either."

Really, Theo thought, *'cause that was kind of a bitchy thing to say.* "I never said you were."

This time when Rob breathed in his shoulders were relaxed, his face soft, and his smile genuine. "I'm sorry, that was a rude thing to say."

Only if rude is heterosexual for bitchy. It was Theo's turn to take a deep breath before he spoke; he didn't want the rest of their conversation, the rest of their meeting, however long, wherever it might lead, to be a series of rude, nasty comments. "Forget it," Theo said, but he couldn't, he would never be able to forget and from the tone of Rob's voice he wouldn't be able to forget either. "It's no mystery that we share a history."

Did Rob just glance around to see if the people at the next table heard Theo's comment? Are words, indisputable facts, more condemning than handholding? As if still able to read Theo's mind, Rob answered, "I'm not ashamed of what we had."

Looking at Rob's still youthful face, the cluster of soft, long lashes whose sole purpose it seemed was to spotlight his beautiful blue eyes, Theo held his gaze for a moment, but then he felt the pull of a distant memory and traveled south to the little scar on Rob's chin, almost unnoticeable unless you knew where to look. A little piece of mended flesh, not even a quarter of an inch in length, the result of a diving board accident when they were thirteen. Rob's parents had gone away for the weekend, an early December getaway before the hustle and bustle of Christmas took over, and they reluctantly allowed Rob and his older sister, Corinne, to stay home without a babysitter. Corinne, being sixteen, not-so-bright, and blond, had a boyfriend, and the two of them occupied most of their time in her bedroom, so Rob and Teddy had decided it was the perfect time for a midnight swim, which quickly turned into skinny-dipping.

The Christmas music and the airport noises faded away, and all Theo could hear was the rippling of the pool water as Rob climbed out of the deep end, then the soft pounding of his feet as he scurried to the diving board. Rob's family was one of only two in town that had an indoor pool; the room was built as an extension of their garage and had big sliding glass doors on two sides that could open up in the summer to let the sun in or remain closed in the winter to keep the cold air out. All year round, however, the room was filled with a stifling smell of chlorine. Treading water in the middle of the pool, Teddy looked up; his eyes stung a bit from all the chemicals in the pool, and the only light came from the stars and moon outside, but nothing could prevent him from seeing Rob standing on the diving board, his toes touching the edge, his arms stretched out to the sides, his naked body, exposed, almost glowing from the moonlight that invaded the room, and Teddy felt a hand enter his chest and literally snatch his breath away. Even at thirteen Teddy recognized this was a defining moment, a moment that would comfort and haunt him forever.

Droplets of water raced down Rob's body, along his arms, across his flat chest, stream after stream of running water stopped and disappeared into the small forests of hair that accumulated in his armpits and above his privates that hung in the air unashamed, curious, willing. "Watch this," Rob had whispered before turning around. Rob didn't have to give Teddy any instruction, there was no way he was going to turn away; the new and exciting sensation in the pit of his stomach would make sure that the only thing Teddy looked at was Rob's naked body regardless of which side was on display.

Inch by inch Rob moved backwards on the diving board, his arms still outstretched, hands flat, palms facing the ground. He moved with the precision of an Olympic high diver, not that Teddy cared how he moved as long as he moved slowly. Mesmerized, Teddy watched Rob slide one foot back, then the other, until only the front pads of his feet and his toes were attached to the board, the splendid arches of his feet and the heels were suspended above the water, and he stood so strong and tall Teddy thought he could take a step backwards and still hover over the pool.

Uncontrollably, Teddy's eyes traveled up Rob's legs, the mixture of water streams and matted-down hair becoming a dizzying array of lines and curls, two slim canvases of abstract art, his eyes only stopping when the two pieces of art met and merged together. Unlike his legs, Rob's ass was smooth, undecorated, and in Teddy's mind absolutely perfect. Even though the room was enclosed it was still winter and the air was cool; even still his stomach, his chest, and his brain were on fire—it was like his whole body was exploding, like the firecrackers that had laid dormant within his loins and his mind for his entire life were finally ignited. The match had been struck, the blaze had begun, and not the cold pool water, not the December draft, not the harsh warnings from society and church and family and strangers that one boy shouldn't look at another boy with such passion and desire, none of that could extinguish the fire. Teddy finally understood what he had been feeling for years about Rob and other boys; he finally understood who he was, and it was exciting and frightening and glorious all at the same time. It was such a powerful feeling that it remained despite hearing the thud as Rob's chin crashed into the diving board.

The attempt to do an inverted backward dive or whatever Rob called it had failed. Teddy had no idea if Rob's foot had slipped or if he couldn't get enough bounce from the board or if the darkness caused him to miscalculate the distance between the board and a safe landing; he had been staring at Rob's backside.

When Rob emerged from the water, however, Teddy was waiting for him, and from the way that Rob reached out to grab onto Teddy's arm, he knew that Rob had expected him to be there. That simple movement born from instinct and not thought made the fire in Teddy's belly expand to consume his whole body, extend beyond his fingertips and toes, filling him, the pool, and his entire world with beauty, joy, hope, every good thing possible even as the blood started to gush down Rob's chin.

Knowing that the warmth was not being created by the pool water, Rob touched his chin and looked at his red fingers. "Guess I'm no Greg Louganis."

Teddy held Rob with a tighter grip and smiled. "Who needs an Olympic gold medal anyway?"

Unexpectedly, Rob descended under the water to rinse away the blood, but didn't let go of Teddy; in fact, his hand pressed into Teddy's shoulder harder, making the connection between them even stronger. Slowly treading water, Teddy's toes brushed against Rob's knee, gliding all the way down to his calf. He was grateful that Rob was under the water so he didn't hear him sigh. He knew it was a weird sound no matter how good it felt.

For a brief moment after Rob was back above the water he looked perfect, he reached out with his other hand to grab Teddy's other shoulder, and they held on to one another, floating in the pool, swathed by the moon glow and the light from the few stars that were strong enough to break through the harsh blackness of the New Jersey sky, and they were just two boys, naked literally and figuratively, in a moment of innocence. A moment that was broken by the insistent presence of reality.

"You're bleeding again," Teddy declared, trying not to sound scared, more like an adult, in charge. "Tilt your head back."

Rob did as he was told and gazed up, through the top part of the glass doors and into the night sky. He kept staring at the immensity that hung above him as he felt himself floating forward, his legs dangling in the water. He felt Teddy's hands on his body; one was pressing into the center of his back while the other was holding his own hand against his chin to stop the flow of blood. He didn't resist; he allowed Teddy to take charge. He couldn't define how he felt, except that it was nice to have his friend, his friend who always made him laugh, who always made him feel good about himself, take care of him in a way that only another adult had ever done. He felt protected.

When they got to the ladder, Rob only climbed out of the water because he knew that Teddy was right behind him. He kept his head tilted back, his hand still pressed against his chin, and shuddered a bit when the cool air wrapped itself around his wet, naked body; he was cold, but he felt alive.

A step below him Teddy felt the same way except he never felt the cold. When the water dripped off of Rob's arched body and landed on Teddy, he felt like he was being engulfed by flames; he felt as if the water was being sprinkled down from heaven to anoint and scald his skin, to burrow underneath the surface to make him feel what he had never known existed. His body was practically aglow with the burn, and he felt himself grow, but this time he wasn't ashamed. How did that old song go that his mother loved? "It can't be wrong when it feels so right, 'cause you, you light up . . ." Amazing, even thinking about his mother couldn't make him feel bad; he didn't think anything could make him feel bad ever again.

The feeling of invulnerability only deepened as the night lingered on. Sitting next to Rob on the cold cement next to the glass doors, Teddy held a towel against Rob's chin. The bleeding had slowed down considerably, but neither boy wanted the connection to end, and so they sat there, silently, towels wrapped around their shoulders, listening to the sounds of the night, maybe thinking about what they would get for Christmas this year, or maybe just thinking about each other. In a move that stunned them both, Rob turned and slowly positioned himself so his head was resting in Teddy's lap. He kept the towel pressed against his chin even though they both were pretty sure the bleeding had stopped, and he looked up and saw that Teddy was looking down, and suddenly the only thing they could see was each other's eyes and that was enough, but quickly it became too much and neither boy knew what to do next. So they stood still.

Teddy's body finally shivered, not because of the temperature, but because of the flurry of his own unanticipated emotions: His mind was racing; just when he thought he understood everything about himself, Rob, the world around him, everything changed. Tentatively he touched Rob's forehead and caressed the side of his head, his fingers shaking slightly as they felt his damp hair. Rob closed his eyes; gone was the beautiful blue and in its place long, black lashes, intertwining, like an intricate lock, and Teddy felt an irrational fear that he would never see those eyes again, that this moment, this series of unexplainable, yet inevitable moments would be gone forever. When he spoke he heard the fear in his voice, "Look at me."

Rob unlocked his lashes and opened his eyes as if the sound of Teddy's voice was the key that opened them. They were still beautiful and blue, and Teddy was thankful that it was dark and he was wet so Rob wouldn't know that tears were starting to fill up his eyes. He blinked and the tears didn't betray him; they didn't fall down his face, but he felt as if they were. He tried not to think about them and concentrated on his friend, his best, sweetest friend whose head was resting in his lap, who was looking up at him, smiling, not confused at all, but content. Teddy tried to mimic that expression and clouded by the darkness he thought he was successful, even though he was just as bewildered as he had always been. Nothing made sense and yet everything did, as long as Rob would stay where he was right now, nestled in his lap, looking up at him like a baby, like a boy, like someone who would one day grow up to be a man. Like the man Theo was staring at right now.

"Your scar never fully disappeared," Theo said.

Tracing his chin with his thumb, Rob smiled. Theo couldn't

tell what the smile meant though. Had Rob retreated back to the same memory; did he remain silent as he tried to remember how the scar got there in the first place? "Guess I'm like Michelle Kwan and was never meant to win Olympic gold either," Rob said.

He did remember! Theo hadn't made it up; there was a pool and a moon and spilt blood and Rob willingly lying in his lap, it all happened. Theo felt like the Grinch when his heart grows three times too big, and he wished there was a Who-ville nearby so he could join in a festive celebration because he was so excited. It was silly, he knew it, it was silly to feel so ecstatic simply because someone else shared a fond memory, and yet he was thrilled to know that Rob meant what he said, he wasn't ashamed of what they had had, what they had once shared. If that were true maybe, just maybe . . . Theo felt his chest tighten again and his neck grow warm; he was filled with a profound sense of wisdom, and he realized if this conversation was going to continue he would need more courage. "Refill?"

Waiting for another round of drinks at the bar, Theo looked over at Rob. How weird was it that he felt like this was where he belonged, here with Rob, a man he hadn't seen in over a decade, and he felt that Neil was the one who seemed like a distant memory. Was the time he had spent with Neil all a waste? Was it all a colossal mistake? He knew the relationship wasn't perfect; he knew he should have confronted Neil more about certain things, but he hadn't wanted to rock the boat. He stayed silent, and so he got tossed overboard. He had been crushed, devastated, but more so because the relationship had ended and not that Neil was out of his life. Wow, that was a major confession. Clearly, Scotch is good for the soul.

So are ex-boyfriends, or old friends, or whatever the hell he should call Rob. Love of his life? That would probably fit. Oh God, what was he doing? Theo glanced at the clock on the wall, just five o'clock, he still had another hour with Rob, another full hour, who knows what could happen in that time.

He looked over at him and was surprised to find that *he* wasn't checking his watch or his BlackBerry; he wasn't making a phone call or doing something to fill up the silence or worse, something to end the silence and plan his escape. He was waiting, just waiting for Theo to return. Maybe he was hoping something magical would happen too?

Theo felt his head swirl and knew that he was beginning to feel the real effects of the Scotch, and a voice in the back of his head reminded him of why he only drank beer when he went out. But it was Christmas Eve and Rob was here; it was a special night so to hell with the voice in his head. The voice continued to sermonize, but he ignored it; instead he stared at Rob.

He was leaning back in his chair, making the two front legs become airborne, his fingers lightly touching the edge of the table, more for balance than security, just like he used to do in Mr. Hesterfer's Spanish II class sophomore year. Theo had sat right behind Rob, and when he leaned back like he was doing now, Theo always felt it hard to concentrate on Mr. Hesterfer's lecture; he was more interested in how Rob's hair fell, straight down and then with a little curve to the right.

Once when Teddy was imagining what it would be like if Rob was a giant and he could slide down his soft, brown hair, Mr. Hesterfer surprised him by asking him a question. The teacher had a knack of knowing which student was daydreaming, not paying attention while he was talking, and always asked that wayward pupil a question. On this occasion they were conjugating action verbs in the conditional verb tense, and Mr. Hesterfer wanted to know how you would ask someone "Would you like to go ice skating with me if the lake turns to ice?" Since Theo hadn't been paying attention but was, in fact, wondering how wonderful it would be to glide down Rob's hair as if it were a huge, soft, brown-haired sliding pond, he had no idea, so he did what he always did when he was unsure of an answer: He made a joke. And since he was in Spanish class he made what would become his standard Spanish joke.

"*Comé me pantalones, señor.*"

It roughly translated to "Eat my shorts, man" which was Bart Simpson's extremely popular catchphrase at the time. In this instance, it really didn't make sense as a logical reply, but Theo was desperate to say something, and so he said the first thing that popped into his head. Rob found it so hilarious in its absurdity that after a moment of shocked silence, he laughed so hard and so heartily that soon the entire class, including a reluctant Mr. Hesterfer, was laughing along with him. For the rest of the year whenever Teddy didn't know an answer to one of Mr. Hesterfer's questions, he would reply with the Spanish version of Bart's bon mot, rousing laughter would ensue, and Teddy was guaranteed an A for classroom participation.

As Theo handed Rob his drink and sat down across from him, he wished he was back in Spanish class and could spend all day listening to his classmate's approving laughter as he gazed into Rob's hair imagining what it would be like to live there, to hide from reality instead of have to face it head on. Then he realized adults could hide too. "Remember when I was the breakout star of Mr. Hesterfer's class?"

Rob laughed and almost choked on his Scotch, but managed to swallow without spitting any into Theo's face. "It's the main reason why you didn't get beaten up sophomore year."

It was Theo's turn to almost choke. "What?!"

Nodding furiously, Rob replied, "Yeah, no one ever wanted to beat you up because you made everybody laugh. We had meetings about it."

"Meetings?!" An image flashed into Theo's mind: Rob and his buddies sitting around a conference table underneath the bleachers at the football field discussing the pros and cons of beating him up. "You had meetings to decide whether or not you should beat me up?"

Head nodding was replaced by head shaking. "No, of course not."

Well that's better! Theo heard his familiar nervous laughter and hoped Rob didn't think he was crazy for taking his comment literally. As it turned out he had nothing to worry about, he had interpreted the comment correctly.

"Not just you," Rob corrected. "A bunch of guys."

Theo knew that he had the beginnings of a Scotch buzz, but he also knew he was far from drunk and was capable of following a conversation even if it involved traipsing down the twisted, complicated path that led back to high school. But this he was having difficulty comprehending: clandestine meetings of the popular set to discuss organized attacks on those who populated the more undesirable factions of high school society. It was absurd, and yet Rob looked completely serious. "Are you serious?" Theo asked.

"First Wednesday of every month, give or take," Rob explained. "Me and the guys would get together during free period in the library and figure out who should get beaten up or, you know, just shoved around a bit."

It was like finding out that Santa Claus didn't exist, sad, disturbing, but not that much of a surprise. "I can't believe this was something that was debated."

"Vigorously," Rob declared. "Phil Kleiber usually got a lot of votes, mostly because of the book thing."

Another image flashed into Theo's mind, this one real: Skinny Phil Kleiber being pushed into a locker by some burly football player simply because he made the unfortunate mistake of carrying his books propped up in his arms like a girl instead of tucked at his side like a normal guy. It didn't matter that Phil's way was smarter and it was really much easier to hold your books that way; he had violated the gender laws governing book transportation and had to pay for it.

"I usually voted for Larry Stanetsky," Rob confessed.

This shocked Theo even more than the disclosure of the group meetings. "I thought you liked Larry? You said he was the only one who was better than you at Qbert."

Shocked, Rob couldn't reply fast enough. "He was not better than me at Qbert!"

"Then why did he have the high score at Arcade-A-Palooza?"

Rob contemplated this new piece of information and then offered a piece of his salesman skills: He changed the subject. "What I do remember is that one day in algebra he told Mrs. Inzintarri that he wanted to be addressed by his given name, Laurence, which I found to be incredibly pompous, so I voted for him to be that month's punching bag."

Theo thought for a moment and remembered a brief time when Larry was indeed called Laurence by his teachers; he couldn't remember, however, if this time had coincided with his also being pushed into a locker or having his books knocked out of his hands. Maybe he was closer to being drunk than he thought; maybe there was a whole secret part of high school culture that he never knew existed, or maybe the crinkles around Rob's blue eyes were growing deeper because he was trying not to laugh out loud. "You, Rob Colangelo, are such a freakin' liar!"

Theo emphasized his claim by pointing his finger at Rob, but forgot that he was holding his tumbler. The emphatic gesture caused a little tidal wave to erupt within his glass and allowed a few errant drops of liquid to escape into the air and land on Rob's knee. "Oops," Theo squealed. "Scotsman overboard!"

Grabbing a cocktail napkin, Theo pressed it into Rob's knee to absorb the liquid. He pressed down hard, completely disregarding the fact that he should have been pressing lightly to blot the liquid, and felt the muscles just underneath the worsted wool. Before he allowed himself to think about it or Rob to protest, he moved the napkin an inch or two north and pressed down even harder, discovering an even more solid muscle mass. Obviously the former track star was still disciplined and frequently used the treadmill; the muscles Theo was being introduced to were not created by walking up a few flights of stairs every day.

It might have been another slick sales tactic or it might have been an innocent move, but Rob took the cocktail napkin from Theo's hand, pressed down one final time on his knee, crumbled the paper napkin into a ball, and tossed it onto the table, all the while laughing at being caught in a fib. "Maybe not every month," he said. "But we did have the occasional powwow, and you lost out every time."

Rolling the napkin ball in his hands, the napkin that had just been dangerously close to a hidden part of Rob's flesh, Theo raised his eyebrows, his mind, his emotions straddled in both the past and the present. "I guess it was the one time that it was good that I was a loser."

Leaning forward, Rob snatched the napkin from Theo's hands and playfully tossed it at his face. With perfect aim as always, it hit him right on the tip of his nose and bounced off. Before Theo's reflexes could even kick in, Rob swooped his hand in front of Theo's face and grabbed the napkin while it was in midair. "You were never a loser," Rob corrected. "You were funny, and nobody thought you'd be funny with a black eye or, you know, a cracked rib. Except for Matty Czarnecki, he always voted to beat you up."

That name! It was like a pudgy fist reaching out from the past and punching Theo in the stomach, like the pellet from a Red Rover BB gun ricocheting off a tree and into his eye. Like a warning that no matter how content his life got, no matter how happy and fulfilled, there would always be a reminder that he was closer to loserville than unadulterated adult success. "Oh my God, Matty Czarnecki!" Theo exclaimed. "I hated that fat prick!" Both men were stunned by Theo's outburst, Rob by the still obvious level of hatred Theo felt for his former nemesis and Theo by the still obvious level of dishonesty. "What am I saying? I *still* hate him!"

Downing another gulp of amber-colored alcohol, Rob grimaced, then spoke. "He hated you too, all through high school, but I could never figure out why."

Raising his arms like an angry Evita, Theo shouted, "Because he was jealous of me! I was funnier than he was."

Rob nodded his head. "Yes, you were."

"I was smarter than he was."

Another nod. "He was no rocket scientist that one."

"I was better looking than he was."

No more nodding. This time when Rob spoke he focused on the empty space in between his two hands, in between the crumbled up napkin and his drink. "That you were."

Riled up, racing down the cold, stone path that was more commonly known as Memory Lane to meet a former foe, Theo didn't see Rob's expression, apprehensive, cautious, as if he was about to plunge down his own rabbit hole to another time, a hole that had been securely locked and barricaded for over a decade. A hole that had been closed up for so long, its contents were no longer fully remembered; what remnants of the past lay down there were anybody's guess. Theo was privy to none of that; he was too keenly aware of his own fat ghost that had suddenly reemerged from the depths of his own private darkness. "But I was funnier, smarter, and better looking than a lot of kids," Theo announced. "Why the hell did Matty hate me so much?!"

With one eye gazing down the rabbit hole and another staring straight ahead at Theo's still-handsome face, Rob said, "Maybe he was a closet case and had a crush on you too." His voice was softer, like falling snow when it finally finds a safe landing. But there was nothing safe about what Rob had said or how he had said it, not in Theo's mind; he said the word "too," and he said it quietly—it was something so important that it needed to be heard. It was an admission that they had been more than just friends, they weren't just friendly with each other, they had had a relationship, not just the one-sided courtship that Theo imagined every waking moment of his life. It had been something real.

While Theo was processing this information, however, he remained silent, and in the real world silence usually makes another person talk, which is what Rob did. When Theo was finally prepared to listen once again to what Rob was saying, he was surprised he was still talking about that Czarnecki asshole, this time in the present day. "Corinne's got a place near him down Long Beach Island," Rob said. "He's married now, bunch of unruly kids, I think he's a fireman."

"That fat thing is a fireman?!"

So much for quiet, important speech.

But sometimes loud, unimportant remarks are just as welcome. Rob's pensive gaze was replaced by an unshy grin. "I haven't seen Fatty Czarnecki in years. But I assume he lost some of his baby fat in order to pass the fireman test."

"The only way he can ever redeem himself in my mind is if he lost enough weight to be in one of those hot fireman calendars," Theo declared. "And Mr. July or August so he's only wearing a fire hat and his naked body is drenched in that white, foamy fire extinguisher stuff!"

As Theo's words sunk into his brain, humiliation rose from his toes. Eerily, Whitney Houston was singing "Do You Hear What I Hear?" over the airport loudspeaker, and Theo wanted to scream at her, "Yes, Miss Whitney, you did hear me make a fool out of myself, Rob heard me, the pilots circling the tarmac probably heard me too because I'm loud and I'm tactless."

Suddenly it was Mr. Hesterfer's Spanish class all over again, clumsy silence followed by effortless laughter. Just as he did when they were kids, Rob saved the day: He rescued Theo simply by letting him know he understood, he was on his side, he shared in the joy. And just like when they were kids Theo was grateful, relieved that he wasn't on his own, stranded alone in the spotlight, burned as a result of his own foolish, reckless behavior.

I don't like being alone. For a second Theo wasn't sure if he thought the words or spoke them out loud. Watching Rob, still laughing, mumbling something that sounded like "Fatty Czarnecki and his little fat, red dick," Theo figured the comment had gone unspoken, but spoken or not, why did it pop into his head? *Maybe because it's the truth.*

While Rob continued to make himself laugh by imagining their fat high school friend as a naked fireman, Theo took a sip of Scotch. The alcohol no longer burned harshly and made his face scowl; it wasn't nearly as delightful and tasty as a peppermintini, but he was getting used to the taste, and he was also getting used to being in Rob's company. It was as if the past fifteen or so years of no communication had never happened, as if Rob had been in his life every day since the last time they met, like Theo dreamed would happen, like their adulthood was merely a continuation of every year that had come before. As if Theo's life was completely different and nothing had changed.

"You are still the same, dude!" Rob exclaimed. "I mean Teddy, uh sorry, Theo."

Just listening to Rob trip over his words made Theo smile. *He is still adorable, no matter what he says or does, he can't help but be adorable.*

"I can't wait to tell Audra that I bumped into you."

"Who's Audra?"

"My wife."

Except that. Theo had been having such a surprisingly fabulous time revisiting the past that he had forgotten about Rob's present; he had forgotten even that he had brought up the subject of Rob's marital status before they accidently drove off course. Or perhaps it wasn't an accident at all, perhaps Theo deliberately steered them into the right lane so they could take a U-turn in their conversation. Now that he thought about it, he really didn't know which it was. The Scotch and the Christmas music and the memories and staring at Rob's face, manly, yet still clinging on to its boyhood, were starting to have an intense effect on Theo. "Oh that's right," Theo said, sounding as nonchalant as a person who wasn't at all nonchalant could sound. "You have a wife."

Rob didn't respond verbally. Instead, he nodded his head, sipped his drink, waved his hand in the air, multitasking furiously so he didn't have to speak. So of course Theo did it for him. "I always thought you'd marry Debbie Testa."

"Debbie Testa," Rob mumbled, the name muffled by the crunch of an ice cube. "Oh God, I haven't thought about her in years."

Disbelief took claim over Theo's face. "You took her to the prom, Rob."

"Well yeah, I know that, but the only reason I took her was 'cause *you* took her best friend, whatshername, Stephanie. . . ."

When it was clear that Rob was not going to be able to remember Stephanie's last name, Theo supplied it for him. "Ott."

"Who was really, really hot!" Rob accentuated his point by slamming his hand down hard on the table.

"Um, okay, if you say so."

"And Debbie was not!" This time Rob slammed his hand down even harder, making Theo jump a bit. He wanted to continue speaking, but he was laughing so hard he couldn't. Theo didn't want to laugh, he was unhappy that Rob had brought up his wife, but Rob's laugh was contagious. But then it dawned on Theo that he might have something to laugh about where Rob's wife was concerned; each time she was brought up, the conversation reverted back to a pre-wife, pre-heterosexual topic. Maybe there was hope after all.

"Stephanie was hot, and you knew it too," Rob said. "She was one of the hottest girls at the prom."

That's not what I remember about the prom, Rob. I remember me, you, your father's flask filled with peach schnapps, and sneaking out into the woods behind the Fiesta to drink and make out before heading back to our dates. "Maybe, but I wasn't really interested in her," Theo admitted.

Before Theo finished his comment, Rob interrupted, eager to continue the saga of the hot girl from the prom. "I remember Cliff Degelman asked me if your parents paid Stephanie to go with you."

What?! "He did not!" Theo said, clearly insulted.

"God's honest truth," Rob replied. "He said there was no way somebody as hot as Stephanie would go to the prom with somebody like you." This time Rob interrupted Theo before he even opened his mouth to speak. "And let it be known that I told Degelman you were way hot enough for a girl like Stephanie."

And there's the sweet Rob Theo remembered. "You said that?" Theo asked. "You really told Cliff Degelman that I was hot?"

For the first time Rob blushed as red as the Santa hat the old lady next to him was wearing. With his twinkling blue eyes and red cheeks, he looked like a real-live Christmas decoration; more than ever Theo wanted to take him home and put him on his tree. Even though he hadn't put up a tree this year. Or any decorations. He still wanted to take him home, and he felt that way even after Rob backpedaled. "Well, I may have said that you were way cool," Rob confessed. "But, well, you know, I meant hot."

Although there was noise all around them, impatient travelers singing along with the Christmas music, rowdy barflies making one holiday toast after the other, the air around Theo and Rob was suddenly quiet. They maintained eye contact for as long as they could, then eyed their empty glasses wondering what to say or do next. Theo acted first; when in doubt, joke. "Well Stephanie did have an amazing time," Theo said. "Just read page sixty-seven of my yearbook, she wrote it right there, in red ink, 'Thanks, Teddy, I had an amazing time at the prom.'"

"She wrote the same thing in my yearbook!" Rob declared.

Theo kicked Rob playfully under the table. "She did not!"

"I don't know, I don't even know where that thing is," Rob said, kicking Theo back, the side of his foot finding Theo's calf. "I do remember Debbie wrote about three pages in the back, she wrote so much she had to continue on the page with the lunch ladies' photos."

Sometimes men, gay or straight, could be so ignorant. "Because she loved you!" Theo declared. "You guys could have been a perfect couple."

"Why? The prom was our only date."

"That's how things start," Theo explained, then began to rattle on, not fully aware of every word that was rattling out of his mouth. "I just remember being jealous, I mean really jealous of her 'cause you guys looked great together, you were both Italian, for a while there you both had the same haircut, that grungy kind of post–David Cassidy shag thing, your parents knew each other, you both loved English class, you sat next to each other in the back and were always whispering. One day when she kept passing you notes all freakin' class, I swear to God I was trying to figure out a way to cut off her hand with my Teenage Mutant Ninja Turtle ruler, but I didn't want to risk detention so I . . ."

"You were jealous of Debbie?" Rob interrupted.

I can sort of accept that you're this happy heterosexual now, but I cannot accept that you're stupid. "Rob, come on, you must have known I was jealous."

"Why must I have known that?" Rob asked.

"Because . . ." Theo started, but couldn't figure out how to finish all the screwed-up, complicated feelings that were his teenage mind and heart.

"I thought you knew me better than that?" Theo thought Rob looked hurt, but that couldn't be true. "Debbie meant nothing to me, you were closer to her than I was, especially when she was in that show."

"Oh my God, *Gypsy!* Her Mama Rose is still talked about!" Theo gushed. "I can still picture her ripping through 'Rose's Turn,' and Mr. Marsch knew somebody who knew somebody and he was able to get the huge 'Rose' light they used for one of the national tours of the show. Every night when that light came on and Debbie belted out that song, the audience flipped out!"

Rob was amused by Theo's excitement, but he didn't share in it. "You see, I wasn't jealous of you and Debbie. Maybe it's 'cause I never got into the whole musical theatre thing."

Well if that isn't proof that you're not a poof. "You missed out on some great experiences, my friend."

Shaking his head, Rob smiled. "No, I had some great experiences, thanks to you, my friend." Theo fought every buzzed urge in his body not to bring up the peach schnapps from prom night, and just when his resolve was growing weak was shocked to hear Rob mention it first. "And yeah, I do remember the peach schnapps."

Bing Crosby and David Bowie were singing a duet; if that wasn't a sign that miraculous things could happen, Theo didn't know what was. Holding on tight to that sign of the Second Coming or the apocalypse, Theo forged ahead, saying things he had only said in his mind for the past fifteen years. "I remember exactly how it tasted on your lips."

Again Rob smiled, which completely unnerved Theo. Why wasn't he getting uncomfortable? Why wasn't he dashing out the door into the snow to flag down a plane and demand it fly him back to Fairfield? Why was he acting like a gay man?

"Despite being forced to sit through one lame musical after another, that was a very sweet time," Rob admitted. "All of high school was very sweet, thanks to you."

"Then why . . ." Theo felt the courage leave his body, float away like a snowflake in a storm. But a wind came and blew the snowflake back, making it swirl until it landed safely in Rob's waiting hands.

"Did I marry a woman?"

"Yeah." It was all Theo had the strength to say.

Rob slid the empty tumbler closer to Theo so it was less than an inch from his fingers. He looked down at Theo's hands, and he may have wanted to reach out and grab them, but he didn't; he didn't pull away, but he kept his grip on his glass. When he looked up at Theo his bangs fell to the side, his hair looked so soft, like his skin, Theo wanted to test them both, see which one was softest, but he didn't dare move, he felt like he was sitting next to Rob's indoor pool again, with Rob's head in his lap, afraid to breathe. This time at least he didn't have to ask Rob to look at him. "When I was finally away from you, in college, I changed," Rob said. "I hadn't really given it that much thought when I was with you. I mean, I know that some of the kids talked behind our backs and called us The Gay Boys."

"One of the more kind remarks," Theo added.

A tilt of the head, a conspiratorial smile. "I honestly have to say those remarks, those words, they didn't really bother me."

"Because down deep you knew you weren't the gay boy everybody was talking about?" Theo asked, with more than a hint of sarcasm.

Oddly, Rob didn't bristle from the comment, nor did he sprinkle onto the conversation his own serving of sarcasm. He leaned in closer, touched Theo's hand, and kept looking right into his eyes. "No, they didn't bother me because I didn't care about them," he corrected. "I only cared about you, Teddy, you know that, don't you?"

Like a child who for weeks had been begging to sit on Santa's lap only to retreat to the safety of his mother's side when the moment arrived, Theo pulled his hand away from Rob's gentle touch. Slightly embarrassed, he rubbed his hands over his thighs and then like a pouting child sat on his hands. And like a pouting child he remained silent for a few seconds while he thought about it. Finally he replied, "Yeah, I do."

Bing and Bowie were rudely interrupted by a loud female voice that demanded attention from all Lambert-St. Louis International Airport passengers. When she started to speak in the flat, nasally Midwestern tone, sounding like Madonna did before she got all Anglophiled, a part of Theo wanted her to announce that his flight was ready to depart, pluck him from this reunion that was getting increasingly harder to deal with, from this ghost he was finding it increasingly harder to face, but no such luck, the Madonna-esque airport voice simply reminded everyone to "watch your luggage at all times to ensure every passenger's safety." If given the choice right at this moment, Theo wasn't sure what he would choose to deal with: a terrorist or the truth. Unfortunately, he wasn't given that choice.

"Look, before I started dating Audra seriously, I thought long and hard about what we had," Rob said. "I loved you."

Theo was impressed. There was no hesitation, no fear, no worry that what he was about to say was going to be scoffed at, no worry that he was going to appear less of a man after he said those three words. Maybe it was because he used the past tense, maybe it was because he was skilled at lying to customers and getting them to believe whatever nonsense came out of his mouth or maybe it was because those words were true.

Unable to remain still, Theo's hands sprung free, floundered a bit, until they found each other and created a tightly woven fist that shook a little. "Rob, please don't say what you don't mean."

Rob placed two fingers on top of Theo's fist; the touch was soft, but the result was warm and calming. "Listen to me, I loved you. And I was in love with you. I didn't spend endless hours trying to define it, I didn't give it a name or classify it as something specific, but I know how I felt." Slowly, Theo's fingers loosened, and the fist melted away to just two hands, folded together, being touched by a couple of other fingers. Those fingers grew even warmer, and Theo almost sighed when Rob grabbed one of his fingers and rubbed the smooth nail as he continued to tell him things Theo had never imagined he would hear. "I cried the day you left for college. I had never cried a day in my life and all of a sudden there I was on your porch and in the driveway was your dad's Honda packed with all your stuff and I had to run from your house so you and your parents wouldn't see me crying like a baby."

Rob's touch, his words, felt wonderful; it made Theo feel ten, sixteen, twenty, thirty-six, all at the same time. "You never told me this."

And then the touch was gone. "Because I was afraid." Rob surveyed the room, taking it all in, but not really seeing any one thing, but Theo couldn't take his eyes off of him. "Once I understood what being gay really meant and how half the world, including my father, was against it, I got scared; I figured if I didn't mention it to anyone, including you, it wouldn't be real, none of it really would have happened."

Put Theo away in a box and store it with the other Christmas decorations. Shove it in the back of the closet, we'll see if we want to use them next year, probably not though. "The odd thing was the longer you were out of my life, the less I thought about it, and the more I thought about girls."

"So what are you saying, you really were just gay for me?"

"I told you, I could be myself around you, I didn't have to act like some popular jock, I didn't have to pretend to be smart and happy and all put together, because I was none of those things, but you made me laugh and you made me feel good about myself and the world."

"I wish I would have known all of that."

"Now who's being stupid? You knew all that, you just wanted more from me, more than I could give you, so you got mad." Rob took a moment for Theo to digest his words as he sipped on another piece of ice. "After graduation, when we were separated I started to understand more, I started to figure things out, and I knew that for all our similarities we had one primary difference."

"I'm gay, and you're straight."

"Yeah. For a while there I wished it wasn't so, I wished I was gay because we had so much fun together. I tried to fool around with this one guy at college who, uh, kinda looked like you, but it totally didn't work out."

"So then you called me to use me for one last test run."

Rob looked at Theo like the parent who looks at the child who refuses to crawl into Santa's lap. "You're kidding me right? I wanted to see if I had made it all up; I wanted to see if maybe I was just one of those people who loved a person and didn't worry about their gender. I wanted to see if I still loved you enough to say the hell with it, you're the person I want to spend my life with."

Anger was starting to mix in with nostalgia. "But clearly that's not the way it turned out."

"You remember how it was, Theo, that last time: It was awkward, forced, neither one of us really wanted it to happen, but we were both too afraid to stop it."

You want truth, Rob? I'll give you some truth. "I wasn't afraid, Rob, not about wanting to stop it; I was afraid that you were going to want it to be over too soon, that you were going to go back to school and forget about me again like you did before and that's exactly what happened." *Why stop now when you're on a roll, Theo; throw some more truth into the fire.* "I called you a few times, I even wrote you a letter, a very dramatic one if I might add. Did you read it or did you get bored with it like you got bored with what Debbie wrote in your yearbook?"

Chalk it up to the holiday spirit, but Rob wasn't taking the bait. "I remember every word of your letter," he said. "I read it several times. But I was twenty years old, Teddy; I was a dumb kid, I didn't know how to respond."

"So you didn't."

"No, I didn't," Rob admitted. "And every once in a while I feel like a complete jerk for that. I know I should've said something, but you were in Boston, I was in Jersey. . . . Look, I'm not ashamed of what we had, I've never been ashamed of it, not then, not now, but I think I knew once I met you again that it was all in the past."

Sometimes the past can repeat itself, Theo thought.

"And it was only you," Rob added. "You are the only guy I ever loved."

And despite all the odds turn up in the present. "And for the longest time in my life it was only you too," Theo said quietly. "I'm not trying to interrogate you, and I'm sure as hell not trying to judge you, but you were the one who said hello to me. You must have known what subjects we would talk about, you must have known this was going to be dredged up."

Classic Rob Colangelo emerged; he leaned back in his chair, his bangs bouncing, and smiled charmingly. "Honestly, when I saw you I was just really happy."

Sometimes, however, the classics can still have a new twist. Rob got a bit too relaxed and leaned back a bit too far and soon not only were the two front legs of the chair airborne, but Rob was about to be airborne as well.

Instinctively, Rob reached out his hand toward Theo, and Theo without hesitation did the same; there was no fumbling, no floundering, just one hand being grabbed by the other to be pulled back to safety. Holding onto Rob's hand, pressing into his flesh so firmly, Theo was amazed that there weren't any electric sparks flying out from their skin; he was even more amazed that he wasn't burned by Rob's wedding band. Turns out it was just a piece of gold, it wasn't a token of evil, it wasn't crafted by demonic heterosexual spirits, and it didn't sear and scorch a gay man's flesh. So much for all the hype.

Rising out of his chair, Theo gave a sharp tug and Rob lurched toward him, his bangs bouncing, the crinkles around his eyes smoothing out as his face registered shock at the sudden disruption. Most of the people in the lounge were crowded around the bar making merry and singing Christmas carols off-key, so there were only a few patrons sitting in the vicinity. When they saw Theo pull Rob up to a standing position, his chair no longer airborne, but toppled over, grounded, the patrons kept their distance and remained seated. They had enough problems having to deal with delayed flights; why add coming to the aid of two Christmas drunks to their list. And while Theo and Rob might not have been officially drunk, they definitely looked it.

Wobbling forward, Rob's free hand sprung out and innocently or possibly magnetically found Theo's neck. His soft, blunt fingers dug into Theo's neck, lean, but strong, and Theo shuddered slightly; a memory of the last time Rob had touched him so forcibly pierced his mind, making the pit of his stomach come alive. Theo tried to extinguish the passionate memory, but either it or the Scotch he had been drinking was too strong, and he was unable to do so. Ah well, so be it. Wasn't Christmas Eve all about remembering the past anyway?

Still unsteady, Rob needed to get a better grip to ensure that he wouldn't topple over. He shifted his hand from Theo's neck to his shoulder, pushing away the material of his sweater to expose and touch even more flesh. The move was quick and uncalculated, but it sent deliberate shivers down Theo's spine. In all the countless times that Theo had dreamed and imagined that Rob would once again caress him, touch his naked body, never once did the scenario include being in an airport lounge, with onlookers and with little to no hope of getting completely undressed. It was fa la la la la and bah humbug at the same time.

Rob took a step back in an attempt to become completely vertical, but misjudged the space between him and the fallen chair and stepped right onto one of its legs. Once again he pitched forward, this time unable to resist the trajectory, and he tumbled into Theo's arms. Giggling like a teenager, Rob was oblivious to the stares from the other patrons; some were disapproving, others borderline titillated from the display of man-on-man action. "Guess I can't hold my peach schnapps like I used to."

Holding Rob like this, close, securely, knowing he was the more powerful one, that if he let go, Rob would plummet onto the table and possibly crash onto the floor, filled Theo with an array of emotions. Cluttered, complex, contradictory. He felt like he was a little boy again, and there were just too many presents underneath the Christmas tree; breathless and pajama-clad he stood motionless, not knowing which one to open up first. Should he open up the biggest box with the reddest bow because such beautiful wrapping could only be used to wrap a sensational gift? Or maybe he should rip open the odd-shaped package that he was certain contained the skateboard he had been begging for? But isn't Christmas all about magical surprises? Yes! So why not unwrap the gift that was sitting in the corner, hidden almost out of view, the one not elaborately wrapped, the one that was hoping against hope that it would be opened? Theo could see his much younger self inch closer to that package, his eyes illuminated by the Christmas tree lights, filled with wonder and just as bright, but the current Theo shut his eyes tight; he wasn't sure he could open up that package. Just let it lie there for a while longer until I'm ready.

Abruptly, Theo pulled back, letting go of Rob, forcing him to stand on his own even if he wasn't capable or ready or willing. The sudden movement surprised Rob, but he knew it was the only appropriate course of action; just like not responding to Theo's letter or his phone calls, it was harsh, but necessary. Even though he knew it was inevitable, he wasn't prepared for it.

Sloping to the left, Rob slapped his palm down onto the table to keep from falling all the way over. It was a halfway successful maneuver: he didn't collide into the floor, but the glasses on the table did.

Simultaneously, he and Theo bent down; separately they moved in opposite directions. Theo descended upon the two glasses that miraculously hadn't shattered, grabbing them before they rolled out of view and possibly got stepped upon by some elderly and most likely inebriated patron who would wind up celebrating the holiday in the emergency room. Rob, meanwhile, made sure that his bag of presents was unharmed by any falling ice cubes. It was ice cube-free, but of course when Rob went to pick up the overstuffed bag to inspect it he only grabbed one handle, so it toppled over, most of its contents spilling onto the linoleum. When Theo saw one of the gifts, he almost let both glasses that he was holding fall back onto the floor.

"Coach Bob!" Theo cried, his voice ripe with sentiment.

Placing the glasses on the table, Theo genuflected slowly and reached down to pick up a box that contained what looked like a G.I. Joe doll if he were off-duty and volunteering his time to coach a boy's soccer team. And if he was bisexual. "I can't believe you have a Coach Bob doll."

"It's an action figure," Rob corrected, stuffing the bag with the rest of the gifts that had fallen out.

Theo held the doll / action figure reverentially like it was a baby Jesus and he was about to place it inside the empty manger to complete the nativity tableau. "It's Coach Bob," Theo said. "Where in the world did you find him?"

The bag repacked, Rob turned his overturned chair upright and sat down. "I found it in an antique store in Chicago," he explained. "I was downtown in between customers and thought I'd do some Christmas shopping."

Theo resumed his seat and placed Coach Bob on the table, never letting go of him and never taking his eyes off of him as he inspected every inch of the doll visible through its plastic covering. "He's just like I remember, the same blue and white tracksuit, the same big *B* on his jacket, the black high-top sneakers, oh my God look at his hand!" Theo shrieked and turned the box to face Rob. "He's wearing the varsity ring!"

Rob brought the box closer so he could inspect it more carefully. "You're right," he said. "I hadn't noticed that."

The moment Rob let go of the box, Theo turned it around so he could gaze on the prized inanimate object once more. "How I loved Coach Bob," he said out loud, but to himself.

"Me too," Rob agreed. "I thought my son might like it as much as I did."

Oh right, you have a son. "How old is he?"

"Joe just turned eight," Rob said.

That's a coincidence. "The same age as we were," Theo remarked.

Momentarily lost in the same memory, Rob took a moment before responding. "Yeah, we both brought the coach in for show 'n' tell right after Christmas and decided right then and there that we had to be the best of friends."

I decided the first time I saw you in the school playground at the start of school that we had to be best friends, but I was too nervous to say hello. If it wasn't for Coach Bob, we might never have been introduced. "We had everything," Theo said. "The workout gym, the trampoline, Coach's van."

"Don't forget Varsity Todd," Rob interjected.

Tracing a finger over the plastic that encased Coach Bob, Theo added, "How could I forget the Coach's star athlete. Todd was my personal favorite."

Rob shook his head at the silliness and profoundness of the memory and said, "He had blue and white shorts and a big *V* on his tank top right?"

"Exactly!" Theo nodded. "And his hair was longer and plastic, not like the Coach's peach fuzz buzz cut."

Theo ached to open up the box and rub his fingers over the Coach's fuzzy head, which sort of reminded him of Mr. Tom, maybe that's why he had liked the security guard so much. Could the night present any more coincidences? He recalled the many hours he and Rob had spent playing with Bob, Todd, and all their gear and accessories. Sometimes they were just a coach and his athlete in the gym working out, preparing for the next big game; other times they were out in the mountains or in the desert utilizing their natural surroundings to strengthen their natural-born abilities and athletic prowess. Theo's favorite times had been when he and Rob forgot about sports and games and practices and imagined Coach Bob was actually a spy and Todd was his protégé and their sports personas were merely camouflage. The two of them would fight side by side against the enemy in some exotic locale that they had seen on TV or heard their parents talking about like Hawaii or Russia or Theo's favorite, Czechoslovakia; he loved the sound of that name and was devastated when the country split up and became three or four new little countries, none of which had a name that sounded as interesting or was as challenging to spell.

The boys had spent countless hours playing in their fantasy world together, content to be on the outside of the outside world. They embarked on wild adventures, overcame oppressive odds, survived the most devastating accidents because, like Rob once said, "they were the perfect team." "You and me can beat anybody, Teddy," Rob had whispered so their enemies wouldn't hear.

"That's why we always have to be a team," Teddy had whispered back.

"Remember when we had to save Santa?" Rob asked.

Images as quick and furious as a sudden blizzard filled Theo's mind and took over. The airport lounge, the piped-in Christmas music, the spirited, semi-drunk patrons were all gone, and in their places were him and Rob as eight-year-old boys on the morning after Christmas, wrapped in their comfy pajamas and holiday joy. They each had gotten additional pieces of the Coach Bob play set as presents, and Rob had begged his parents to let him sleep over Teddy's house so they could wake up in the morning and not waste a single moment before starting to play with their new toys. Their parents were getting used to their mutual desire to be inseparable and happily agreed to the sleepover. That night, Christmas night, Rob had slept in the bottom portion of Teddy's really cool trundle bed less than a foot underneath Teddy. And just like he did every time Rob slept over, Teddy woke up a few times in the middle of the night and immediately looked over the side of his bed to make sure that Rob was still there, that he hadn't gotten homesick and made his parents pick him up or worse, but way more exciting, that he hadn't been kidnapped by some unknown menacing foe.

The next morning they woke up before Teddy's parents and ran downstairs to the living room where they had laid out all their toys the night before. Theo plugged in the Christmas tree lights so the room was twinkling red, blue, green, making the fake white branches of the tree glow even whiter. It looked like it had snowed indoors, and underneath the tree there was indeed an avalanche of presents.

Rob had gotten the snowmobile and Arctic explorer ski outfit, and Teddy had gotten the all-terrain vehicle, scuba diving equipment, and mountain camping gear, which came with its own Styrofoam mountain and rock climbing kit. Surrounded by all their other Coach Bob toys the boys transformed Teddy's living room into the North Pole and set out on an expedition to save Santa Claus, who was being held hostage by a group of mutinous evil elves. It was Rob's idea to set their adventure way up north since he had gotten the snowmobile, but it was Teddy who gave it the sinister twist after watching the classic holiday special, *The Year Without a Santa Claus*.

Holding Varsity Todd, Teddy had made him run into the gymnasium to fill Coach Bob in on the most diabolical scheme the world had ever heard of. "Coach Bob!" Teddy as Todd had yelled.

"What is it? Why aren't you at practice?" Rob as Bob had replied.

Teddy had moved Todd's arms up and down so it looked like he was either frantic or had AFTS—Action Figure Tourette's Syndrome. "It's Santa Claus, he's in danger!"

Danger!? Rob had made Coach Bob grab Todd's flailing arms to get him to focus. "What are you talking about? What kind of danger is Santa Claus in?"

Ever the student, Teddy/Todd had explained, "Jingle Bells, the head elf, is still angry with Santa for trying to call off Christmas this year, and he wants to make him pay."

The Coach immediately understood the severity of Todd's message. "He wants to kill Santa Claus?"

"Yes!" Teddy/Todd had cried, his little plastic arms reaching out to his coach for help, guidance, comfort.

Like a good coach, Bob had been there for his star athlete. He had raised one plastic arm and placed it on Varsity Todd's shoulder to reassure him, make him realize that no one could ever want to kill Santa, no one could ever be that diabolical. "No, Todd, that can't be," Rob/Bob had explained. "If he kills Santa there won't ever be a Christmas again."

"No, Coach, Jingle Bells wants to take over," Teddy/Todd had replied. "*He* wants to be the new Santa."

Rob/Bob had been stunned; he even fell back into the miniature pommel horse and had to hold onto the handgrips not to fall over. "Only an evil elf could come up with a plan so evil!" he had shouted. "We can't let him get away with this! We can't let him kill Santa Claus and change Christmas for the rest of the world."

"And we won't, Coach, not on our watch!" Teddy/Todd had exclaimed.

"But how, Todd! How can we stop someone so evil?"

Teddy and Todd had both taken a moment before speaking, a moment filled with pride, a moment to allow Rob and Bob to prepare themselves because they were going to be amazed. "I've got a plan."

Todd had cartwheeled on top of the pommel horse into a perfect handstand before lowering himself to straddle one side of the horse. Extending his hand, he had hoisted Coach Bob up so he could straddle the other. Face to face, their plastic thighs pressing into the plastic sides of the pommel horse they had each gripped one of the plastic handgrips and leaned into each other to discuss how they were going to save Saint Nick.

"What's your plan, Todd?" Rob/Bob had asked, impressed, but impatient. "Tell me! We're wasting precious time!"

Understanding the urgency, Teddy/Todd had spoken as quickly and clearly as he could. "Santa's number two elf, Jangle

Bells, is a double agent; he doesn't believe in what Jingle Bells is doing, but he's going along with him because Jingle Bells threatened to hurt Jangle Bells's family. Jangle Bells was able to get word out to Rudolph, who was able to get word out to the lower continents by using his blinking red nose as Morse code. But Jingle Bells found out and broke his nose, but I alone was able to intercept the SOS message while I was cross country skiing, training for the triathlon."

"That's why you're my star athlete, Todd!"

Teddy/Todd had been proud. "Thanks, Coach."

"But wait a minute," Rob/Bob had said, noticing a glitch in the plan. "Why can't Rudolph and the rest of the reindeer just fly south for help?"

If Todd could have smiled he would have, but he couldn't so Teddy had done it for him. "That's why you're the smartest coach around," he said. "You think of everything."

It was Rob/Bob's turn to feel proud. "Thank you, Todd, but why couldn't they fly south?"

"They tried to the day after Christmas, right after Jingle Bells imprisoned Santa, but Jingle and the rest of the evil elves caught them and force fed them anti-flying pellets."

"No! That can't be true!"

"Yes, I'm sorry, sir, it's all true," Teddy/Todd had said, Todd's little plastic hand reaching out to touch Bob's little plastic knee. "And it gets worse."

The Coach put his plastic hand on top of Todd's. "How in the world can it get any worse Todd?! How?!"

"Those pellets weren't just to stop them from flying," Teddy/Todd had begun. "In five hours they're going to explode, all of Santa's flying reindeer are going to be killed, burst open like a bag of potato chips with all their insides and everything spilling out onto the snow like potato chips when they spill out onto the rug. And once that happens, even if Santa survives he'll never be able to bring Christmas to the world ever again, he'll be stuck in the North Pole forever."

"No!" Bob/Rob had cried. "Jingle Bells must be insane. If he kills off the reindeer, then he won't be able to be the new Santa either."

Todd had sat bolt upright on the pommel horse. "He wants to be the new Santa, Coach, but he doesn't want to give away any of the toys the elves make. As sick as it sounds he wants to keep them all for himself."

The astounding news had almost made Coach Bob fall off the horse. "Which means there will never be Christmas again except for that one evil elf."

"That's right, Coach, but I have a plan to save Santa and save Christmas for every kid in the world," Teddy/Todd had declared. "Are you with me? But before you answer me you have to know that you'll be risking your life. Jingle Bells is diabolololical!"

"I'll be with you forever, Teddy, I promise you that."

Even as an eight-year-old it had registered: It wasn't the Coach talking, it was Rob, and he had called him Teddy, not Todd. It had registered, but Teddy had made no comment. He hadn't corrected his friend, he hadn't tried to find out if he really meant to say Teddy instead of Todd or if it was just a slip of the tongue, a moment where he confused reality with playtime, he hadn't mentioned it at all.

That's what I've been doing my entire life, Theo thought, *ignoring instead of confronting, letting life unfold around me instead of controlling it and taking an active role in my destiny*. Varsity Todd would not approve, and for the first time in his life neither did Theo.

Words were tumbling out of Rob's mouth; Theo heard a few of them, but he didn't catch full sentences. It was partly because he didn't want to focus on what Rob was saying; he wanted to focus on what he wanted to say. Sure it was wonderful to hear that Rob had a great relationship with his son and doted on his daughter or how he couldn't wait to be with them on Christmas Eve, but honestly Theo didn't care about any of that. All those details were part of Rob's life, and Theo wanted to talk about his own or more specifically about the life that he thought he and Rob were going to share.

The eerie, soprano wailings of the group, Celtic Women,

direct and seemingly innocent, but Rob
'ore."
swer Theo had expected or had wanted to

efore, but we didn't start dating until, you

dge, Theo's hands had unclasped and sep-
ıed to find that they were pressed firmly
urning red in some places, others white,
andy canes as gloves. There was no wed-
finger or any finger; there never had been
y would never be one. Neil hadn't wanted
didn't need anything to remind him how
which Theo believed, even though the
n't want to wear anything that would ad-
nt and get in the way of his sexual adven-
ands and the nonexistent wedding band,
know?"
ad before he spoke, his voice straining
tempt to remain casual. "I told her there
ool, I didn't go into details, but she under-

vere still begging the civilized world to
understand that peace and love are the
planet, not tanks and armies and nuclear
head to the side and looked as if he was
s and their lyrical melody, but Theo was
stening to a word the gals were singing,
the disembodied female voice would
flight so he could return to the safety of
nbrace of the wife he had chosen over
e wouldn't be rescued, Rob swallowed
ll, like I said, I didn't go into details, I
"

"But you weren't."

Rob understood by the tone of Theo's voice that he wasn't going to get off easy; he also understood that he didn't deserve to. Just because more than a decade had passed since they had last seen each other didn't mean their last meeting or the time in between had been forgotten; on the contrary it meant that it was relived and dwelled upon during all that time because there had never been closure, there had never been a good-bye. "No, Theo," Rob said, "I wasn't honest with her and, honestly, I probably won't ever be."

Crossing his arms, Theo leaned back in his chair. He didn't mimic Rob's usual stance, he didn't want to be like him, but he needed some distance to examine this guy who sat across from him, this guy who had suddenly become a stranger to him. "If you want to lie to your wife that's fine with me," Theo admitted. "But could you finally do me a favor and be honest with me?"

To Theo's surprise, Rob answered immediately. "I was a coward and selfish and I realized that I wasn't gay and you were. And more than that I knew what you expected from me."

"I expected you to return my phone calls," Theo huffed. "To answer my letters, that's all I expected from you."

"Come on, Teddy, you expected way more than that and you know it," Rob said. "And I don't blame you, I expected more from myself too. I thought it was going to be me and you forever even though I was shit scared and I knew my father was going to be disgusted and probably disown me. I still expected to wake up one morning and finally admit to myself that I was a gay man, but that never happened. Not even after that night with you."

Theo heard himself laugh. "Which just happens to be fifteen years ago today in case you forgot."

"I didn't forget," Rob said firmly. "I threw up after I ate that Christmas 'cause I was so upset, guess my body knew before my head did that I had lost you."

Theo reached out and grabbed Rob's hand. This time Rob flinched, more because of the surprise than because of the touch, and he quickly tried to salvage the moment by holding on to

ı tight harmony about the disharmony of the
:ed by the same female voice over the loud-
d she wouldn't announce the boarding of ei-
Ie had wasted enough time reminiscing and
when what he wanted to do was ask Rob
estions. If either of them got on a plane now,
d spend the rest of the holiday season and
his life dwelling on the fact that he once
ity slip away.

nnounce that the inclement weather in the
st Coast has finally subsided, and all our
arting shortly," she said. "All of us here at
s International Airport thank you for your
a safe and happy holiday season."

ob asked, "Do you think we have time for
ive to shove off?"

ad. "I've had enough, thanks. I do have
ı."

:d, but the rest of his face and body froze.
ıat was coming and he was silently cursing
a few minutes earlier. "Sure, shoot."

the table, his hands clasped, creating a
l Coach Bob, Theo felt some heavy air es-
hing out fear so he could speak. "We've
hour now and you've hardly told me any-

d, visibly relieved. "Her name's Audra."
ne," Theo said. "But what's she like? Is

e, Rob continued, "No, she's French so
ier so much at first, but now, you know,

'How'd you two meet?"

Theo's hand, but the moment had passed. Theo's hand was now a fist, clenched, protecting itself. "You didn't have to lose me," Theo protested. "You didn't have to disappear, erase yourself from my life. Do you have any idea what that did to me?"

"Yeah, Teddy, I do know! Look I was young and I was stupid, it wasn't the right thing to do, but it was the only thing I could think of at the time." Rob ran one of his beautiful hands through his beautiful hair, though Theo thought they looked just a little less beautiful now. "I didn't want to lead you on, I didn't want to hurt you, and yeah, I didn't want to be with you like that anymore, now that I knew I wasn't that way."

"Gay."

"Yes, Teddy, gay."

"Which is this horrible, disgusting thing?" Theo said, fully aware of how petulant he sounded.

"You want me to be honest, Teddy? Yes, at the time I was greatly relieved that I wasn't gay, I was thrilled to know that what we shared had been beautiful and sweet, but was safely in the past and it wasn't going to ruin my future. But I was twenty years old, I was a jerk, and I knew that you and I couldn't be friends any longer because you wouldn't accept friendship, you would want way more than that. Isn't that right?"

Theo nodded.

"After a while, when I understood that being gay doesn't mean you're disgusting or repulsive, I mean really believed it and just wasn't relieved that I wasn't gay, when none of that mattered any longer, I wanted to call you, I wanted to, I don't know, try to explain everything, but . . . by then too much time had passed, and I figured you didn't want to hear some lame-ass apology from me."

Tracing Coach Bob's name on the box with his finger Theo felt like he was tracing every lonely night he had spent hoping that Rob would call him, every hopeful morning that he imagined he would open his front door and see Rob waiting on his doorstep. "It would have been really nice to hear from you, Rob."

"Well you're hearing from me now. I'm sorry, Teddy. I never meant to hurt you. I just grew up into somebody different than you did, and I just assumed we couldn't still be friends instead of talking to you about it. I stayed silent and took the easy way out."

Which is exactly what you did too, Theo; can't really put all the blame on him without putting the same amount on yourself. "Guess I did the same thing."

"No, don't blame yourself; it was all my fault."

"I'm not going to argue with you there," Theo said, not stifling a smile; "But it's not like I fought that hard for you; I called a few times, wrote you that very Joan Collinsy letter damning you for destroying my life and vowing to never, ever not even if you came back to me . . ."

"Crawling on your hands and knees begging for absolution."

"Would I ever make you feel better by forgiving you," they both finished in unison.

Theo shuddered. "I really used the word absolution, didn't I?"

"Oh yeah," Rob said laughing. "Luckily I'm Catholic so I knew what you meant." Rob picked up Coach Bob and stared at him tenderly. "You may not believe this, but when I found this old guy in that store I took it as a sign that I might see you."

Theo had wasted time believing in worse things, why not this. "How did that make you feel?"

"Happy," Rob replied. "That was my immediate thought. I remembered how much fun we had playing with him and Todd and all the made-up adventures. We spent whole days practicing for some imaginary competition and then jetting off in a helicopter to save the world from some evil Russian."

"Or save Santa from an evil elf."

"Jingle Bells!" Rob exclaimed. "The last time I watched that show with my kids I almost told them about how Jingle turns evil, but I figured Audra would kill me. She doesn't even like Joe playing with guns."

"Oh you better watch out," Theo said. "Little Joe might turn out to be like his long lost Uncle Theo."

Rob placed Coach Bob on the table and looked at his friend.

"And I can finally say with complete honesty that it wouldn't matter to me one bit," Rob said. "I would be proud if he turned out to be like you."

"Well let's not get carried away."

"Teddy . . . Theo, whatever, I mean it," Rob said. "You made me feel invincible as a kid, you made me so glad just to be me, do you have any idea what kind of a gift that was? You were my very own Santa Claus." Rob laughed first. "And yes, I know that sounded really corny, but I mean it."

It suddenly dawned on Theo that it was Christmas Eve and by this time he was usually seated around his mother's table eating appetizers, drinking eggnog that his father spiked with a bit too much rum, making small talk with his parents and his aunt and their friends who he only saw once a year, but about whom he knew every detail of their lives thanks to his mother's endless, boring monologues about them. He didn't care about them, and while he loved his parents, he didn't care to be in their presence. He wanted to be seated at his own table, next to a man he loved, creating his own memories and traditions, not piggybacking on those of his parents.

"You know I guess I have Neil to thank for this," Theo said.

"Your ex?"

"Yeah, if he hadn't dumped me, I wouldn't have flown out to be with my parents. We were planning on staying home for the holidays."

"Well as sorry as I am that he dumped you, I'm glad that he did," Rob admitted. "This has been the best Christmas gift I've gotten in a long time."

Theo knew that he meant it, but he also knew it meant their time was coming to an end, and he was starting to realize how much he dreaded the next part of his journey.

"You deserve to be with somebody though, Teddy, you really do."

Part of me believes that, and the other part just knows that I'm thirty-six years old and flying across the country alone to spend Christmas Eve with my parents, which is going to make me feel even more alone. "It's funny," Theo began. "How do you go from loving Christmas to loathing it?"

"I don't know."

"I wouldn't expect you to hate the holiday," Theo said. "With the kids and all, must make for a pretty special time."

Reluctantly Rob had to agree. "Yeah, it does. It almost makes up for the craziness of the rest of the year." Before Theo could ask, Rob answered, "I mean I don't regret my life, the path I chose or the path that chose me, whatever it was, but there are times that I wish my life was more like yours."

Theo made a face that looked as if it had just been announced that Justin Bieber was going to star in a remake of *Miracle on 34th Street* as a young Natalie Wood. It made sense since he wouldn't need to change his hairstyle, but it was still wrong. "Like mine? You've got to be kidding me. I'm on my way to hotter than hell Phoenix to spend a few boring-to-miserable days with my folks, and you're flying home to your wife and kids."

"I just mean that I don't have a choice, but you do."

Such a simple statement and yet so powerful. Once again Theo invoked an image of the Blessed Mother and hoped she would conjure up another miracle. He imagined how she must have felt when the angel Gabriel told her about the Immaculate Conception; it was a simple concept, and yet she knew it was about to change her world. So did Theo.

"I never thought of looking at it that way."

"It's the truth," Rob confirmed. "And I have to tell you every once in a while I imagine what it must be like to be like you."

"Gay?"

"No, you doof," Rob said, laughing. "To be single, with only yourself to think about."

"Don't go stereotyping. . . ."

Rob groaned and extended his arms, shaking his hands as if they were wrapped around Theo's neck. "No, I'm not saying that just 'cause you're gay means you're irresponsible or that you don't want a relationship and commitment, children and all that," Rob clarified, then picked up Coach Bob. "All I'm saying is you can go out and buy something like this, buy it for yourself, and not have to lie and say you bought it for your kid."

Theo had a picture of Rob turning the corner of some antique shop and coming face-to-face with the square-jawed, hyper-masculine face of Coach Bob, standing frozen and looking back in time, unprepared to be visited by a once-friendly ghost and yet unable to shake free from its grip. "You bought Bob for yourself?"

Cupping his chin in the palm of his hand, Rob smiled. "I scoured that stupid store for the gym play set, the equipment, but all they had was the coach propped up on some old board games in the front window like it was waiting for me. We really had a lot of fun with him."

"No," Theo corrected. "We had a lot of fun together."

Gently, Rob pushed Coach Bob across the table until he was looking up from behind his plastic covering into Theo's eyes. "I want you to have him."

Theo looked down at Bob's blue eyes, practically the same color as Rob's, and felt some happiness break out across his chest, but no, he couldn't take a gift out of Rob's kid's hands. "No," Theo protested. "You were going to give this to your son."

Swiping the air with the back of his hand, Rob smirked. "I told you I lied, I bought it for me, but let's face it, my kid isn't going to like it because it doesn't have a computer chip and my wife'll only make fun of me," Rob said, smiling reflectively. "Marriage is all it's cracked up to be, you know."

Fighting the urge to grab the package and stuff it in his bag before Rob changed his mind, Theo gave him one more opportunity to do so. "Are you sure?"

"Yes," Rob said. "I have a feeling I was meant to give it to you anyway."

"Oh come on now," Theo said. "Don't tell me that you've found religion along with a family. Or is it just the time of the year?"

Rob paused to shrug his shoulders, but Theo could tell he was really trying to choose his words carefully. "I wouldn't say that I found religion, but when you have kids you're reminded that there is a higher power of some sort. The same power that brought the two of us together."

I can't remember when I've received a more perfect gift. Neil never even came close; he only bought me things he *thought I'd like, never anything that he picked up just because it reminded him of me.* "Thank you," Theo said. "This is really very sweet." Suddenly, he was back in Mr. Hesterfer's class and he didn't know what else to say, nor could he think of a joke. "I'm only sorry that I don't have anything for you."

But there was no more need for jokes, only honesty. "Just seeing you and having the chance to chat after all this time is gift enough."

Theo was about to agree when their space was once again invaded by the disembodied female voice. "Attention passengers, Flight 717 from St. Louis to Newark airport is now boarding at Gate 5."

No one moved, but they both knew that their meeting was about to end as suddenly as it had begun. When Rob spoke he sounded disappointed. "That's me."

They both gathered their coats and bags and began their figurative descent. Theo followed Rob out of the bar, Coach Bob securely tucked into his bag peering up at him as if silently urging him on to say good-bye like the champion he knew he was. Rob was fumbling in his coat pocket for his ticket, which gave Theo a few seconds to compose himself, but still when Rob looked up and at him he felt his heart beat a little bit faster. How he wanted to lean over, brush Rob's bangs off his forehead, stare into his eyes, and softly kiss him on the lips. He wanted this, their good-bye, to be romantic, important, worthy of something from a classic movie, and then he realized that was one of the stupidest thoughts he had ever had. Almost as stupid as Rob's. "You know, I'm in New York a lot for business," he said. "Maybe I could meet you there for dinner or something."

Obviously somebody wasn't listening. "I, um, live in Boston," Theo repeated.

"I know, I just thought, you know, that you might get to New York some time, and we could meet up and have another drink."

Wary, Theo decided to reply honestly. "Well I do get to New York from time to time."

"Perfect!" Rob declared. "Why don't we exchange numbers? What's your cell phone?"

Reconnecting with an old friend who was much more than an old friend, that's not exactly how Theo envisioned he would be starting off the New Year. He could agree, allow life to sweep him along as it had always done, or he could make a choice; he could do what was best for him. "I don't think that's such a good idea."

Shoving his cell phone back into the pocket of his coat, Rob tried to maintain his composure. "Oh I'm sorry, I didn't, you know, mean . . ."

"I know you didn't mean anything like *that*," Theo said, interrupting him, acknowledging that he understood Rob didn't mean that they should hook up on the sly. However, he also didn't think hooking up in the open in public was a very good idea. "This has been wonderful, it really, really has, not to mention long overdue."

"Yeah, very long," Rob concurred.

"But it's over," Theo said. "And I think we should keep it that way."

Unable to hide his disappointment, Rob opened his mouth to talk, but closed it without saying a word. He might not agree with how Theo felt, but he couldn't disagree with it either. Being the salesman that he was, however, he couldn't resist one final pitch. "It's just that don't you think we bumped into each other for a reason?"

Absolutely. "Yes, I do."

"So do I!" Rob exclaimed. "I think we were meant to see each other again, to reconnect, build up our friendship again."

Theo couldn't explain it, but he hadn't felt so strongly about something in years, he just knew that he needed to say good-bye and for it to be final. "I can't speak for you, and I'm not going to try, but I can say for myself that I was meant to see you again so I could move forward," Theo said. "We had a great friendship and you have always and will always be special to me, but we haven't had any kind of relationship for years and as you've explained there've been reasons for that."

Once again the female voice boomed throughout the space overhead and urged Rob and his fellow passengers to board at Gate 5. "Sounds like it's time for you to go."

And like the good salesman he was, Rob was able to admit defeat. "Yeah, it is."

The effects of the Scotch long gone, Theo knew that when Rob hugged him tightly it was because he wanted to, not because his inhibitions were lowered; he was just as grateful for this impromptu meeting as Theo was. "You make sure you take care of the coach," Rob demanded.

"I will, I promise."

They didn't fill the air with pleasantries, no "say hello to your parents, give your kids a hug for me"; it was as if they didn't want to clutter their last few moments together. Theo watched Rob leave toward his gate never once expecting him to turn around to wave one more time or steal another glance at the man who held a small place in his heart. He remained standing looking in his direction simply because he didn't feel the need to move; he didn't feel the need to do anything, and it felt liberating.

After Rob disappeared into the throng of the other passengers who had been anxiously waiting to board their flight and even after all those passengers disappeared, Theo still stood there in the middle of the terminal, just staring. People walked around him, some said "excuse me" but politely since it was Christmas Eve, and no one told him to sit down or move out of the way. It was a good thing too because he wouldn't have listened.

He dug into his pocket for some unknown reason and pulled out a candy cane severed in two, and an image of him and Rob standing next to each other, but not touching, flashed in his brain. He couldn't figure out why for the moment so he stared at the candy cane more intently; anyone who saw him would have thought he was a little bit drunk and a little bit crazy, especially when he cried out, "That's it!" He was the red stripe and Rob was the white, or vice versa, it really didn't matter, it simply mattered that the two lines never connected, they continued on in circles next to one another, around and around and around, never connecting, never becoming one. For the first time it was clear that that's the way they were meant to be.

Judy Garland was telling him to have a merry little Christmas, and that's really all that he had wanted. And maybe that's what he should do, make it really little, just him and Coach Bob. Noticing some empty stools at the bar, Theo sat down on one and put his coat and bag on another. He positioned Coach Bob so he could see the small silver Christmas tree in the corner of the bar that had obviously been decorated in a rush with a few strands of tinsel thrown onto its branches haphazardly and a few plastic red balls that as his mother would say "had seen a better day." His mother, hmm, suddenly he felt depressed. He could see her face and hear her voice, hear her talking, never asking him important questions, questions that mattered. He could see his father looking through him, laughing at his own jokes; he could see his aunt and their friends and he just felt paralyzed. What had Rob said? *He* didn't have a choice, but Theo did.

He had a choice, but had taken a job that fell into his lap and stayed there long after it had ceased to be enjoyable. He had found a man, Neil, who on paper was perfect, but in life was terribly flawed and not committed to building a life with him, but Theo chose to ignore the signs and allow their life to continue instead of choosing something better for himself. He had let life take him for a ride instead of the other way around.

Philosophy and self-examination had never been Theo's strong suit, but he knew he had to make some changes in his life if he wanted to capture any of the happiness and joy and freedom he had felt when he was a little boy. He had no idea how he was going to do it, but he had to start thinking like a man who was free and could make his own choices. He waited for the guilt to come, but it didn't, which made sense because he made his choice out of love. Love for himself.

The female voice returned to the air. "Flight 422 for Phoenix, Arizona, now boarding at Gate 27."

Theo turned to look at Coach Bob, content, sheathed in his box, covered in plastic, and Theo longed to feel the same way. He stopped thinking and took action.

Catching the eye of the bartender, he said, "I'll have another."